The Korr Stigmata

A NOVEL

BY TIM DUGAN

Table of Contents

1. Grace Arundel

September 1940.

In the south of England, at the time the German war was reaching British shores, a young woman ran along an empty beach. She was raven haired and tall and ran with the long, measured strides of a competitive runner. Even though woman athletes were frowned upon by polite society, Grace Arundel still loved the experience of running down the wide, lonely strand outside her hometown of Stokehill. But at that moment on that empty beach, running races was the furthest thing from her mind.

Stokehill had been bombed three times by the Germans, and everything was chaos. For most of the summer, the war had taken place in the air, the German planes against the British planes, or on the ground against military targets, like the radar station just outside Stokehill. That week everything changed. It was the beginning of the Blitz, and the Germans were bombing cities and towns, trying to terrorize the British people and force a capitulation from Great Britain without the need for a messy invasion. And since Stokehill was one of the first cities a German pilot saw after crossing the Channel, Grace and everyone in town were suddenly in the middle of a war.

A seagull cried overhead as she picked her steps between clumps of seaweed. The bombs and the air-raid sirens and the daily droning of aircraft engines had been a nightmare. The first attack had seemed no more than a misfire: two bombs dropped in a field outside town. But the second and third bombings had not been misfires, and the destruction had devastated Grace. Five houses in the neighborhood of thatched cottages known as The Oaks had been destroyed, and ugly piles of wood and brick and glass were heaped in their place. In the town center two 16th Century timbered buildings that over time had come to lean against one another like an old married couple were leveled by a German bomb, and the shopkeepers in both had been killed. And the oldest building in Stokehill, the Norman church, which had witnessed countless christenings, weddings and funerals over nearly seven centuries, was missed by only a few feet, and a smoldering bomb crater lay in the lawn next to it like an open grave.

Grace stopped to pick up a beautiful, green-speckled seashell lodged in the sand. In all, four people had been killed, and in a town as small as Stokehill, Grace had known them all. It was as many as the town had lost in the whole of the first war. She felt the shell slip from her fingers and heard a soft thud as it hit the sand.

"The first war," she shook her head. "Now we're numbering them."

There was a saying in town that there were Arundels in Stokehill before there was a Stokehill. The family cherished the local legend that the nearby castle and town had taken their name not from the valley of the river Arun, but from them. Whatever the case, they knew for certain that the first entry in the baptismal book in old church library was for one William Arundel dated Christmas Day 1287, and they'd had an unbroken line residing in or near the Stokehill ever since.

Grace had always felt that her roots to her home were not only deeper than most—they went beyond her ken. It was as if she stood over a deep, dark well whose bottom she could not fathom, but whose water nourished her in a mysterious way. But Grace was an only child without cousins or other relatives, and when her days were done, the Arundel name was destined to vanish from Stokehill forever.

She stepped over a piece of dark driftwood half-buried in the coarse sand. Grace's mother, Mary Arundel, had been devastated by the attacks that week as much as anyone, especially as a nurse at the hospital. In one week she had gone from bandaging household mishaps and biking injuries to treating severed limbs and third degree burns. The severity of the injuries was bad enough, but what made it worse was that Mary knew all of the injured: friends and neighbors she had known her whole life, merchants and shopkeepers from town, even the vicar, Mr. Phelps. Each one became harder to treat than the one before, and Grace could see the strain growing on her mother each day.

And as is if the war wasn't enough, Grace had ended her engagement with Roger the month before. Even though she had told herself it was the right thing to do, the sudden break after four years together—four years that seemed to be building to something—left Grace feeling like some part of her inside had been rudely severed. And now she was alone. She stopped in her tracks as a rogue wave just brushed her shoes. *Was it really the right thing to do, or am I not in my right mind because of this war?*

Then she noticed a low drone, barely piercing the sound of the crashing waves at first, but unmistakable, and becoming louder by the minute. The drone was soon joined by a wail that began to rise from the town center, growing in pitch and volume. Grace froze.

"The air raid siren!"

She dashed up to the road above the beach as the aircraft noise became oppressive, and began to jog back toward town. All the terror from the previous three bombings seemed to pick up exactly where it left off on Grace's nerves.

"This isn't getting any easier," she huffed.

The siren had stopped but the airplane noise was now overwhelming, and Grace could see a vapor trail trace an arc in the sky far above her. She thought of her mother and her grandfather as she ran up the road.

"God, I hope they're both somewhere safe!" Grace felt that her grandfather would be alright, but Mary Arundel had become so agitated that week that Grace could no longer have a quiet conversation with her. It was as if her mother's nerves were damaged by the bombings, and all she could do at home was snipe and shout. Only Mary's best friend Elaine seemed to calm her down.

Grace heard an explosion somewhere across town as she was turning onto the high street. She heard someone scream from up the street as she watched people she knew scurry about like mice, and saw a cloud of smoke rise above the row of shops.

A blast off to her right, barely a hundred yards away, made Grace lurch to a stop. She felt the tremor pass through the pavement under her feet like she was standing on a ship at sea. She froze again and her mind went numb. *Is it better to stay in one place, or run for cover?* She saw the Norman tower of the old church on her left, the only shelter in sight. There was a blonde woman frantically waving at her from the arched doorway where several people were huddled together. It was Elaine Ashley, her mother's friend, beckoning her as the others she was with were struggling to unlock the church door.

Grace felt a glimmer of hope, but as she started toward Elaine she saw the church lawn with the gaping bomb crater, and she stopped. A shrill whistle came from the sky overhead, and a bright flash, and suddenly Grace was on her back in the middle of the street, knocked down by another blast. Her ears were hammered by the explosion and she looked up, dazed and momentarily deaf, at the rising cloud of smoke silently surrounding the church. A pile of rubble slowly came into focus where the doorway had been, and Grace could see no one moving.

"Oh God!"

As she tried to move, Grace was suddenly aware of a tall, young man with dark brown hair and blue eyes bending over her, offering her a hand up. She took his hand as her mind tried to reset itself, and though he looked familiar, all Grace could think of was how fortunate she was not to be alone. Then as her hearing began to return she realized who was helping her.

"John! John Perceval," she blurted out. "Thank you."

"Are you alright, Grace?" he asked, as she brushed herself off, but it sounded to her like he was speaking with a pillow against his face.

Grace had gone through most of her schooling with John, including graduate school where they were both enrolled. He was always the tall, occasionally outspoken young man in class or on campus, his hands perpetually in his pockets, but Grace was surprised that she had not noticed until then how handsome he had become.

"Yes, yes." She looked at the ruined smoldering church, and the color ran from her face, but her mind started to clear.

"Come on, they need help."

That evening John Perceval sat at the Arundel's kitchen table, a cup of tea steeping in front of him. His tall frame was hunched over the teacup and he was distractedly watching the steam curl up around his outstretched index finger. Across from him sat Grace's white-headed grandfather, Mr. Fisher, fidgeting with that day's unopened newspaper as they both waited patiently for Grace to return from her mother's bedroom.

Elaine Ashley had survived the bombing with a severely broken leg and some bruises, but when Mary Arundel saw her best friend wheeled unconscious into the hospital with her mangled limb and Grace at her side, she fainted dead away. She had what the doctor described delicately as 'a bit of a breakdown'.

At the sound of Grace's footsteps coming down the stairs both men turned toward the open door, and sat up in their seats.

"How is she?" they asked in unison as Grace came into the light of the kitchen.

"She's out like a light. The sedatives they gave her must have been really strong. I think I could use one." Grace smiled at the two men seated at the table, but she was only half joking. She was clearly shaken.

"That's the best thing for her," Mr. Fisher said with some relief, as he opened the newspaper. "This past week has been—"

"I know," Grace answered softly.

"Then it's just as well she doesn't know I'm here," John added. "She didn't seem too fond of me."

"Oh John, she's been like that with everyone lately," Grace said, looking up at him, "besides, she doesn't know you very well." Unlike most of the town's inhabitants who were born in Stokehill, John's mother moved them to town when he was a teenager following the death of his father, to live with John's grandfather, the professor.

Grace poured herself a cup of tea and sat between the two men at the table, then turned to John.

"I know I said it earlier, but I appreciate your helping me get my mother home. You've been a tremendous help. Where were you when the bombing started...in the library?"

"Actually, I'm a little embarrassed to say I was at Lady's Well, fishing." John answered.

"Good for you!" Mr. Fisher said kindly, a pair of reading glasses perched on the end of his nose. "Catch anything?"

John suddenly perked up.

"As a matter of fact I did," he replied, his eyes growing wide. "A trout that was twice the size of anything I've ever seen in that little pond. It was two foot long if it was an inch!"

Grace's grandfather took off his glasses and studied John's face.

"Did it have greenish-gold speckles on its back?"

"Yes, it did."

Mr. Fisher looked at Grace for a moment, then returned to John.

"John, my friend, that's the Lady of the Lake, and you're only the second person that I've known that's seen it." He looked at Grace. "The other was your father, Grace."

John's eyes grew wide.

"I'd heard about the Lady of the Lake when I was in grade school, but I'd forgotten it, or didn't believe it. Anyway, the strangest thing was how easy it was to catch—almost like it wanted to be caught, or have a look at *me* maybe. Those big eyes seemed…" He sat staring at the tea cup in front of him like he was seeing the fish again.

Grace thought it was strange they could both show such interest in fishing with everything else that had just happened, but then she recalled her own daily running habit, every day whether rain or shine, and now in peace and war. She knew most people thought it very strange.

"What did you do with it?" Grace asked.

"That was when the first bomb hit, so I released the fish and started back toward town. When I heard the next bomb I was running up the high street. I saw the big brick house on the corner of Lake Street and the high street had been hit, and as I turned the corner the church exploded and I saw you in the street." He looked anxiously at Grace, whom he had always studied from a distance as she and Roger strode arm in arm through school or town. Now he was sitting in her home looking at her green eyes, and despite the war and the bombing, all he could think about at that moment was that she was unattached.

"This is all an absolute nightmare," Grace replied, holding her hands over her still-ringing ears. "I just want all of this to end. How do we make it stop?"

"We all want it to end, Grace," her grandfather said with more exasperation in his voice than Grace had ever heard from him. "But it won't just stop—not now." He stopped and tried to smile at her.

"Stiff upper lip, Grace!" But his smile didn't last, and he returned to his newspaper. "They've invaded France, now they're having a go at us."

The next afternoon Grace was on the beach for her daily run, which was now beginning to feel to her like a daily patrol. She was unhurt from the blast the day before, and although her ears were still ringing, the waves and the crying gulls sounded the same as ever. But all Grace could think about was her mother's breakdown.

"Where will all this lead? What will I do if she gets worse?"

She thought of the grey gothic sanitarium near Southampton, and it made her feel ill in a whole new way.

Grace came to a stop, as if to keep her world from further unraveling, and a tear rolled down her cheek. She looked back at her trail of footprints in the sand. It was all catching up with her at that moment. Everything was welling up in her at once—fear, disbelief, anger—and Grace suddenly couldn't stand it anymore.

Now they're having a go at us. Her grandfather's words would not let her go. She looked up as the tears flowed freely down her face.

"God, I ...I haven't been to church very often." She was not in the habit of praying, especially out loud, but at that moment she was barely aware of it.

"But please, *please* protect my family, this town, this country. It's getting worse and we need help now. Please...we need a helping hand." As she said it Grace remembered looking up at the tall form of John Perceval with his outstretched hand. Did fate bring him to her there, in the street, someone she had barely known for so long, when she really needed it? How would that work? Maybe fate brought his grandfather, the Arthurian scholar, to Stokehill, and that started it. Maybe...

Oh, who knows. She let out a sigh to the whole sea and sky, and for a while she felt better.

Suddenly she saw through her tears a sailboat a half mile out where there had been only white-capped waves a moment before. It was heading toward her.

"Where on earth did that come from?"

Grace watched the boat reach the shore and saw a man climb out and wade into the surf. The two figures who remained in the boat quickly turned it about with little apparent effort and headed quickly back out to sea.

The man was walking straight toward her, and she noticed that something was different about him. He was wearing a dark brown cloak that fell down below his knees, and it was now soaked up to his waist. Grace looked to see if the two figures in the boat were similarly dressed, but strangely, the boat had already disappeared.

"Mustn't let a stranger see me crying," and she wiped her face again and began blinking her eyes. He was about forty yards away when Grace looked again, and the closer the man got, the more unusual he looked. He wore the brown cloak and his trousers were tucked into unusual-looking boots, and he had a full beard.

"Looks like he's in costume!"

They were perhaps twenty yards apart when Grace realized the man was tall, six foot three or so.
Dad's height, she thought.

He stopped and looked at Grace like he wanted to ask her something.

"Good afternoon," the man said in a Welsh or perhaps an Irish accent. He spoke in a dignified and yet a familiar way, as if he knew her, but Grace was sure he was not from Stokehill.

"Hello." Grace tried not to stare at his clothes.

"I'm wondering if you could help me. I'm looking for a small lake nearby, fed by a spring," the man said, smiling, then suddenly looking more serious. "Do you know where that is?" He spoke as if there wasn't a moment to lose.

Grace looked at him, standing dripping wet in his theatrical attire. What in heaven's name could be so urgent about the old fishing hole? But he seemed desperate, and Grace felt sympathetic toward him.

"Yes, that's Lady's Well," she answered. "It's on my way home. I can show you where it is if you like."

"I would be very grateful," he replied courteously.

Grace waited for a moment, expecting the man to introduce himself; when he didn't, she turned and led him off the beach and up to the road. She could not help peeking at his clothing as they walked along the winding path.

"Are you . . . new to the area?" she asked.

"No, I am from here originally, but it has been a very long time," he said, choosing his words carefully. "I am returning because of the war."

Grace sighed. "A lot of people are leaving because of the war."

The man turned toward her with a smile. "You haven't left."

Grace thought of her father, and her grandfather, and she seemed to see the line of her ancestors going all the way back, and it suddenly occurred to her that it if the bombing continued much longer, the town of Stokehill could end up sharing the same fate as her family name.

"This is my home. It's the only place I know."

As they continued walking, it occurred to Grace that when the man said he was returning, he meant he was only *just* returning—on that small boat.

That's odd, she thought. Where in the world was he coming from? She looked again at his clothing, wet to the waist.

"Those are . . . unusual clothes you're wearing," Grace observed, as if for the first time.

It's also a little unusual that he hasn't introduced himself, she thought. *Should I?*

"Yes, do you know where I could get something more appropriate? More like what you're wearing, perhaps," he replied innocently. He was looking at Grace's scarlet track uniform.

What *I'm* wearing? Grace was caught off guard, and could only stammer, "Uh, well, this isn't really appropriate either, it's just for running. Alfred's in town has men's clothing."

He smiled. "I suppose that was a strange question," he offered with a disarming chuckle. Grace smiled with relief.

He's eccentric, she thought, but in an engaging way.

She continued along with him to Lady's Well. Most of her friends would have simply given him directions to the pond and left him to find his own way. But Grace enjoyed the company of older men; she seemed to find a comfort in their presence that she didn't find with other people, and she was sometimes slow to part company with them.

Sunlight began to puncture the gray wall of clouds as they continued up the old road, leaving the salt air and the sounds of the surf behind them. They finally came to the dirt path that led to Lady's Well. Grace had fully intended to send the stranger down the path and continue on her way home, but she stopped. Something seemed to be pulling her down the trail, an attraction of some kind that was hiding deep in the shadows of the oaks and the hemlocks. Her head started to spin a little as she stood on the roadway.

"Lead the way!"

And to her surprise, Grace found herself walking down the woodland trail and away from the safety of the road, past the clutching undergrowth and deep into the woods. A strange feeling began stealing over her, a sense that she was approaching an historic or holy site. She had been to the old fishing hole a hundred times, and she knew she never had that feeling before. Her heart began to race.

The woods opened before them and there was the small, shaded lake, lying like a sheet of glass amidst the wall of trees.

"There it is," Grace said, but she could barely hear herself. The silence of the surrounding woods was ringing in her ears. She shook her head, but it was no use. The air was heavy and dead still, as though someone had laid a heavy, invisible blanket over the whole area that stifled all sound.

Grace was about to leave, but she hesitated. She saw the man approach the edge of the water; he stood rigid, like a soldier at attention. His gaze was focused on the middle of the pond, as if he were searching for something in the water.

Suddenly, out of the depths a shining metal object began to rise slowly, emerging from the center of the lake.

A sword! thought Grace. The hair on the back of her neck bristled. As the sword emerged, the hand thrusting it became visible.

"There's someone under the water!" she cried, and everything seemed to move in slow motion.

It appeared to be a woman's hand, draped in some shining white garment, holding the sword straight up toward the sky. The man made no reply; he seemed rapt by the scene. Something stirred deep in Grace's memory, something vague, from long ago.

Just then, the man, his clothes still wet from the surf, started wading into the lake. He was soon in water up to his waist.

He's going in to get the sword! Who is this man?

The water was up to the man's chest when he reached the hand with the sword. Grace's head was swimming as she watched him take the sword and hold it aloft, then slowly wade back to shore, while the hand disappeared silently into the water.

Grace knew why it all seemed so familiar. She watched the man emerge from the lake, water pouring off him as he held the sword aloft. She felt herself fall to her knees. Grace felt the tip of the sword lightly touch first the top of her head, then one shoulder, then the other.

"I am Arthur. I have returned."

2. The Korr Stigmata

"Rise . . ." Arthur said with an inflection in his voice.

He wants me to say my name.

"Grace. Grace Arundel," she replied as she stood up, her heart pounding.

She stared open-mouthed at the tall, soaking-wet man holding the massive broadsword. He had clear gray eyes, a strong bearded jaw and dark disheveled hair, and even though there was something familiar about his face, there was only one name that came to her mind, and she knew it was utterly impossible.

Arthur, something inside roared, *King Arthur?* She felt her life had suddenly been cleaved into two parts by the great sword: everything up to that moment, and everything that would follow.

"What's happening?" Grace asked, as if in a dream. "Why are you here?" For a moment she didn't know if she should let the dream play out, or try to snap herself out of it. *Snap out of it, of course!* But try as she might, nothing seemed to be changing.

Arthur lowered the sword to his side.

"What was promised long ago has finally come to pass. I am the champion of the sovereignty of this land, the Pendragon, and I have waited all the long years for this moment. I only hope that I have not waited too long. An enemy is gathering himself for an invasion, and he grows stronger every day."

"B-but there have been enemies before…"

"Yes, there is something much different this time—something else that this enemy wants." He looked at Grace.

"I need your help, Grace Arundel." Grace was awash with fear, and she felt her knees begin to tremble. It was moving too fast and she had to do something.

"Wait, please…who is that in the pond?" With a great effort she turned her head slowly back, and the water was calm again.

Arthur smiled patiently. "I know this is not easy for you. But this is all real, as real as the threat that is looming." He took a breath. "As for the pond, she for whom it was named."

But Grace's mind seemed to have slowed down, like her brain had turned into concrete, and she did not understand. It was all weighing down on her, slowing everything down, and she couldn't speak.

"It was not by accident that I came to you on the beach just now. There is much about you that I know. I asked you to state your name just now, but not because I did not know it. You will be of..." he hesitated, "...importance to me, and to this land at this most desperate hour."

Importance? Grace understood the word, but she was miles away from knowing what it could possibly mean for her. She racked her brain but only the dream part of her mind seemed to be working. It was too much, and she knew she had to find a way to snap out of it.

"I'm sorry," she finally managed to find the words, "I hope you don't think I'm being rude, but this is all—I don't know—I can't—*importance?*" She realized she was starting to babble and she stopped. *I need to leave.*

Arthur smiled again, and waited for a moment. "I understand. But if you change your mind, I will need some regular clothes."

Grace felt herself actually give a little laugh. "*Clothes?* I'm sorry, but..." That was it, and she tried to take a step back but tripped awkwardly. Arthur continued to smile placidly as he reached out his hand to her, touching her elbow.

"Careful!" he said gently. "We need you in one piece." She looked at him incredulously for a second, then managed to turn and slowly start down the path back to the road. But each step was still an effort, and her mind was not yet back to normal.

"I'm sorry, but *really*..." she said over her shoulder.

Then he called to her. "If you do change your mind about the clothes, can you meet me back here at dawn?" Grace looked back at him, even more incredulous, and he was smiling at her, ever patiently. She could only shake her head, and she forced herself down the path.

"Thank you, Grace Arundel," he called out.

Grace's heart was still racing and she began to run as soon as she reached the road. She did not stop until she arrived at the front gate of her red brick home, and as the evening star shone overhead she stood frozen with her hand on the latch. Grace did not know what to make of what she had just witnessed at Lady's Well, and the dreamy daze was still thick in the air around her, so that none of the familiar things—the white gate, the house, the curving street—looked quite the same.

An elderly woman out for an evening walk with her perfectly groomed Yorkshire terrier waved from across the narrow street.

"Hello, Grace," she called. "Been out for a run?"

"Oh, hello, Mrs. Davies," Grace said with her bravest face, as she tried to catch her breath. "Yes, a run usually helps clear my head, but this time it seems to have made things worse."

"Oh, I'm sorry dear," replied Mrs. Davies. "I hope you're all right."

All right? Far from it, Grace thought. She seemed to be seeing everything at Lady's Well, like she was still there.

"I say, Grace, are you alright?"

Get inside or she'll have you here chatting for half an hour.

"Yes, thanks!" Grace called over her shoulder, as she edged up to the house.

She opened the front door, and immediately Grace could make out the familiar voice of her grandfather from the kitchen. He sat at the oak kitchen table wearing the same green plaid shirt Grace had seen countless times, drinking tea and visiting with Grace's mother. His kind old face lit up when Grace entered the room.

"There's my granddaughter," he smiled. He noticed her scarlet tracksuit. "Out for a run, Grace?"

Grace walked over to her grandfather and mechanically kissed his wide forehead.

"Yes, granddad," It was still taking an extra second for Grace's mind to process anything put to her.

Mary Arundel looked up from the stove, wiping her hands on her apron. Her dark hair was streaked with gray, and her face still bore the stress and strain of her recent ordeal. Hanging from her neck was her familiar squared cross necklace with the five dark gems.

"*Running*? I suppose that's so she can get away from all the men that are chasing her," she cracked. Mr. Fisher cowered in his chair.

Grace stood stunned for a second, but her mother's remark was like a whip that shot out and snapped her out of her daze. Her jaw tightened, ready for battle. But her grandfather's presence, cringing at the kitchen table, combined with her mother's condition, weighed on her and she hesitated.

"I need to go wash up. I'm going out with John," she fumed, and she stormed indignantly out of the kitchen and upstairs to her room, closing the door with a bang.

Her mother stopped her cooking and turned around at the stove, making a loud, protracted sigh as she did, like the sound of air coming out of a tire.

"Dad, she's driving me crazy," she said, simmering. "There's a war on, and she's either running, or out with her friends, and now it's John *Perceval*—like everything's as normal as you please." She said his name like it pained her.

"Yes," he replied calmly, as a smile started to grow on his face. "I think she could do a lot worse."

"But what was wrong with Roger?" Mary jabbed the spatula in the general direction of the large estate to the northeast. "The Harrolds are one of the oldest families in England, and people in their class don't marry down very often. Grace may *think* she didn't love him, but..." She turned frustrated back to the stove as her thought evaporated. Her father sat with the smile straining on his face as she continued.

"Marriage is a sacrifice, let me tell you. If it's not one thing, it's something else. But don't tell Grace that. To her it has to be all fairy tales and Camelot."

That evening, despite a steady stream of commentary from her mother and a good case of nerves, Grace went on her first date with John. He was anxious to see the new Vivian Leigh picture at Stokehill's only movie theater, and so for the very first time in her adult life Grace found herself dating someone other than Roger. She was surprised how quickly she felt comfortable with John, and almost as soon as they sat in their seats they were holding hands, watching the newsreel reports of the war with Germany.

The images of the destruction in London horrified them both: fires raging in the jagged skeletons of buildings and houses. And as film footage ran of people being pulled from the rubble, the narrator spoke about the trauma people were experiencing, even those who weren't injured. Everyone was affected in some serious way, the voice said, every man, woman and child.

"Maybe it's time to quit working on my thesis and enlist," John agonized as he watched the flickering screen. Grace said nothing, but she noticed she was squeezing his hand tighter.

Then the newsreel changed to older footage from the King's coronation. The narrator spoke about the king in a rousing, patriotic voice, as he sat in the Coronation Chair receiving his crown.

Grace wasn't listening; she was wondering what the King was really like in person. She always watched older men keenly, most of the time without being aware she was doing it. She couldn't really remember her father, since he had died when she was four, but Grace had always wondered what he was like and what he would do in given situations. *Would Dad have sat that way?* part of her wondered as she watched the king. Then Grace thought of what she had witnessed that afternoon at Lady's Well.

Did I really see that? *Or am I going through some kind of war trauma?* She knew the answer. Of course it must be trauma—she was reacting to the war just like everyone, especially her mother. The apple doesn't fall far from the tree. But this strange Arthurian twist had Grace spinning–something about it was different. She needed to tell someone.

Grace looked at John sitting next to her, his blue eyes and handsome face illuminated by the movie screen.

"John, you've studied…the Arthurian material a great deal, haven't you?"

He turned to her from the screen.

"Of course," he smiled, "only full time for the past three years." He knew everyone at the small university knew his field of study, including Grace.

She wanted to say more, but just then the newsreel ended and the feature began to play, and Grace hesitated.

The apple doesn't fall far from the tree. But that wasn't it, and she knew it. Deep inside Grace knew that she didn't hallucinate—she saw the sword rise from the water. She was no longer looking at the movie screen, but at all the people in front of her, their heads silhouetted by the screen.

What if this is it, the thing that will save all of them--save the whole country? And even as she was telling herself how impossible it was, she found herself turning again to John.

"John," she whispered, "he didn't die, did he?"

Only after a moment did John realize that Grace was speaking to him. "What? Sorry, who didn't die?" He was engrossed in the larger-than-life face of Vivian Leigh on the screen. Grace moved closer to his ear.

"Arthur," she whispered, "King Arthur. He didn't actually die, did he?"

With some effort John turned his attention away from Vivian Leigh.

"Yes, that's right, at least if you believe Sir Thomas Mallory." He forced a polite smile at her.

"Of course," Grace replied as she turned back to the screen. The movie had gone at most another minute before Grace returned to John's ear.

"What else did they call him?" she whispered. "Arthur, I mean...it was Pen-something." John turned quickly, then he smiled.

"Pendragon," John answered patiently, keeping one eye on Vivian Leigh. "He was called the Pendragon, which basically meant he would always and forever be on call to protect the country in her most desperate hour." He waited politely; still anxious to return to Vivian Leigh but wanting to be sure he had satisfied Grace.

"I wonder what's keeping him!" he added with a grin. He expected at least a chuckle from Grace, but she only sat back in her seat, lost in thought. Only after a minute did she force a smile and mumble.

"Thanks."

That night, Grace lay in her bed wide awake, churning over her deteriorating relationship with her mother. It came to a head that week, but it really all began the month before, the day she broke her engagement with Roger. She had done a good job of putting that whole episode out of her mind, but it had not set well with her mother, who thought she had squandered her best chance at marriage. Grace couldn't picture herself becoming one of the Harrolds, and if the truth were told, she couldn't picture giving up her name at all, not to mention giving up running for good—running simply wouldn't do with *that* family. All of it would hasten the end of the Arundels in Stokehill, and it felt to her as if the last link with her late father would be severed. She remembered when it had all come out during their first really big fight, and the words were still ringing in her ears.

"You just want me to have all that money, and to hell with my name, *our name*."

"And you're twenty-five now, and do you know what they call unmarried women at that age? *Spinster.*" The word still dripped with venom.

Grace turned over and finally managed to drift off to asleep. After a time, she had a vivid dream of King Arthur riding into Stokehill on a white horse and in full armor, holding Excalibur aloft as a crowd of people gathered around him. Grace froze, not sure whether or not to follow. She was staring at Arthur's strangely familiar face when suddenly she realized it was her father's face, not Arthur's, and he was standing in front of her, close and full of passion. Was it the same face?

"Go, Grace! Follow him! It's the best thing you can do," he implored.

Suddenly she woke up, his voice still ringing in her ears. It was morning, much earlier than Grace usually awoke. And although she was normally a slow riser, Grace was wide awake.

"What if he's gone?" Grace said to the empty room. She dressed and hurried downstairs to the spare room, where her father's old clothes were kept.

Dawn had broken cool and clear over the woods, and Grace found herself again at Lady's Well. Across the still lake stood Arthur, tall and motionless at the water's edge, his brown cloak drawn around him and his inscrutable face locked onto the surface of the water. Grace stopped. He looked like a yogi in a meditative trance, and she dared not disturb him.

What in the world can he be thinking? She had no idea, so she waited in the silence of the woods, holding the paper sack full of her father's old clothes, for some signal that he was ready to receive her. As she waited, she began to feel anxious, and nagging fears began to whisper to her.

Who *really* is this man? And what did I really see yesterday, anyway, that I let myself get all worked up? Grace peered into the murky water, not sure exactly what she was looking for. She saw nothing, but she felt her hope beginning to deflate like a balloon.

"I need to end this silliness right now and part company with this Arthur, whoever he is," she puffed, straightening herself up.

Then the cloaked figure began to stir, and Grace saw his face fix on her. It startled her and she nearly dropped the sack of clothes. He was looking at her with the same intensity he had shown during his meditation, and Grace had the urge to leave the bag and run home as fast as she possibly could. His hand emerged from the cloak and began to wave her over.

"He wants me to go over there—I'll just hand him the bag, then leave."

As she started over, her knees began to shake so that she had to take care not to trip and fall on the sloping lakeshore. Grace knew the only other time her knees shook like that was in the national championship meet, in her last year as an undergraduate. Somehow she managed to fight through her nerves and finish a respectable third place.

You're being ridiculous, she told herself as she approached him. Now speak up like an adult and get this over with.

But when she reached him nothing came out of her mouth, and she stood mute in front of the towering figure with the intense countenance. Then his face changed, and he was suddenly looking on her in a kind, fatherly way.

"Good morning," Arthur said, as his gray eyes studied her face.

"Good morning," she answered. *Now what do I say?*

"Did you—were you all right—did you sleep well last night?" He must have slept right here last night! She couldn't imagine spending the night in the woods.

"Fine, thank you."

Grace handed him the paper sack with her father's clothes, and she was surprised how good it made part of her feel, but the rest of her was in turmoil. Part of her accepted this man as the help she prayed for, and there was hope again in her heart, but her intellect could only regard the whole notion as not only ridiculous, but insane. She was torn, and to make matters worse she was now handing over the clothes of her departed father to this stranger.

"Here are some clothes. I hope they fit." Then she added softly, "He was about your size."

"Thank you," Arthur smiled at her, with all of the intensity in his face as before, only now radiating kindness. It illuminated Grace, and again she felt her doubts about Arthur begin to fall silently from her like leaves from a tree. She had crossed a line that she wasn't aware of, that she didn't know she had crossed. Whatever it was, this man was more real and more sane than anyone she had ever met, and Grace felt her resistance was simply not necessary.

"Can I ask you something?" she began.

"Of course."

"Yesterday you said you are the Pendragon. Are you still the king, too, after all this time?"

"I am Arthur," he replied. He spoke his name with such a power that it seemed to ripple out through the woods in concentric circles, like the water in the pond. Even though Grace was standing on two feet, it felt like part of her was kneeling before him. "What was is no longer important."

Finally she spoke again. "And you have come back to help us? In the war?"

"Yes."

Yes. Grace felt the warm glow again in her very center, but Arthur's brow began to look troubled.

"But I will need your help, as I said last evening," he added.

"Anything," Grace heard herself say. *Anything?* Why did I say that? What can I do?

"We will not be fighting on the front lines," Arthur said with a smile, sensing her discomfort. "Our fight will take place behind the lines, in the world of shadows and spies. But it will be dangerous, too."

"Shadows and spies?" She swallowed, she wasn't expecting that. "How will fighting there help us in the war against the Germans?"

"By keeping something out of the enemy's hands that he most keenly desires," Arthur said as he looked down the dirt path to the road leading back to the beach, and across the channel to the continent.

"Is it a weapon?"

"It can be, in the wrong hands. It is something of great power," Arthur replied. "Great, mysterious power, of which I know precious little."

Grace flashed back to a dream she had the month before, around the time she broke up with Roger, when every day the newspapers were full of stories about the German conquests. She'd dreamt that they had made a bomb that would destroy the world, and everyone and everything in it. She remembered how the dream had ended: from her bed she was somehow watching the bomb going off across the Channel, and the explosion kept getting larger and larger until it crossed the sea to England. She remembered how she had woke up in a cold sweat, filled with dread, thinking it was the worst dream she'd ever had.

Arthur continued. "However, there is someone who can help me—help us," he said, looking at Grace. "But he is a long way from here. It would be well if we had some means of getting there."

Grace was confused. "Means of getting—do you mean a car?"

"If that is what they are called, then yes."

She thought of John picking her up that night in his father's old car. "I think I know someone that can help us," she said as she felt hope well up again in her heart.

Some weeks before, on a hot dry summer day in the south of France, the war came to the mountain village of Montsegur. The remote town of dirty stuccoed buildings had eluded the conflict that had rocked Europe and left France split in two. But the inevitable arrived that morning in the form of a convoy of trucks emblazoned with the Iron Cross, and full of SS soldiers in black shirts.

A dark-haired boy perched in an olive tree watched the line of trucks drive purposefully up the mountain. He had never seen trucks like that before, but somehow he knew what it meant. He fell out of the tree and staggered into the village, as the trucks were already engulfing everyone and everything in a deafening din and a billowing brown cloud of dust.

"Germans!" he gasped. He tried to scream, but his small voice was drowned in the all the noise.

"Wake up! The Germans are coming!"

A few days later, in the cellars beneath Montsegur castle, one of the two ranking *SS* officers watched over the excavation with an older gentleman. Otto Rahn was a heavy man with a handlebar moustache and weak eyes that squinted through wire-framed eyeglasses. He was not in an *SS* uniform, but wore a plain black suit and tie. Only his lapel pin revealed his allegiance: the double lightning bolt of the *Sig*-rune, the ancient Germanic rune of power, and insignia of the *SS*.

"Please don't worry, Monsieur Perelles, we will clean up before we're done," Rahn smiled, as they both watched the patchwork of square holes being dug by the black-shirted *SS* troops. Perelles, the stooping, gray-headed patriarch of his family and owner of Montsegur, only coughed and spat on the ground before storming off.

At the far end of the cellar, a senior uniformed officer smoking a cigarette started toward Rahn. He was tall with graying blonde hair and sharp blue eyes, and he strode across the cellar as if he, and not the old stooping French man, was the real owner of Montsegur. As he walked by, the soldiers one by one stopped their digging to watch him.

He passed an arched alcove that was screened from view by canvas sheets on wooden frames. An armed guard was posted in front of it, and no one but the two senior officers were allowed to enter. The uniformed officer stopped in front of Rahn.

"We have been here two weeks. There's nothing else down here but dirt, Herr Rahn, and General Koln is due in the morning," he said, squinting through the cigarette smoke. "And if you knew the General as well as I do, you would know how disappointed he will be that we have fallen behind schedule." All the soldiers were now watching, anticipating another confrontation between the two officers.

"I am well aware of the General's schedule, Colonel Streicher," Rahn snapped. "We have seen something of the highest importance here," he motioned toward the alcove, "so the likelihood is that there is more that cannot be seen. And I am tired of telling you that this kind of work does not lend itself to scheduling. So the sooner you continue, the happier we both will be."

Streicher began to look amused. "I am only trying to help you, Herr Rahn. We are peers, after all." He said the word *peers* with a lilt that brought a chuckle out of some of the men.

"Yes, we are both colonels, and I wish you would accord me the respect due my rank, Herr Colonel."

Streicher laughed, then took a step closer to Rahn. "Your *rank?* You have an honorific, Herr Rahn, not a rank! Who do you think these soldiers would listen to, you in your suit or me? If I told them to lock you up, what do you think they would do? If I told them to shoot you, do you think they would hesitate?" Perspiration formed on Rahn's brow.

"Please, Colonel," Rahn pleaded softly, "please get back to work."

Streicher began to look bored.

"As you wish, Herr Rahn," he sighed. He took a drag on his cigarette as he turned and worked his way back through the excavation, waving at the men to resume their digging.

Rahn wiped his brow with his handkerchief. His book *Croisade contre le Graal* had caught the eye of the head of the *Schutzstaffel* himself, Herr Himmler. It was Himmler who had personally invited Rahn to join the *SS*. Rahn's book laid out his theory on the existence and the actual physical location of the

Holy Grail, which fed Himmler's seemingly endless appetite for the mystical and the occult.

But just as Himmler wanted more than simply an army of soldiers, Rahn wanted to do more than write arcane books. He saw an opportunity to grab a position of power and influence in the *SS*. He had boldly convinced the Reichsfuhrer that the Holy Grail was more than just a legend, that it did indeed exist and that *he* could find it. And if it could be found . . .

"It would be a sign that God himself was conferring his blessing upon the Thousand Year Reich," Rahn said to himself as he watched all the activity before him, reliving the moment when he had persuaded Himmler to begin the search for the Grail. But now he must deliver something new—anything to show progress. He knew the *SS* was not an organization that tolerated failure, and he had heard that the Fuhrer himself was watching with interest.

Rahn finally realized that some of the soldiers were not working.

"Dig! Dig!" he roared, his voice echoing off the stone walls and ceiling.

The next day two open-top German staff cars stormed through the village and up the road to Montsegur castle in a whirlwind of dry, brown dust. The whole town collectively stopped what it was doing and watched the two cars fly by, as the cloud of dust slowly rolled toward the sky.

Near the road by the corner of an abandoned, shuttered storefront, a tall stranger in dark glasses and a broad-brimmed hat studied the two cars as a cheroot dangled from his fingers. He had arrived in Montsegur the same day as the Germans, but he was barely noticed in all the excitement. He watched intently as the two cars wound their way up the road and toward the castle gate, squinting through his dark glasses, as if with a little extra effort he could see through the massive castle walls and into the heart of all the activity.

"A general! Has Professor Rahn found something? If he has, then *my* general will surely want to know about it."

He took one last drag, cast his cheroot away with a flick of his thumb and forefinger, and slowly began to ascend the road to the castle.

Herr Rahn, Colonel Streicher, and a makeshift honor guard of four of his men were standing in the courtyard of the castle as the two open staff cars came through the gate and made a wide arc, pulling up within a few feet of where they stood. A thin, older officer in a uniform caked with dust, and a grim expression on his face got out and Streicher and the honor guard snapped to attention.

"Welcome, General Koln" said Rahn, with a strained smile.

"Thank you, Herr Rahn," Koln replied. "At ease, Colonel," he said to Streicher, and the general wiped his brow and his neck with his handkerchief.

"So this is Montsegur?" he sneered, unimpressed by modest-sized, ancient stone building, in need of some repair. "It is very...hot." Rahn shifted his feet nervously as Streicher stood motionless in the hot sun.

"Yes, Herr General, this is Montsegur," Rahn muttered. "Please come inside," he added with more enthusiasm, hoping the conditions indoors would improve the general's mood. He extended his right hand to the open doorway in the shadows behind him, and the three men walked inside. They entered a dark, cool stone entrance hall, sparsely furnished and quiet as a tomb.

"Would you like to see the activities and the—" Rahn began.

"Yes, yes," Koln interrupted. "Let's see what you have."

Rahn led them through a doorway on their left, which opened to a long hallway that ended at a round swelling in the wall, with an ascending staircase on the right and a descending staircase on the left. The swelling was the interior of one of the two castle towers.

They descended the staircase on the left in silence, save for the sound of their boots echoing on the stone steps.

Rahn's anxiety was growing by the minute. He didn't know General Koln well, except that the general was more pragmatic than Reichsfuhrer Himmler and less interested in mystical subjects. At *SS* headquarters, Rahn had never given the general's attitude a second thought, but here he suddenly felt vulnerable, and the fear of saying the wrong thing left him choked with silence. And the presence of Colonel Streicher on his heels only added to his anxiety.

The stairway opened to a large basement that consisted of innumerable stone arches, where twenty *SS* soldiers were digging in large, square holes with rolled-up shirtsleeves, as artificial lights blazed. The men stopped working when they saw the General and came to attention.

"Tell them to continue their work, please, Colonel," Koln said to Streicher as he carefully surveyed the cellars.

Streicher took a step forward and called out, "Back to work!"

He stepped aside so as not to obstruct the general's view. Rahn anxiously studied the general's grim countenance as he looked around.

Suddenly the general's gaze fixed on something and his expression brightened noticeably. Rahn felt himself relax for the first time since the general's arrival, and he looked to see what had captured Koln's attention.

Of course, Rahn thought. He was looking at the alcove behind the canvas partition.

"Is that it?" Koln asked after a moment, in a hushed tone.

"Yes, Herr General," Rahn announced in a proud voice. "The Korr Stigmata. Would you like to see it?"

And it seemed to Rahn that General Koln looked him in the face for the first time ever.

"Yes!"

Later, when the tour was completed, the three men were smoking cigarettes in the baronial dining hall. The windows overlooked the rugged, forested mountains, and the setting sun streaked through the large windows and across the huge oaken dining table. Rahn excused himself, and when he was gone, General Koln immediately put down his cigarette and went over to the window where Streicher was standing.

"Colonel Streicher, has anything else been found?"

"No, Herr General," Streicher replied. The room got suddenly darker as the sun disappeared behind the mountains.

"And Herr Rahn already knew the Korr Stigmata was here, correct?"

"Yes, Herr General," Streicher replied. "It was in his book."

"I did not read his book, Colonel," he sneered. "It has been two weeks, do you think he is close to finding anything *else?*"

Streicher knew he was being led by the general's questions but he did not hesitate.

"No, Herr General, I don't think he will find anything else."

"I didn't think so," Koln said as he turned to look out the window at the range of mountains. "The Reichsfuhrer is anxious to begin the English phase of the search before *Operation Sea Lion* begins."

He turned back to Streicher.

"Colonel, we would like you to begin work immediately on the English phase. You and I will leave after dinner. I have a plane waiting at the airstrip."

"Yes, Her General," Streicher responded with a click of his heels.

Outside the castle, the dark figure in a broad-brimmed hat was moving in the twilight toward a small, unguarded door in the wall. He slipped silently inside, softly closed the door behind him, and entered a small tool shed, where he made himself comfortable on a short stool.

"I am very interested to see what you have found, Professor Rahn," he said. "Could it be that which has been lost all these years?"

3. Ankerwyke Hill

Grace sat dumbfounded in the cramped office of her academic advisor amidst the dusty stacks of papers and books. Professor Markson's normally benign face was wrinkled with worry, and his usually wild gray mop of hair hung limp and tired around his head. It was her monthly progress meeting for her dissertation, but they never even began talking about her paper.

"I'm sorry, Grace, but the university cannot operate safely. It's only a matter of time before it must close." He looked at her, and Grace realized that she had never seen Professor Markson truly sad until that moment.

"This war is changing everything."

Ten minutes later, Grace was walking down the grass-bordered pavement under a row of chestnut trees toward the center of Stokehill. It was one of her favorite parts of town, but her anxiety was making her uncomfortably hot, and she could not enjoy it.

She hopped over the gurgling Culvert and stopped, bending down to dip her hand in the cool water. The Culvert was a trickle of a stream paved in cobblestones that meandered its way under and through the center of Stokehill until it emptied into Lady's Well. It was only a few feet wide in most places, not much different from a large drainage ditch, but its flow of spring water was ceaseless. Moss and green water plants flourished in it, and even though it occasionally flooded during heavy rains, the inhabitants of Stokehill were extremely fond of it. Grace loved it more than she knew.

She stood up, shaking the water from her hand, and turned a corner onto the nearly empty high street. There she saw the blackened remains of one of the bombed buildings. She stopped and stared dumbly at it for a moment, as Professor Markson's words rang in her ears.

This war is changing everything.

She couldn't bear to look at it any longer, and she moved on. She was already late for her meeting with John and his roommate, and Grace knew that looking at the destruction would only make her more upset than she already was.

Grace went into an open doorway set in a wall of green ivy. Above the door was hung a large wooden sign: The Waterway. The pub was normally full of students at that time of day, but now it was nearly empty, and she had no trouble spotting John and his roommate Dennis, at a table by the window, each with a pint of beer in front of him.

"What light through yonder doorway breaks," Dennis said puckishly, "The last of the Arundels."

John turned around to look, and a smile broke out on his face. He stood up as she approached their table.

"Grace!" He gave her a kiss on the cheek. He had had his dark hair cut earlier that day, was wearing a smart-looking jacket, and Grace was struck for a moment by the fact that he was the best-looking man in the place. But her meeting with her advisor was still weighing on her.

"Hello, John," she replied, somewhat distracted. "Hello, Dennis," Grace said to the thin, blonde-headed man across the table.

"Hello, Grace…" Dennis began, but Grace's pale expression made him go silent. John waved to the waitress, who soon brought Grace a pint.

Grace stared blankly at her glass full of beer.

"My advisor just told me it's only a matter of time before they close the university," she began.

Dennis' puckish mood began to flicker out, and he lit a cigarette.

"A good portion of the undergraduates have already moved away, and now members of the faculty are beginning to leave. There is hardly anyone left."

"What do you suppose it would take to get us out of this mess?" Grace asked no one in particular. "This war, I mean."

"A bloody miracle," Dennis answered, his voice dropping low. His two friends inclined their heads toward him. "I hear they're sizing us up, you know, taking inventory of all the good bits, art and such," he whispered, trying to sound flippant but looking quite pale. John's head hung down; the war was all the talk in the barber shop that morning. Grace recalled Arthur's words at Lady's Well. *The enemy is gathering himself for an invasion.*

Maybe they're wrong, she thought, groping for anything to keep the unraveling feeling from returning. But she looked at Dennis smoking his cigarette, and Grace knew he was right. He was working on his thesis in political science, and although he occasionally spent too much time in the pubs, his knowledge of current events was better than anyone she knew. Grace felt her hope deflating again.

"Of course, they're bombing us in hopes that we'll capitulate," he added. "But that will never happen, not with Mr. Churchill."

"Good for him," John interjected with a mixture of pride and anguish.

Grace looked at Dennis.

"So we're back to needing a miracle," she sighed. She suddenly wanted to bring up the subject of her experience at Lady's Well, but she didn't have the slightest idea how to do it, and it was frustrating her. Her fingers began drumming the table.

"Right," John said to her with a smile, trying to be cheerful.

As Grace smiled weakly back at him, she had an idea.

"And who believes in miracles these days?" she asked. She was careful to maintain her somber tone, but she was eyeing her companions' reactions.

"It's all fine stuff for fairytales and legends, but it doesn't happen in the real world," she added.

"Of course," John agreed quietly as he looked out the window, while Dennis simply nodded.

"Even if *King Arthur*, say, was to show up on our doorstep, what could he really do?" Her fingers began to fidget more nervously and she hid her hands under the table.

"Right," Dennis agreed with a sigh. "A medieval king with a sword and shining armor wouldn't be much help against the German planes." Then he turned half-heartedly to John. "Of course, that's more your field, old boy."

But John was looking curiously at Grace. He remembered her bringing up Arthur the night before at the cinema, and it was unusual for anyone, especially anyone he was *dating*, to show so much interest in the subject. He stared dumbly at her.

"That's the *second* time you've mentioned King Arthur," he said finally, more as a question than a statement, although he still managed a smile.

"Oh, is it?" she replied, and she tried to nonchalantly sip at her beer.

"Yes!" John answered emphatically. He sensed Grace was up to something as she sat next to him acting strangely nervous. He was beginning to find it charming, and he gave her a squeeze around the waist. Grace gave him a kiss on the cheek in return, but inside she was stuck.

Now what do I do? How do I talk about it without sounding like a lunatic? Try as she might, Grace could not see a way, and she grudgingly let the matter drop.

"I guess I've been thinking about miracles a lot these days," she finally replied. "Quite all right," Dennis offered.

"Yes, you're forgiven," John said to her with a smile, and for a moment they all returned to their beer. Then John realized that this was a chance to talk about one of his favorite subjects.

"The real Arthur lived in the absolute depths of the Dark Ages," he began, as he glanced at Grace. She was listening. For the first time, here was a woman who appeared genuinely interested in his subject, and John couldn't quite get over it. He felt his pulse quicken.

"He indeed had his sword, but there was no shining armor or idyllic castles, only wooden and brass shields, drafty forts, and leather jerkins," he continued, sitting up in his chair.

Grace was vividly picturing the man she had met on the beach.

"And he would have had a long brown cloak," she added absentmindedly. John stopped and looked at her, completely perplexed.

"Now *how* in the world did you know that?"

Grace's green eyes fixed straight ahead in panic. She quickly picked up her beer and took another sip.

"Uh, lucky guess," she mumbled. It was time to change the subject.

"Before I forget," she said affectionately to him, "a friend of mine needs a lift this evening somewhere out of town. I told him you might be able to help out. Do you mind?"

"Of course not, if the Germans cooperate," he replied, as he continued to look at her curiously.

Dennis put down his beer purposefully and looked at John. "Are you saying there was no Camelot and jousting and romance? Were all the stories just made up? Was there a King Arthur *at all*, or was it all a just lot of fluff?"

John's jaw tightened as he carefully positioned his beer glass in front of him.

"At the core of all the myth and legend there must have been a truly extraordinary man: a warrior and a leader—in those days the two went hand in hand—unsurpassed, not just in his ability to fight hand to hand or with the weapons of the day, but more importantly, in his ability to lead other men. He literally brought out the hero in each and every man under him, and it enabled him to overcome insurmountable odds time and time again. I daresay there have been few like him anywhere in the world, before or since."

John felt like he had just recited some kind of personal creed that he hadn't known he had, and the faces of his two companions reflected his passion as they sat in silence, listening to his every word. He continued.

"We who are used to daily newspapers forget the tremendous span of time in those days between when events occurred and when they were recorded. It was often decades and sometimes centuries. The Arthurian material that we're most familiar with was written down in the later Middle Ages, much of it in France, when there was jousting and full armor and chivalry and all that, so the stories are set in that time. But if there had been no truth at the core, then mere fluff would not have survived, especially for upwards of fifteen centuries. It must have all started with a great, great man."

Outside, a low, wailing sound was becoming louder and rising in pitch. The pub suddenly became silent. Dennis swallowed hard as he looked at them.

"The air-raid siren. Here we go again."

Colonel Streicher was pacing outside the Reichsfuhrer's conference room at *SS* headquarters in Berlin, nervously smoking a cigarette. An operations review was underway inside, and he was waiting to be called in for the briefing on the next phase of Operation Sangraal. He had heard that Himmler had personally selected him to lead this phase of the operation.

Streicher had been a career officer in the *Wehrmacht*, the regular army, before being recruited into the *SS* two years before. Although he had received choice assignments, including Operation Sangraal, he had grown to detest the way the *SS* operated. The needless butchering appalled him, and he was well aware that after joining, no one ever quit the *SS*. Those that tried either had some sort of bad accident or disappeared entirely. Streicher had come to refer to the change as the 'worst mistake of my life'.

After a long wait, the door was pulled open from the inside.

"Colonel Streicher," someone called. He quickly put out his cigarette and went inside.

When he entered the room, Streicher recognized all the *SS* high command seated at the magnificent round conference table. Himmler was seated across from the door, studying some documents in front of him. There were no available seats at the table, so Streicher stood along the wall near another junior officer.

A bald general with his hair combed over from one ear to the other was just finishing his briefing on Operation Sea Lion, standing in front of an oversized map of the English Channel. A dozen large red arrows pointed ominously to the English coast from various points on the Continent.

"I have every confidence that, assuming the Luftwaffe does its job, the Fuhrer's forces will be occupying London by Christmas Day." The room began to buzz with excitement, and Himmler grinned.

"Thank you, General von Klaus," he said. "Who's next?"

"Operation Sangraal," said the officer seated to Himmler's right. "General Koln."

Koln stood up and began the briefing, beginning with the personnel that would make up the team for the next phase of the operation. Streicher felt vulnerable as his qualifications for selection were presented, including his years studying history at Cambridge. He nervously bit his lip.

"So he's the highest-ranking anglophile we have," one of the generals said, and the room burst into laughter. Even Himmler was chuckling.

Streicher had been in the *SS* long enough not to be surprised. Even when a promotion or a key assignment was given out, someone was always there to get a dig in.

"Let me just say that my years in England provided me with more than ample motivation to want Operation Sangraal and Operation Sea Lion to succeed," Streicher replied as evenly as he could. The room quieted. Himmler looked at him with a smile.

"Very good, Colonel Streicher," he said. "Please continue, General Koln."

Koln continued with the remaining personnel selections, then covered details on tactics, and concluded with the logistics.

"Due to the urgency of the operation and the imminence of Operation Sea Lion, the team will be leaving immediately," Koln said as he finished, shuffling his papers.

"Excellent," Himmler said. "Good luck, Colonel Streicher."

Streicher gave a smart click of his heels. "Thank you, Herr Reichsfuhrer," he replied. He left the conference room and as he walked down a hallway bustling with officers, he reached for his cigarettes.

"Finally, after wasting all that time in Montsegur, we are back on track," he said to no one under his breath. He slowed to strike a match and light his cigarette, and a fire kindled in his eye.

Now we're getting somewhere.

Early that evening, John began the circuitous drive to Grace's house in his grandfather's old car. He tried to think how long it had been since he first took a liking to Grace, and he realized it was when he was thirteen, after his family had come to live with his grandfather in Stokehill following the death of his father. He heard the Arundel stories around town and in school, and he had always fancied Grace very much, as did all the other boys in their class. But since their undergraduate days Grace had always been on Roger's arm, and John had written her off in his mind as unattainable, referring to her among his friends as the future Mrs. Harrolds.

"Now a few bombs go off, and she's on my arm," he mused aloud in the old car as it sped along. "Maybe my luck's changing."

But her sudden fixation with King Arthur had thrown him. Was this an eccentricity of hers? In the past he always had the impression that she found her history classes a chore, when they were done she could never seem to leave them fast enough. He knew that for certain because he could never seem to get a chance to strike up a conversation with her. Then why the sudden fixation? Could this be why things had broken down between her and Roger?

There must have been a pretty good reason for her to give up all that money, he thought. He shrugged his shoulders as his hands gripped the steering wheel.

"Now *I'm* the one fixating."

He turned the corner and pulled up to Grace's house as the sun was just disappearing over the row of brick houses. He flew

up the steps and knocked at the front door, and when Grace
opened it, he was beaming at her.

"Hello, Grace!" He embraced her gently and gave her a kiss.

"Hello, John," she replied, smiling. "Shall we go?"

"After you," he said. He skipped to the car and held the door
open as she got in, then dashed around the other side and jumped
in. He turned the ignition key for a moment, but the engine
cranked noisily without starting. John didn't drive it often and he
had forgotten that it was often temperamental. His face showed
a hint of embarrassment as he turned it off and waited a minute.

"Where is your friend?"

Grace hesitated for a second.

"Lady's Well." She tried to sound like it was perfectly
normal, but she wasn't as convincing as she would have liked.
John looked at her, confused.

"Lady's Well? Is he fishing?" John looked like he was
processing the information for a moment, then he shook his head
and tried the car again. The engine roared to life.

"No—well, he *may* be fishing, I don't know." She cringed as
they drove off.

"He doesn't *live* there, does he? In the woods, I mean."

"Of course not!" Grace replied, almost offended, but her insides were knotting up. She suddenly wished Lady's Well was much further away so she could have time to compose herself. She couldn't believe that she was helping Arthur, first with her father's clothes, and now drawing John into it along with her. She remained silent, but inside she wanted to scream. What if she hadn't really seen what she saw, what if it *was* war trauma? What would John think of her? She would never have dreamed of getting Roger into something as crazy as this, whatever it was. But John was so different—he was someone with whom she wasn't afraid to make a mistake.

Soon they were driving up to the trail leading to the small lake; standing by the side of the road just ahead of them, they saw a tall, bearded man wearing a long raincoat. John pulled over slowly and stopped. They waited for a moment, but the man continued to stand there.

Suddenly Grace gasped. "John! He's never been in a car before."

John looked at her, baffled. Had it been anyone else, it would have put him over the edge. But it was different with Grace, and all he could do was look at her.

"He's never been in a *car* before?"

Quickly he got out and went around to where the man was standing. He could all but see the word *eccentric* in large letters in front of his face as he stomped though the gravel. He reached over and opened the back door for the man.

"Thank you," he said. He smiled at John with a tremendous confidence and presence, and despite his long hair and old clothes, he didn't appear to John to be the least bit eccentric.

"Not at all," John replied, and he found himself shaking the man's hand.

"John. John Perceval," he added.

"I am Arthur," he replied, and John was impressed by the iron grip of his hand. He flashed back to the time as a boy when he shook the hand of an admiral in the receiving line at a naval review in Portsmouth. He remembered how impressed he had been by the towering figure in the richly decorated uniform who looked him straight in the eye—it felt to John like he was meeting the King himself.

Arthur looked at the open door apprehensively for a moment before bending down and crawling awkwardly into the back seat, like he was entering a small rabbit hole. He made a great effort to right himself on the seat, while the car bounced and rocked under his substantial weight. Finally he appeared situated, and he looked back at John holding the door.

"Ready."

John closed the door and shook his head as he returned to his seat. He didn't know what to make of his new passenger. How could someone who appeared to be so noble also be so unsophisticated that he had never been in a car before? He couldn't help shooting a glance at Grace when he sat down, but she was still avoiding his glare.

"Are you all right, then?" she asked Arthur in the back seat.

"Aye," he replied thoughtfully, as he eyed the interior of the car as if he were trying to plan an escape route.

John turned the car around and it sputtered as he tried to accelerate, as if to complain about the extra passenger, but soon the engine smoothed out and they were on their way.

"Where to, Arthur?" As he spoke the name, he remembered Grace's recent preoccupation. He looked sideways at Grace

Now what could that mean? Are they *together* somehow on this eccentricity?

"Over the hill north of town," Arthur replied as he looked out the window, seeming more comfortable by the minute.

"John, what do you do?" Arthur asked pleasantly after a short while.

"I'm a graduate student at the university here, like Grace," he replied, looking in the rear-view mirror as he did. Then he realized his opportunity.

"And you? What do you do?" Grace shifted uncomfortably in the front seat. Arthur seemed to only partly hear the question.

"Me? I'm retired," he answered, as he continued looking out the window. "I had a career in the military."

Grace looked at John with a nervous smile, relieved with Arthur's reply, and decided it was time to change the subject.

"Uh, do you think we'll be back before dark? There's the curfew, and we're not supposed to be out driving then."

"I think that should be enough time," he replied. "If I can remember correctly where we're going."

Up ahead, a car they had been following came to a stop. It completely blocked the narrow lane they were driving on, and John patiently stopped his car to wait.

Suddenly Arthur leaned forward and managed to position his large face at John's open window.

"Make way!" he roared like a lion. *"Make way!"*

John nearly jumped out of his seat, while Grace sat petrified next to him. The car ahead of them finally lurched forward, and Arthur sat back in his seat with a satisfied expression on his face.

As John began driving again, Grace felt him looking at her. She finally smiled weakly at him, but inside she was so full of anxiety she was sure that if one more thing happened, she really would scream. They were leaving town and heading north as the western sky began to turn faintly pink. The road was empty.

"What brings a retired military man out on a night like this?" John asked after a while.

"The war. So I suppose you could say I'm coming out of retirement."

John was so distracted by Arthur and what to make of him that he kept driving, forgetting that he had no idea where they were going.

"Turn here!" Arthur said suddenly, as an old dirt road appeared on their right. John had to hit the brakes and back up the car before he was able turn onto the one-lane road.

"Sorry. It's been so long since I've been here that I didn't recognize the landscape."

"That's all right," John answered. "Do you remember how much longer it is?"

"It's not far now," Arthur replied, peering carefully out the front of the car.

I hope not, Grace thought, as she suffered silently in the front seat. Does John think I'm a complete lunatic?

The evening star began to shine again as Arthur sat up in the back seat.

"Here we are. This is as close as the road gets. Can we stop and walk the rest of the way?"

"Of course," Grace said, smiling at John. He smiled in return and pulled the car over onto the gravel shoulder.

We won't be back in time for curfew now, he thought, but he would have stayed out all night if Grace had asked him. *In for a penny, in for a pound.*

John and Grace got out of the front of the car as Arthur fumbled in the back with the door handle. Grace opened his door for him.

"Thank you." He stood up and looked around.

It was farmland—rolling green pastures in the daylight that were vast sheets of shadow now. The land rose to the east, where it was faintly light around the horizon, and there at the top was a prehistoric stone monument, silhouetted against the evening sky. Arthur studied it carefully.

"There it is."

John's mouth opened as he looked at the hilltop. He had been so preoccupied with Arthur that he failed to notice where they had been going. But he realized now where he was, and he couldn't believe it.

"The Ankerwyke Dolmen!" he said to himself.

Arthur turned to John.

"Is that its name? That is what we're looking for."

He turned back to the hill and immediately stepped through a gap barely visible in the fence and began to march across the field and up the slope to the dolmen.

Grace fell in behind him, then John, who quickly became lost in thought.

Very few people know the history, the legends about this dolmen, he thought, as he plodded along. Is it a coincidence that they brought *me* here?

It was now so dark they could no longer see their feet hit the ground, and it felt to John like he was floating above the dark, silent pasture—silent save for the crunch of their footsteps on the dry grass.

Professor Ashe had mentioned it, he recalled, in *Ley Lines of the Ancient Britons*, as having a connection with Stonehenge, exactly to the west and north. It aligned directly with those stones. A reputable but not widely read book.

Then there was that obscure work of Hungerford, a much lesser scholar, fixing the hill as the sight of one of the twelve battles of Arthur. The legendary Badon Hill, also called Mount Badon, right here in Stokehill, John thought. That was a bit farfetched.

But it was the eleventh century manuscript in the church archives back in town that had been the clincher, now gone forever thanks to the bombing. He remembered that freezing December day, four years before, when he himself had discovered it. A hoar frost had blanketed the area and he'd been huddled in the tiny, frigid church library when he came across it. The old manuscript was stuck between two drawers, and there it was, scribbled on the back, in Old English. He remembered the wonder, then the excitement, then later the pride he felt on making such a find. He felt afterward that his life as a scholar had begun that day in that cold room. How did his translation go?

On Ankerwyke where the bodies heap'd
But for the one knock, his vigil keep
Will rouse him from his chamber deep
There waits Merlin, yet asleep.

John looked up. They had arrived at the dolmen.

4. Glastonbury

When they came to the crest of the hill and the dolmen, there on the eastern horizon was the full moon, just beginning its climb of the evening sky. It lit the landscape in front of them with cool, silver light, and left the fields and everything behind them in darkness. But all Grace seemed to see was the massive, imposing stone monument in front of them.

It was comprised of two large boulders set upright in the ground about five feet apart, with another huge, flat rock laid across the top, forming a massive stone table. It had been there for time out of mind, straddling the hilltop like some ancient, crouching stone giant.

Arthur stepped forward to within arm's length of the monument and stood silently at attention. Grace stayed several paces back and waited uneasily, her nerves frayed. Finally John looked back to Grace and broke the silence.

"You didn't know we were coming here, did you, Grace?" he whispered with a bewildered look on his face.

"How in the world would *I* know?" she snapped, more forcefully than she would have liked. Even though Grace had no idea what was about to happen, she knew exactly why it was upsetting her. It was the same feeling she'd had at Lady's Well the day before.

Just then, Arthur slowly drew Excalibur from within his coat and held it aloft, and it shone like the moon herself. Grace looked at John, who appeared as stunned as she was to see Arthur produce the huge sword.

Where on earth did that come from? She had not noticed Arthur carrying it under his overcoat, and she was sure she would not have missed something so large. John instinctively took a step back, and Grace grabbed his hand. Her heart was now pounding in her chest, and it was all she could do to keep from screaming with excitement.

After a long pause, Arthur slowly brought the extended sword forward and down until the tip touched the topstone with a metallic *clang* that shattered the heavy silence. He then deliberately, almost ceremoniously returned the sword to his side.

A sound of movement came from the moon shadow of the dolmen, just a few feet away. Something or someone was stirring. Grace took another step back as her knees began shaking, and she felt John tighten his grip on her hand.

A figure rose from the shadow on the far side. It was a man wearing a hooded cloak, with his back toward them, looking around; he seemed to be orienting himself. Then he turned and faced them through the stone doorway of the dolmen. He was a large man with flowing gray hair and beard that were silver in the moonlight. Grace looked at Arthur, but he had not moved a muscle.

"Who summoned me?" the figure asked in a booming voice that seemed to shake the dolmen itself down through the earth and up through Grace's spine.

He stared long at Arthur, without giving any notice to Grace or John. Gradually his countenance brightened, and he slowly started walking around the huge stones.

Grace was now completely unnerved and wanted nothing more than to run back to the safety of the car. John was holding steady but he felt his heart pounding like a hammer in his neck and chest. Sensing their agitation, Arthur held out his hand behind him, and spoke very deliberately.

"Don't move." The man came around and stood facing Arthur.

"It has been a long time, my old friend," Arthur said.

"After so many ages, Arthur, you have returned," said the man in amazement.

"And now, so have you, Merlin."

"Merlin!" Grace said in awe.

"Merlin?" John tried to repeat, but had no breath to speak.

Then John looked at the large sword, and then to the man holding it, and he realized who he really was and what it all meant.

"*Arthur!*" John gasped, and though he found himself slipping down, he never felt his knees hit the ground.

Then Arthur turned, and as the stars wheeled overhead, he lightly touched John's head, then his left shoulder, then his right with the tip of the great sword, as he had done with Grace at Lady's Well the day before.

"Arise, John Perceval," he called out to the night sky.

Arthur and Merlin had moved off a few paces and were having a conversation that Grace and John could not quite hear. John continued to watch dumbfounded as Arthur and Merlin talked with each other.

"Do you *see* why I couldn't tell you?" Grace blurted out, still on edge but feeling less inclined to scream. But looking at John, she wasn't sure if he had even heard her.

He could not answer. For the first time in his life, the outspoken John Perceval was struck dumb. His whole life rushed up to meet him at that moment. Those things he had been studying for years now, some of which few others ever knew about, they had led up to this—somehow.

This is no coincidence, he realized. And it all happened through Grace. His head was spinning as he looked at her, and he still felt numb from his knees down.

Grace watched John staring at her, uncharacteristically silent, his eyes wide and his breathing heavy. *Why won't he say anything? Is this it, are we finished? Will he even give me a lift back to town?* But then she saw over John's shoulder the two great men still talking earnestly to each other. And she began to get the feeling that they were talking about she and John.

Yes, I'm not being silly, she thought, *they're looking at me as they talk.* She felt like she was being examined under a glass.

Suddenly the two men began walking over to where Grace and John were standing. Grace flinched, and John reached out and held her hand. She felt perspiration on his palms.

"This is Merlin," Arthur said evenly, trying neither to coddle them nor to intimidate them. Merlin said nothing but gave a short nod of his head.

"We've come to you because we need your help," Arthur continued.

"Aye," Merlin said.

"I'll do whatever I can." She looked at John out of the corner of her eye. He still had not spoken, and she felt sure he wanted no part of any of this. But something inside her would not let her walk away from the two men, whoever they were. She was prepared to do anything to help, even alone. Then John finally spoke.

"Yes, anything," he exclaimed. She turned to him and felt herself slowly smile.

Arthur was also smiling. "We must go to what is now called Glastonbury." He turned to Merlin. "Is that right, Glaston-bury?"

"Yes, Glastonbury," Merlin replied. "It is most urgent."

Arthur looked intently at them both. "Can you help us?"

Grace and John looked at each other, then back at the two men. "Yes, of course," they said in unison.

"Would t-tomorrow be acceptable, around midday?" John stuttered. He would have to borrow fuel coupons from his roommate.

Arthur smiled. "That would be fine. We will be here."

Grace and John both sensed that they were being given leave for the time being.

"Tomorrow, then, at midday," John repeated, and he moved a step backward and Grace did likewise.

"Tomorrow," Grace repeated.

"Thank you both," Arthur said earnestly.

They both waved and started back down the dark hill and got into in John's car, leaving the two great men atop Ankerwyke Hill. Merlin turned toward Arthur.

"I remember the last time we stood on this hilltop together."

"So do I, my friend," Arthur replied wistfully. "So do I."

On the road below, John turned the car around and began driving slowly back toward town, and Grace watched him as he drove with one hand and held the other to his forehead, like he had a sudden fever.

"The manuscript I discovered in the church...the whole reason I got into the doctoral program...I know I'm babbling, but I... I feel like I'm dreaming." He had never been hysterical before but he felt like he was getting close.

"I *know*. So do I," Grace smiled, relieved to no longer have to question her own sanity.

"Arthur came to me on the beach yesterday and said he returned because of the war. He said that he was here to keep something out of the enemy's hands, something that would make them invincible. But he said it wasn't exactly a weapon," she added emphatically.

John listened more calmly, without replying. They were now on the outskirts of the blacked-out town, and he turned off his headlights.

"Glastonbury," Grace said. "That's a long way, isn't it?"

"Yes…" John mumbled. He was thinking about Glastonbury, and the hair on the back of his neck stood up. Still he said nothing as they drove along the narrow, winding road.

"Why do you suppose they want to go to Glastonbury, of all places?" Grace asked, turning to him in the dark car.

"I don't know," John heard himself saying, "but Glastonbury has always been associated with"—he paused to clear his throat "—with the Holy Grail."

Far to the west, on an empty Dorset beach, a man in a black Macintosh stood smoking a cigarette. He was studying the darkening sea in front of him carefully, occasionally looking back behind him to see if he was being watched. It was deserted.

After a time he saw a long dark shape appear in the water a few hundred yards off shore, like a sea monster rising up from the cold depths. The man produced a flashlight from within his raincoat and carefully began signaling the u-boat, shielding the light with his coat so that he could not be seen from the side.

Slowly a smaller shape moved away from the submarine and began making its way toward the beach and the man with the flashlight. The man in the Macintosh continued looking over his shoulder nervously as the small, dark shape inched its way toward the shore. Finally he could make it out: an inflatable raft with three men inside, rowing with paddles. Behind them, the u-boat slowly disappeared back into the sea.

Soon the raft reached the shore, and the man put his flashlight away and went down to help pull the craft onto the beach. The men inside quickly jumped out and one of them immediately began deflating the raft.

The man greeted them with a wave of his hand.

"Colonel Streicher?" he asked.

"Klein?" replied the winded Streicher, dressed from head to foot in black clothes.

"Yes. I have the car waiting. Come this way," he said, and he turned and led them up the beach.

The next day, Colonel Streicher parked his car outside the Glastonbury Inn, got out, and surveyed the quiet town. His two junior officers got out with the bags and went into the inn to make arrangements. Streicher lit a cigarette and watched the smoke drift into the mild morning air.

Can't see it from here, he thought, looking at the skyline.

He quickly jogged across the street and looked back and there, silhouetted against the western sky, was a very tall hill crowned by an ancient tower. The hill was so tall compared to the surrounding landscape that it was like a tower itself, jutting above the countryside. The outline of the stone tower atop it looked like a blunt sword piercing the Somerset sky.

"The Tor," he said quietly and took another drag on the cigarette.

A smile stole over his face.

All those arrogant Englanders at Cambridge, he thought, all of them could use a dose of what we just gave the French.

"This will be a Christmas to remember in England," he added under his breath. He took one last drag, threw his cigarette down, and walked back across the street to the inn.

Late that morning Grace shut her front door with a bang, as John was strolling up from his car parked at the curb. She didn't smile as she picked up the small overnight bag that she used to carry to track and field meets.

"Where's your mother, back at the hospital?" he asked as he greeted her with a kiss.

"I *wish* she was back at the hospital," Grace huffed. Suddenly a voice from somewhere overhead shot through the morning air.

"*Grace!*"

Grace dropped her bag like it was full of bricks.

"*What?*"

"I thought you were going to Beth's? Why is John here?" John could only cringe as he sunk his hands as deep into his pockets as they would go.

"He's giving me a lift, *mother!*"

"Well it's a strange time to pay a social visit to Beth all of a sudden, with this *war* going on."

"I told you, mother, her nerves were shaken. *Sound familiar?*" Grace was seething as she bent over and picked up her bag.

"I'm sorry John, but she and I have been over this," she said in a softened voice. "Can we go?" Without waiting for his reply, Grace went down the steps and let herself into John's car. John stood for a moment by the front door, then decided it would be best not to continue to stand under the open window overhead, since wasn't sure what might come out. He ran down and jumped in the car.

"I had to borrow some petrol coupons from Dennis. He was gone by the time I got up so I had to leave a note. Hopefully he wasn't planning to drive his old wreck anywhere very far."

Grace looked at him as a grin formed at the corner of her mouth. "Then we should have enough fuel for *your* old wreck."

"The old girl has character!" he said, half-heartedly. "Besides, she runs like a top." Grace laughed and they drove off.

They were soon turning onto the one-lane road to Ankerwyke Hill, and standing waiting for them on the shoulder were the imposing figures of Arthur and Merlin. Even though they were both now dressed in Grace's father's clothes, they stood nobly, like two classical marble statues from antiquity. Grace began to feel again like she was dreaming and she could not take her eyes off them. The more she looked, the more two-dimensional they appeared to be, as if she were looking at a picture in a book. She rubbed her eyes uneasily.

As John stopped the car on the shoulder, he and Grace were both studying Arthur to see if they could discern Excalibur concealed within the raincoat. It didn't look to Grace like anything was in the coat but Arthur himself. Merlin carried a small gray bundle that appeared to be his own clothes, but it was not much bigger than a loaf of bread.

"Has he hidden it somewhere? Excal—the sword, I mean." John asked as he got out to help them.

"I have no idea," Grace responded, but he was already out of the car. John heard the drone of aircraft engines, and he instinctively looked up, but saw nothing except blue sky.

"Good day," Arthur said.

"Hello," John replied as he opened their door. Arthur shot an apprehensive glance at Merlin, then, with much effort, bent down and crawled into the back seat. Merlin quickly followed him, and soon the two large men were sitting shoulder to shoulder in the small car.

"Are you ready for a long drive?" Grace asked pleasantly from the front seat.

Merlin looked with curiosity around the interior of the car. "I honestly don't know."

Arthur laughed and slapped him on the knee. "You'll be fine, once you get used to the noise."

Grace turned around with a grin. "They're not all as noisy as this one," she said, looking at John out of the corner of her eye. John laughed sheepishly and turned the car around, heading north toward London, then turned left onto a hedge-lined road that disappeared into the west.

They were silent for the first few minutes as the car wound its way through the rolling farmland. Finally Arthur was ready to speak, and he turned his gaze from the window to the front seat.

"I suppose you would like to know why we are going to Glastonbury, is that right?" he asked.

Grace and John looked at each other, before Grace stammered, "Um, yes."

"Well, the short answer is that we expect to find German spies there, and we must do whatever we can to frustrate their efforts."

Grace and John looked at each other again anxiously. "Why do we expect to find German spies there?" she asked uneasily.

Arthur looked at Merlin, who smiled through his mass of gray whiskers.

"Ah, now for the long answer," Merlin said.

Colonel Streicher squinted at the countryside from atop Glastonbury Tor, seemingly oblivious as the wind blew his hair across his eyes. His two junior officers were beginning their ascent of the tower as part of their investigation, slowly carrying two bags of equipment and a stepladder up the stone staircase. During more peaceful times, there would have been a tourist or two at the Tor, but the only witnesses that morning were a few sheep grazing on the windy hillside.

After some time, one of the junior officers approached Streicher.

"Herr Colonel!" began the large, dark-headed young man, with a click of his heels.

"English only, Werner!" replied Streicher sharply, without turning around. "What is it?"

"Everything is as our intelligence said it would be, except…"

"Yes?" Streicher replied, still not turning around.

"We have found what appears to be a Korr Stigmata."

Streicher spun around on his heel.

"There are no Korr Stigmata catalogued here! Are you sure?"

"Yes, Colonel. It has been obscured by lichen." Werner grinned.

"Very well, show me at once!"

They dashed into the old tower and started up the wooden stairway, taking two steps at a time. The cold wind howled through the windows, but they took no notice of it in their excitement. The lower floors had all been lost to decay and rot over time, and the steps wound around the inside walls of the empty tower. Finally they came out to the top room, where Lieutenant Dunst was on a small stepladder in the center of the rough wooden floor, photographing the ceiling. He got down when Streicher came up the stairwell.

Werner was out of breath and spoke in fits and starts.

"All the lichen in here has obscured it, Herr Colonel. I noticed the pattern when the camera flash went off." Streicher immediately climbed the small ladder.

There, in the very center of the wooden-beamed ceiling, was an image barely three inches across. It looked like four dots forming the corners of a square, with a fifth, larger dot in the center.

Streicher was wide-eyed with disbelief. He lightly touched the marks. They were small indentations carefully chiseled into the dark, mottled oak that just fit his fingertips, and they looked like they had been there a very long time. Finally his excitement won over.

"Ah ha!" he cried, clapping his hands together.

When Arthur had finished speaking, Grace looked silently at John clutching the steering wheel.

He was right about Glastonbury, she thought. The Nazis, in addition to everything else they are doing, are trying to find the Holy Grail! She felt numb and confused and frightened all at the same time, and it took an effort even to ask a simple question.

"If it *was* there, wouldn't someone have found it by now? If they go to Glastonbury, will they even find it?"

Arthur and Merlin looked at each other briefly before turning back to Grace.

"The power that sent Merlin and I back after all this time is a mystery, even to us," Arthur replied. "But it would not have done so if the enemy were not getting close to what he seeks."

"And the Grail is a power much greater than mine that I cannot penetrate," Merlin added with a hint of a chuckle, like the situation was amusing . "Much greater. I won't know its exact whereabouts." He studied Grace from the back seat, carefully watching her reactions.

Grace sat in the front seat in silence. *The enemy*. The word itself was adding to her anxiety. She had the intense, sour feeling in the pit of her stomach that she used to get before big track meets, only now it was magnified many times. The thought crept into her mind, like an assassin penetrating the defenses of some sleeping castle, of being captured and tortured by a dark, faceless enemy. The feeling in her stomach was becoming so severe that she couldn't stand it.

That won't happen, she thought, and pushed it out of her mind.

By the time their car pulled into Glastonbury late that evening, Grace and John were famished. The streets were nearly empty, and there were not as many lights on in the small town as they would have liked.

"I'm afraid we need to get something to eat." John said cautiously, not sure if their two passengers needed food at all.

"Yes. This will do," Arthur said as they were passing a public house.

John pulled over and backed up the car before parking at the curb. As they were getting out with much effort and stretching, Grace noticed the sign overhead: The King's Head.

It was getting cold, as if autumn had arrived in Glastonbury before it arrived in Stokehill, and Grace had to keep herself from dashing indoors before the others were out of the car. Finally the four of them went in.

A small wood fire welcomed them as they entered the old room crisscrossed with brown timbers. They sat themselves close to the fireplace, over which was mounted a stately set of deer antlers. The rotund proprietor shuffled up to take their order but before he could open his mouth, Arthur spoke.

"I would like a ploughman's and beer, good man!" he boomed gregariously. The other patrons looked up momentarily before returning to their drinks.

"The same!" Merlin added with glee, rubbing his hands together.

John smiled. *Beer!* Of course it stands to reason they would like beer, he thought.

"Make it four." John added.

"Except make mine a half pint, please," Grace added as she looked at her smiling companions. *Men and their beer.*

"Very good," said the man, and he shuffled back and disappeared behind the bar.

Arthur looked around the room.

"These places haven't changed too much."

"No, thank goodness," Merlin replied with a smile.

The pub was quiet, and there were only three other people in the place: a gentleman with a black beard at the bar nursing a glass of red wine and two young men sitting by the window drinking lager beer.

As she watched the firelight flicker softly on their faces, Grace felt like their companions were simply two friends with whom they had shared a ride and now a meal. She sat back more comfortably in her chair and her mind began to fill with questions.

"Do we know who we're looking for?" She asked with keen interest. "I mean, what kind of persons? How will we know them if we see them?"

Arthur and Merlin remained silent as the proprietor returned with their glasses of beer on a round tray.

"Thank you," they said as the man shuffled off.

Merlin watched him leave before he responded, then leaned forward. "There are at least two places that would be of extreme interest to them, possibly more. Those are the Tor and the Chalice Well. We are looking for someone showing an unusual interest in those places."

Grace began watching the two young men by the window more closely.

What about those two? she wondered. They look like they could be German. *Are they listening to us?* But she shook her head and turned her attention back to the table.

Don't be paranoid, Grace.

John looked at Arthur.

"I hope we're not asking too many questions," he began carefully, "but, where have you been all this time, that you know so much of what is going on? Is it—?" His voice trailed off, unable to speak the name that he well knew.

"The Isle of Apples, it has been called," Arthur answered, finishing his sentence. "It is a place where time does not pass the same way."

He paused and then whispered, "It is Avalon. And it has a window on this world."

Grace looked at Arthur and listened to his answer, but between the soft firelight and the beer and the long drive, she didn't react nearly as strongly as she might have otherwise. It was as if part of her mind had already begun to drift off to sleep—even though she was still sitting up and eating and drinking—and it was all the beginning of a dream. Finally she roused herself.

"And you, Merlin?"

A smile came to Merlin's face, but it was a sad smile. Immediately Grace knew she had brought up the wrong subject. *Now I've done it.*

He looked at her kindly.

"Not Avalon, not I," he said quietly. "There have been few indeed worthy of that reward. I have been in the roots of the land--where it is dark and dripping and there are no windows--neither alive nor dead, not awake nor asleep. I am very glad indeed to be out and here with you now."

Grace decided she had said enough, so she nodded politely and had a sip of her beer. John spoke up again.

"Your speech," he said. "How did you learn modern English?"

"We did not learn it," Arthur answered thoughtfully. "Rather, we have been given it as a gift—something we would need for the task set before us."

Grace had decided only a moment earlier to stop asking questions, but already she had to ask another.

"Um, what else can you tell us about the Grail? You searched for it in your day, didn't you?"

Arthur looked like a painful subject that had been avoided was finally brought up.

"I can tell you we spent our best years searching for the grail, or what we thought was the grail, until I realized that what I was chasing was an illusion, and I had the real thing all along." He looked sadly at Merlin, who simply nodded silently.

"But now we don't have years to find it, we have days or a week or two at best, and we *must* find it before the enemy does."

Suddenly the young men by the window got up and left. Grace thought for a moment about pointing them out, but decided against it.

Don't be paranoid, she reminded herself, and she returned to the conversation at her table, but it had stopped for the moment. The only sound was that of a wooden match being struck across the room.

Grace looked over to the bar. The dark-bearded gentleman was lighting a long cheroot.

5. On the Tor

The next morning the four of them drove up to the grassy Tor. It was overcast and gusty, and they parked and began the hike up the steep, lonely hill. They climbed in silence. Grace felt uncomfortable sleeping in her clothes, and she wished she had brought a warmer jacket, while John ached from sleeping on the floor of the room above the pub that he had shared with Grace.

"I should have slept in the woods with Arthur and Merlin," he grumbled to himself. "They seem as right as rain."

The wind was blowing hard as they reached the top, and a magnificent view of the surrounding area opened up to them. At the very center of the hilltop was a very old Norman tower, standing sentinel over the hill and town. It was stone with occasional window openings around its sides, and it stood perhaps forty feet above the hilltop.

Merlin went immediately into the tower while Arthur went around the outside of its massive stone walls. Grace and John took in the panoramic view as the wind blew their hair all about their faces. No one else was on the hill except for a few grazing sheep.

Suddenly the sun broke through the clouds, bathing the hilltop and the tower in radiant sunlight, and it brightened Grace's spirits. She embraced John, but he was preoccupied.

"The Tor," he said as he stared at the tower. The idea that somehow, at that very moment, the Holy Grail itself could be in that tower or perhaps buried in the earth beneath his feet made John feel like he was standing on holy ground. The hill itself seemed alive, and he walked carefully on its surface, half expecting it to move if he stepped the wrong way.

Arthur joined Merlin inside the tower and was surprised to see him standing still, looking intently at nothing in particular. He was listening. Then he pointed upward. Suddenly Arthur heard a slight clang coming down the stairwell, followed by a voice. Someone was above in the tower, with tools or something. Immediately Arthur started up the stairs with Merlin immediately behind him.

Up and up they went until the stairs ended at the top room, the wind howling through the window openings. When they emerged into the room, there were several pieces of equipment on the old wooden floor, and on a step ladder examining the ceiling stood a thin blonde man in his late twenties, with a magnifying glass in his hand and a startled look on his face.

"What are you doing?" Arthur demanded, as if the young man were trespassing on his personal property.

It was Dunst, who blanched for an instant, then regained his composure. The fact that no one in the whole country would ever suspect what he was really doing filled him with confidence, that and the fact that he had a pistol in his jacket. But the command in Arthur's voice left a lingering doubt in his mind.

Could he be the landowner?

"I am a student in architectural history at Oxford," he recited. He had an impeccable English accent and his cover story was well-rehearsed. "I am afraid you gave me a start," he added with a smile.

Dunst finally recognized Arthur and Merlin from the pub the night before, the very ones he and Werner had overheard talking about the Tor and the Chalice Well. They had reported it to Streicher as a precaution when they returned to the inn. Streicher had told them to avoid the group, and now he was face to face with them.

"Let me ask again: what are you doing?" Arthur raised his voice only a degree, but its power filled the room, and the smile froze on Dunst's face.

"I study Norman architecture. I am interested in the woodwork, and I have a lot of work to do, so if you don't mind, I really must get busy," he replied, allowing his own impatience to show.

I ought to teach these two old codgers a lesson, he thought. Dunst was a brilliant historian, but he still felt he had to prove himself in the SS. He did so by becoming deadly with a luger.

Arthur walked over to the stepladder and faced him.

"Get down, please," he ordered, as one who was used to having his commands obeyed. Dunst became irate.

"Now look here, I don't know who you think you're talking to, but I have a legitimate academic need to be here!" he shouted. Suddenly Arthur grabbed Dunst by his jacket and threw him to the wooden floor. Shocked, Dunst fumbled inside his jacket for his pistol, but Arthur was on him before he could find it. Arthur pinned him with a knee on the chest and grabbed the gun from Dunst just as he found it.

"Is this what students carry at Oxford these days?" Arthur asked, and he tossed the gun to Merlin, who examined it with a mixture of curiosity and distaste.

"I hope not," Merlin murmured.

It hit Dunst all at once that his cover was blown and that he had been disarmed by two English civilians as old as his father. He flushed, and began thrashing as much as he could in Arthur's hold, but the strength of the man on him was far superior to his own. Finally he stopped struggling and tried to regain his composure.

"Now, perhaps you can tell us what you're really doing here," Arthur continued.

"I told you! I am a student, and I have a permit for the gun!" Dunst snapped. "You can't treat me like this. I'll be contacting the police, you can be sure of that!"

Merlin began to pace anxiously. He could be telling the truth, he thought.

"Perhaps I should try my methods," Merlin suggested.

Arthur hesitated; his instincts told him the young man was the enemy, but it had been a long time since he had had to rely on his instincts. He stopped struggling with the young man and let him up. Merlin went over to the stepladder and carefully climbed up.

"Let us see what part of the architecture was so fascinating."

Merlin squinted up at the ceiling beam in the very center of the room. He stood balancing on the small ladder for a moment, then he looked down at Arthur and spoke carefully in a low voice.

"They have found the sign."

Arthur's eyes grew wide and he towered over Dunst, grabbing him by his lapels and lifting him off the floor. Dunst felt like a little boy in some fairy tale in the hands of an angry giant. Arthur took him to the window opening and, still holding onto fistfuls of Dunst's clothing, thrust him outside the window and suspended him kicking and screaming in the open air, thirty feet above the ground.

"Now, what are you looking for?" Arthur shouted to him as the wind whipped both their clothes.

"The Grail!" Dunst cried, *"We're looking for the Holy Grail!"*

With that, Arthur pulled him back in and threw him on the floor. Dunst was hyperventilating as he scrambled desperately for his equipment.

"Go tell your leaders what happened!" Arthur boomed. "You won't find the Grail, and you'll never invade this land as long as I am here!"

Arthur and Merlin towered over the scurrying Dunst, who disappeared down the stairs with his stepladder and the bag of equipment. Finally Merlin looked at Arthur.

"I could have gotten that out of him much more peaceably than that," he said with a sigh.

"I know, but I wanted to make an impression on him," Arthur replied, breathing heavily.

"Perhaps we should have turned him in to the authorities," Merlin added.

"Perhaps, but even if we could convince the authorities he was a spy, they would lock us up in a mad house if we told them we were here to protect the Holy Grail," Arthur answered.

"Well, I don't think we've seen the last of him or his comrades." Merlin's voice trailed off as he looked intently up at the sign in the center of the ceiling.

Down below, outside and on the other side of the tower on the sunbathed hilltop, Grace and John could just hear what sounded like shouting. They looked at each other.

"Should we go in?" Grace asked with an alarmed look on her face.

John hesitated, then ran inside the dark tower. He was momentarily blinded; his eyes took several seconds to adjust to the dark chamber from the bright sunlight outside. Finally he could see the stairway winding its way up the tower.

"Is everything all right?" he called up from the bottom of the stairs.

Just then, Dunst came charging down the stairs, trying to carry his equipment as he fled in panic. John's eyes widened as he recognized him immediately from the pub the night before. He froze for a second, not knowing whether to let him go or to try and stop him. Dunst tried to avoid him, but his shoulder caught John at the hip as he ducked past, and they both went flying.

Dunst quickly gathered his things and fled down the hill, passing within arm's length of Grace, who was riveted by her first look at the enemy up close. John instinctively got up and ran out of the tower after him.

"Let him go," a voice called from one of the windows above.

It was Arthur. He and Merlin were coming down the stairs.

They rejoined Grace and John, and Grace only just noticed that she was shaking.

"Are you both all right?" Arthur asked.

"Oh, yes," they both tried to reply casually. "Of course!"

"But why did we let him go?" John asked. "Shouldn't we have turned him in to the authorities?"

Merlin answered, "Not yet. We need to find all of them, and learn how close they are. They have already made a discovery here. If we turn this one in, the others might disappear."

"What did they discover?" Grace asked, and as she asked the question, a strange feeling came over her. Merlin eyed her curiously.

"A sign." It seemed to them as if Merlin was going to say something more, but he apparently changed his mind and brushed off the question.

Grace waited for him to say more, and when he did not she felt disquiet stirring deep within her.

"We must go after him; he may lead us to the others" Arthur said. "Merlin and I will follow him on foot. You two please take the car back to the pub and wait for us there. We must hurry!" And with that they were off. They scrambled down the hill after the young man, but he was already out of sight.

By the time Arthur and Merlin got to the bottom of the hill, the German was far ahead of them and had just vanished around a shop corner and into the town. They moved quickly down the road toward the same corner.

"Hurry, he runs well," Arthur said to Merlin behind him.

"And I definitely do not," Merlin puffed.

They turned the corner and looked down the lane lined with shops and small houses, and there, jogging two blocks ahead of them, was the figure carrying a stepladder and shoulder bag.

"There he is!" Arthur said.

They dashed down the lane that curved gently to the left. At the next corner, an old woman bent with arthritis was selling apples from a small cart. She was talking to herself as she rocked back and forth on a wooden stool.

Arthur and Merlin came to the corner and stopped to let a lorry drive by. Suddenly a premonition flashed in Merlin's mind, of Grace in the back of a car headed into the middle of an apocalyptic war scene. In a moment it was gone.

"Perhaps I should have stayed with the two young ones," he said suddenly. Arthur turned to him.

"They should be safe for now," he said, eyeing him. Merlin shrugged his shoulders and smiled.

"You're probably right. I wish I *knew* more," he added. The lorry passed and they both started across the street.

"Be careful what you ask for," someone said with a laugh. It was the old woman peddling apples. Her face was ravaged by skin disease so that she was not easy to look upon, and she had the fog of senility about her. Arthur turned to her and smiled kindly, then began to cross the street.

"We must take greater care of our young ones," she said more clearly. "They are our future." She was no longer rocking, and her voice was suddenly as clear as a bell.

Arthur and Merlin both stopped and looked at each other. Even though they knew the German was getting away, they walked slowly back to the old woman, who was once again rocking and mumbling softly to herself.

Merlin studied her carefully for a moment, not sure what to make of her as she sat rocking on her stool, now seemingly oblivious of the two men standing in front of her. He was about to say something to Arthur when the clear voice returned.

"Especially the girl. Take great care of her. She must undergo an ordeal, but if she does not survive it, all is lost."

They both stared open mouthed at the old woman, whose eyes were suddenly deep wells filled with the wisdom of ages. She looked directly at Merlin.

"Who am I?"

At that Merlin knew who was sitting before them, and his voice left him and the color drained from his face.

"There is much more you can learn," she continued, in her clear, ageless voice. "The Old Master still lives. Seek him."

Merlin swallowed. "I will."

Then she smiled placidly at Arthur.

"You were both great men in your day, especially you, Arthur, but the world has changed. To champion this land as you have done in the past, you will be called upon to do more than ever before."

Arthur spoke. "I welcome the chance to fight again, to live again, to walk this land again." Then he looked at his hands as if he were seeing them for the first time.

"But I, too, am somehow changed…"

"Yes, you have been given more gifts than just your speech," she smiled.

Then the old woman nodded and slowly stood up, placing her stool inside her cart. She grasped the cart handle and gingerly began pushing it down the street, its big wheels creaking as they turned. Then she stopped the cart and turned back to them.

"Hurry," she said clearly. "Even now there is danger." She returned to her creaking cart and pushed it slowly away, mumbling softly as she did.

Arthur watched her for a moment, then looked down the lane. The man they were following was long gone.

"We must return to the pub," he said desperately, and they ran across the street and down the lane.

Colonel Streicher stared blankly at the wall in front of him as he tried to decide what to make of Dunst's encounter on the Tor. Dunst continued to stand nervously in front of the Colonel, trying to catch his breath, unsure if Streicher was done questioning him. Streicher looked back at Dunst silently, almost clinically, as he tried to decide what to do.

Dunst may be a little too much of an intellectual and not enough of a soldier, but he is not one to lie, he thought, as Dunst fidgeted in front of him. I must rely on what he said.

He rolled his eyes toward the ceiling. "We blew our cover on the *second* day."

Streicher had thought it so unlikely that anyone from the sleepy English town would notice them that he had left Dunst alone to continue at the Tor while he and Werner went to the Chalice Well.

"That was a mistake. I should have checked out the Englanders myself before I put Dunst back up in that tower—especially alone." Werner and Dunst stared mutely at him.

To make matters worse, he had made an unscheduled radio report to headquarters, gloating about their discovery and gushing about how well things were going. To have to report the very next day that their cover was blown would not go well for him with the High Command. He thought of himself enjoying Herr Rahn's torment in Montsegur; now it was his turn. Streicher felt sick to his stomach.

"A *stupid* mistake."

Dunst, agonizing as he stood in the center of the room, assumed Streicher was referring to him.

"I'm very sorry, Herr Colonel. I should have kept my wits about me," he apologized. He thought of Arthur up in the tower and he swore to himself he would avenge himself if he got the chance.

"I should not have insisted on leaving the pub so soon last night. We could have learned more about them," Werner offered. He was standing behind Dunst but towered over him. "But they did not fit the profile at all: two older men accompanied by a young couple. We thought they were just villagers, but they knew exactly what we were up to."

"What?" said Streicher, who had not been listening to them. "No, no, I meant me. But, yes! You should have kept your wits about you. You're in the SS for God's sake!"

He stood up and began to pace in the small room. Dunst and Werner tried to give him as much room as they possibly could.

"I must think!" he said, talking to himself. "They knew about the Korr Stigmata; very few people would know about that. They must have been on to us for some time. What will they do now? They did not try to detain Dunst," Streicher said as if Dunst wasn't there. "That is most unusual." He stopped pacing.

"Unless they wanted Dunst to lead them to us." His voice trailed off as he looked at the window, then the door.

"They could be here any minute. There's no time to lose. Werner, get this equipment packed. Dunst, bring the car around back. Quickly!" Streicher put on his jacket and headed down to the front desk to check out.

John and Grace had climbed down the hill and returned to the car. They started back to the pub as the sun disappeared once again behind the clouds. On the way they were delayed by a large group of uniformed school children on an outing, crossing the street like so many ducklings, but soon they were back at the curb in front of The King's Head. John parked at the curb and turned off the engine.

"What exactly do you think happened up in the tower?" Grace blurted out suddenly, and she realized that she was more upset than she thought.

"I assume Arthur and Merlin caught him red handed, looking for the Grail, although I don't know how in the world they knew that. But he looked like he was running for his life," John said.

They sat without speaking for some time, watching nervously as pedestrians went up and down the street. Suddenly Grace sat up in her seat.

"Look there!"

A car was coming out of an alley across the street and down a short way, and as the car turned, they could clearly see the driver's face. It was the young man from the Tor, and he was driving straight toward Grace and John. There were two other men with him.

"What should we do?" she gasped.

"Get down!" John said, and they both ducked as low as they possibly could in the small car. They could hear the engine get louder as the car approached them. Suddenly there was a slight squeak of the brakes and they heard the engine idling just outside their car window. The car had stopped in the street next to them, blocking them in.

"Oh my god!" Grace choked, trying to stay as low as possible.

"Keep down!" John gasped under his breath. His hands were perspiring, and the steering wheel prevented him from getting as low as he would have liked.

Then the engine revved and they could hear the car driving away. Grace didn't budge from her position, but John cautiously peeked through the rear window. The car was turning right at the corner.

"Thank god!" Grace exclaimed as she finally got up. But Arthur and Merlin were nowhere in sight, and when she realized that they would not know where the spies had gone, fear started to grip her once more.

"We've got to follow them," John said. Then he looked at Grace as he started the car. "In for a penny, in for a pound."

"I know," she gulped, and they were off.

Arthur and Merlin crossed several streets, then turned left at a corner that looked familiar, and stopped to look for a landmark they would recognize. They saw nothing. They quickly retraced their steps and continued to the next block and there, halfway down the street, was The King's Head. They carefully studied all the parked cars on the street for signs of Grace and John as they walked toward the pub.

"These things all look alike," Merlin grumbled. Soon they were standing in front of the pub, but there was no sign of them anywhere.

"They must have run into the enemy," Arthur said, winded and exasperated, "and they're either following them or they've been taken by them." He looked gravely at Merlin.

"And we'll never catch them on foot," Merlin added.

Arthur looked up at the sky in anguish.

"Why must it be like this? I'd rather face the enemy in battle than play cat and mouse with spies."

Merlin remembered being in the same situation in ages past, and he felt again the pressure to provide good counsel to Arthur when he needed it most.

"We must take solace in the fact that she is in good hands, better hands than they both yet know," he replied. He paused and then added, "Perhaps it is time for me to seek the Old Master. The place is not far from here."

Arthur was reluctant to leave, but he knew they had to make good use of the time. He let out a heavy sigh and looked at Merlin.

"I hope you can find it, my friend. Let's go." And with that the two turned and headed back up the street.

"Don't follow too close! They'll see us," Grace said.

They were quickly out of the small town and heading east through green pastureland. A few hundred yards ahead, the black car would come into view, then disappear again around a bend in the road. Occasionally another car or a lorry would pass going the other way, but for the most part there was little traffic on the road. Soon the sun started to peek through the clouds again as they continued through the rolling farmland.

Up ahead, Dunst was looking in his rearview mirror.

"Herr Colonel, the same car has been following us since we left town." Streicher turned around from the passenger side and looked back. He could make out two figures.

"There are only two," he said as he studied the other vehicle carefully. "Slow down a little."

John noticed the gap between his car and the black car closing, so he slowed down.

"They're slowing down. Do you think they've noticed us?"

"Oh God, you're right! Turn here," Grace exclaimed as another road was coming up on their left. John made a quick turn and pulled over to the gravel shoulder just fifty yards off the main road. They were screened from the main road by a tall dense hedge.

"We can't let them get away. I'll wait here for a moment, but then we have to resume," he said.

"How far will we follow them?" she asked anxiously. "They could be going to London, for all we know." But it felt to Grace like they were taking a break, and she began to relax.

Then they heard the sound of another car pulling onto the gravel shoulder just behind them. John looked in his mirror and saw a black sedan immediately behind them. It was the Germans, and there was no place to hide.

He looked palely at Grace. "It's them."

6. The Old Master

Merlin and Arthur passed some old church ruins and continued on the pavement until it ended, then walked single file on the shoulder of the road going north out of town. They stopped where an old worn footpath ended at the road. Merlin scratched his head.

"I think this is the one." He turned to Arthur and gave a wry smile. "But it's been a while."

Arthur slapped him on the back.

"Let's try it. Lead the way, old man!"

They left the main road and started down the footpath, bordered by an old wooden fence on the left that had wire fencing added to it. The path was ancient, having been used before the Romans came to Britain, but that had been long forgotten.

The late summer sky was now mostly blue again, and the green fields on either side of them shimmered in the September sun. A small flock of birds flew playfully just overhead and down the path ahead of them, leading the way to their destination.

"Well, whatever happens, I am glad for the chance to walk in this land again," Arthur said to Merlin ahead of him.

"So am I," Merlin replied lightly, like he could start skipping any moment. "I don't know what gift *she* was referring to, but just being back here now for a walk on a day like this is greater than any gift I could imagine." Then he added thoughtfully, "Although the land has been cleared since our time. I miss the forests."

Arthur looked at his hands again.

"Yes, it looks different," he said to himself. "I *feel* different, somehow. Is that the gift?"

They continued on until the path came to the end of the pasture. There was a small gate, which they went through to the next pasture, and they found that the path turned north and started rising as it met a low hill. They continued to the top of the hill, where they stopped and looked around. The town and the Tor were behind them, and ahead of them the path descended into a dell with a small grove of oak and other trees. In the center, a small church steeple barely peeked through the treetops.

They started down the path into the wood and soon were under its canopy. The air was still and all was quiet. The dappled sunlight on the trees and undergrowth made an altogether different atmosphere than that of the fields behind them. Just ahead, they could catch glimpses of the old chapel through the trees. They continued on and came to the small church, in ruins and overgrown with vines. Next to it was a massive, sprawling evergreen tree that, while not very high, dwarfed the chapel next to it. It was a yew, dark and wizened, and it was the grand old man of the wood.

"There it is," Merlin said in a hushed voice as he looked at the great tree. "The Old Master."

They both studied it without speaking for some time. Merlin walked slowly around it, and Arthur could barely make out some murmuring coming from his friend. He continued slowly around the enormous tree, pausing occasionally to face it directly while he made his breathless utterances, until finally he returned and stood by Arthur's side once again. Merlin was silent for a moment, as if gathering himself. Then he spoke.

"Thankfully this wood has survived. It is the oldest in the country, and this tree was a thousand years old when you and I last walked this land." Merlin paused, "In our day, this was the most sacred of places. This chapel must have been built later, for it was not here in our time."

"I'm afraid I don't remember this place," Arthur said.

"The holiest sites were kept secret by my order," he replied. "It was not possible to keep all such places secret, but we were successful in this case." He paused to listen. "It is well protected."

With an effort Merlin gathered himself once more, and turned to Arthur.

"There is much to be learned here, but it will take some time. Can you come for me in the morning?"

"Of course," Arthur said. "I will return in the morning." He started back the way they had come, but after a couple of steps he stopped and turned around.

"You'll probably want this," he said, and he tossed Merlin a small red apple.

"Thanks," Merlin replied as he caught the apple and slipped it into his pocket.

Grace was panic stricken and gripped the car seat with all her strength as she heard the black car's doors open behind her. John saw in his mirror the three men eyeing them carefully as they got out of the car. He could see that at least one of them had a long black pistol drawn. That was too much for John, and he grabbed the gearshift.

"Hold on!" he said, and he revved the engine but it sputtered badly, and they both feared the car was going to stall.

"*Not now!*" John yelled, and the engine suddenly roared to life, as if to obey his command.

He popped the clutch, causing the rear wheels to spin and throw a shower of gravel and dust on the three men behind them.

The car took off wildly and John had to fight to keep it on the roadway. They heard a gunshot from behind, and Grace ducked down as low as she could. Another shot went off and they heard a metallic *clunk* from the back of the car.

"That one hit us!" Grace yelled.

"Stay down," John cautioned, as he negotiated the winding road going as fast as he could. The black car was now out of sight behind them, but they knew it wouldn't be for long. Behind them Streicher and the others clambered coughing back into the black car.

"After them!" Streicher shouted, and Dunst threw the car into gear and hit the gas. He wanted desperately to make up for his failure on the Tor.

The tires squealed around the first bend as Streicher and Werner held on. Streicher wanted to get to these two Englanders before they joined their more formidable comrades and find out how they knew about the mission almost before it had started. But he also wanted to reach them before they got back to town and created an incident.

"Faster!" he said to Dunst.

Up ahead, John was going as fast as his old car would carry them while trying to keep an eye on the rear view mirror.

"Do you know where we're going?" Grace asked, still gripping the seat.

"No idea," John answered quickly. "More or less north in terms of direction, but I don't know if this road takes us back to town or away from town."

As he was talking, he glanced again in the mirror. The black car had just rounded a bend, crossing the line in the road as it did. It was moving very fast.

"Here they come!" John said as he came onto a straight section of road. He pressed the gas pedal against the floorboard, and the engine labored loudly.

"Be careful!" gasped Grace as the car barreled down the country road. A lorry was coming the other way, and it passed them in a blur. The next bend was coming and John had to brake hard to keep the car from rolling over. Behind them, the black car was gaining. Another road was coming up quickly on the right, and John turned onto it, his tires screeching as he made the turn.

"They have a faster car," he cried, gripping the steering wheel with clenched fists. Almost immediately the road bent sharply to the left, then again to the right before straightening out. The black car was out of sight for a moment, but then it reappeared in the mirror. It was still gaining on them.

Grace looked back. "They're closer!"

Another road was coming up, again on the right. John turned again, taking the corner as fast as he could without rolling the car into the field.

"Hold on!"

Grace glanced at John. He looked at once frightened and thrilled, and she thought he should be flying a Spitfire instead of his old sedan. His face was tense and his eyes were as wide as saucers.

Is he *enjoying* this? She braced herself against the dashboard.

The black car was much closer, now less than thirty yards behind them. Before they knew it, the main road back to town was just ahead of them. John had to slow down to make sure the way was clear, and the black car was almost on top of them. He turned right again and hit the gas, and the black car was still right behind them.

Streicher tried to lean out of the window to take a shot but had trouble positioning his right hand out of the left side window.

"Wait, Herr Colonel!" shouted Dunst, as another car passed them going the other way. "All right now!" He said, as the car disappeared.

Streicher fired and missed. Up ahead, John and Grace heard the shot.

"They're shooting again!" Grace cried as she ducked down.

John began to weave back and forth across the road while still going as fast as possible. The tires were screeching wildly. Another shot fired and just missed Grace's window. John negotiated two more bends in the road as fast as he could, but the black car was still closing.

"How much further till town?" Grace asked as she tried to peek over the dashboard.

"Here!" John slammed on the brakes. Another bend in the road had hidden the outskirts of town, and they were suddenly back on the high street. The town was alive with noontime traffic, and the pavements were crowded with people busy with their lives. Behind them, Dunst also hit the brakes and eased onto the high street. They were now immediately behind John and Grace.

"All right, we'll follow them. Let's see what they do," Streicher said coolly, and he lit a cigarette.

"What do we do now?" Grace asked, exasperated. "We have German spies following us! Arthur and Merlin could be anywhere!"

"I don't know! I'm open to suggestions," John snapped, his heart still pounding.

Up ahead a lorry with a flat tire had stopped traffic in their direction. They came to a complete halt, with no way to move until the road was cleared. Behind them, the black car came up and nudged their rear bumper.

"What are they doing?" Grace cried, not daring to look at the car behind them.

"I don't know, I just wish we could *move!*" John slapped the steering wheel in frustration.

In her side mirror, Grace could see Streicher getting out of the car behind them and coming up to her window. She was frozen. Streicher tapped on the window, but Grace would not look at him.

"Why are you following us?" he asked through the window with a grin.

She never felt more petrified in all her life, and her neck was so rigid she could feel her head begin to shake like an old woman. Streicher tapped again at the window, enjoying the torment he was causing her.

"Where is a police constable when you need them?" John cried.

Just then, a large hand grabbed Streicher on the shoulder and spun him around. It was Arthur, who had come up the street just as the traffic had stopped.

"Why are you harassing my friends? Didn't your servant tell you what I said?" Arthur boomed. His voice carried up and down the street, and pedestrians began to stop and watch the altercation. Across the street, a man in a black mackintosh watched with great interest.

"What's happening?" John asked excitedly, unable to see their faces from his side of the car.

"It's Arthur!" shouted Grace.

Streicher was not intimidated, in spite of the growing crowd of onlookers. Behind him, Werner was getting out of the car to assist.

"Please take your hands off me," he said calmly. "I was only trying to ask them why they were following us. It is they who were harassing us."

"You obviously do not know how much your servant revealed to us on the Tor."

Streicher laughed. "You mustn't believe everything he tells you. He's rather inclined to romanticize things."

Arthur noticed something that looked heavy in the pocket of Streicher's jacket.

"He was well armed for a romantic—as are you." Arthur suddenly grabbed at Streicher's pocket, but Streicher managed to keep his grip on the gun and his finger on the trigger.

"I *will* use this," he with a low growl, his smile gone. Werner had his own concealed gun pointed at Arthur.

"Would you really shoot me in front of all these witnesses?" Arthur asked quietly. "You are a very clumsy bunch of spies."

Streicher moved to within inches of Arthur's face and grinned. "We don't need to bother ourselves being overly surreptitious.

In a few short weeks we will invade this island, and we will take what we want."

Arthur flushed crimson, and he seemed to rise up and tower over Streicher, who blanched for a moment.

"No one will invade this land as long as I am here!" he roared, his voice echoing off the walls and rooftops.

Everything in Glastonbury seemed to stop. The whole town appeared to be riveted to Arthur as he stood in the street facing Streicher. The faces of the people showed a mixture of confusion and hope, as if a long-forgotten voice was trying to wake them from the nightmare of the war.

Arthur felt their attention and he turned, wanting to say more, but then stopped. He saw all their sad faces waiting for something more, anything he could give them. He realized they were no different than the faces of his day.

That is not what I have been sent here to do.

Arthur let go of Streicher's arm and reached into his own coat pocket and revealed the top of Dunst's revolver. He pointed it at Streicher.

"I also have one of those, thanks to your servant," Arthur said quietly. "Would you like to die here, so far from your homeland?"

Werner was becoming increasingly agitated, but Streicher remained calm as the crowd buzzed with confusion.

"No more than you would like to see your young associates here die," he answered, and he pointed his weapon at Grace. But he was struck by the power of the man in front of him and the reaction of the onlookers.

Who *is* this person? He has the whole town ready to follow him.

Grace and John could not follow the exchange from inside the car. The traffic was now starting to move, and vehicles from behind them were going around the two stopped cars. Just then a mustached police constable came up.

"Everything here all right?" he asked as he walked up, looking a bit annoyed. Arthur turned to him in a flash.

"Are you the local sheriff?" he demanded. The constable stared at him for a moment, as Streicher watched Arthur carefully.

"I am a police constable. What's the problem here?"

"What is the penalty for spying?"

"*Spying?* You mean foreign spies?"

"I mean German spies." The constable went slightly pale. Streicher smiled with amusement, as if the game had only just gotten interesting.

"Yes," Streicher broke in, "you know, someone performing military reconnaissance, trying to gain a military advantage in the war—" he gently stressed the word *military*.

"In my day, they were hung by the neck until dead," Arthur interrupted, so that everyone nearby could hear him. The constable swallowed.

"That is still the penalty."

Arthur's expression changed, and he suddenly looked at him like an old friend. The constable's moustache seemed to droop on his face as he stared at Arthur, mesmerized.

"This war is the greatest threat to this land in ages!" Arthur said passionately, and it seemed to the constable that it was only he and Arthur standing face to face on the street, and everyone else had vanished. "You are a protector of this land, as am I. The lives of all of us will depend on what each and every one of us does, or does not do, today and in the days that follow."

It felt to the constable as if the man speaking to him had looked into his soul and examined the whole span of his life up to that moment, and it looked to those watching as if the constable had suddenly woken up. He set his jaw in determination and turned to Streicher.

"Now look here—"

Just then a shot rang out across the street. Klein had produced a gun from his black mackintosh and fired it into the air, and was running down the street. Panic broke out on the busy street, and pedestrians began to run or take cover. Cries and shouts filled the air. Without waiting, the constable bolted after the man with the gun, leaving the three men standing in the street.

Streicher stared at Arthur as he got in the car. He and Werner slammed their doors as Streicher continued to study the tall enigmatic man who was glaring at him. Then Dunst pulled out and around John's car, and they were gone.

Arthur got into the back seat of John's car.

"We have not seen the last of them. Let's go."

John drove off but Grace was still shaken, and she couldn't stop looking straight ahead, as if her neck had froze.

"Where's Merlin?" John asked Arthur.

"He is trying to learn all he can about our business," Arthur replied, as he studied with great interest the pedestrians walking down the street. "He is not far from here, but he must be alone. His ways have always been secret."

To Grace's surprise, John suddenly broke in.

"Secret! Yes, most of their knowledge has been lost to us because they guarded it so carefully." His mind raced back to the fleeting encounters he had had in his studies of the mysterious druidic tradition—the arts, astronomy and astrology, prophecy and conjuring. It had always been the stuff of legend. Now he was tantalized by the notion that not only was the tradition real, it was perhaps being practiced at that very moment somewhere nearby.

But Grace couldn't believe she was still traumatized by their encounter while John seemed to have already forgotten it.

"And tree worship," he continued, as he drove down the high street. "They communed with the spirits of trees—"

"--*Thank* you, John," Grace interrupted, with a strained smile. Then she turned back to Arthur. "Will he be joining us soon?"

"In the morning," Arthur answered. "His is a slow process. In the meantime, there is more we can do."

"More?" She looked at John. More like *that* encounter? Grace knew she hadn't recovered from the last one.

"I'll need to find a telephone, then," she said. "To let my mother know."

John pulled the car over in front of a bright red telephone booth, as the Tor loomed up over the rooftops behind them.

"I'll leave you two alone," Arthur said as he sat up. "I must visit the Chalice Well, then return to the Tor later this afternoon. Can you meet me back at the Tor?"

He opened the door and began to climb out of the car. Grace and John looked puzzled at one another.

"Of course," Grace replied. "But what time? And do you want some lunch?"

"I've brought something, thanks," he replied, and he closed the door with a bang that rocked the car. The slamming door shocked Grace into thinking clearly, and she immediately turned to John.

"John, I don't know what this is that I've gotten us both into, but Arthur and Merlin are….this is just plain dangerous. Don't you agree?"

He looked at her blankly for a second. "I suppose…yes, I think you're right." He scratched his head like he had just woken up. "I think I just really wanted to believe them."

"Me too, and I can't believe how far I went believing it all." She shook her head. "Well, we told him we'd meet him after lunch. Let's meet him as we said and tell him we're going home."

John looked embarrassed but smiled. "Of course."

In the black car on the road heading east, Colonel Streicher was brooding over the encounter on the high street.

"I am sure he is a military man, for he is battle worn. I can see it in his face; he has had a career of leading men into battle— probably many, many men. But why would he just let us go, even if he wasn't acting in any official capacity?"

"And the other older man was not there at all," Dunst added, relieved that Streicher had not fared any better with them than he did earlier that morning.

"What do we do now, Herr Colonel?" Werner asked. The scene on the street was the first time he saw a chink in Streicher's armor, and he struggled to suppress a grin.

"We must find a roadside inn for our scheduled report. It is overdue and I can avoid it no longer," Streicher said with a sigh.

They continued east for almost an hour until they found an old, whitewashed inn with a thatched roof and a gravel car park. Streicher got out and lit a cigarette in the car park while Werner and Dunst made arrangements and unloaded the equipment.

"What an interesting person," Streicher mused as the smoke drifted away with the breeze.

"He knew why we were here, probably before Dunst told him." Streicher took another drag on his cigarette. "But how did they get on to us so quickly?"

After a while Dunst appeared in the doorway.

"It's ready."

Streicher threw down his cigarette and went inside.

7. Under the Tor

At *SS* headquarters in Berlin there was a late meeting in the cavernous office of the Reichsfuhrer. General Koln had just finished briefing Himmler on the events in Glastonbury that day and Herr Rahn, returned from Montsegur, had been asked to join them. Koln and Rahn were seated on a large leather sofa in the dark, wood-paneled room. Himmler was standing, leaning on the mantle and smoking a cigar as he listened, his round spectacles reflecting the glare of the fire. Above the mantel hung the original picture of the Fuhrer as a medieval knight on horseback, replete with full armor and banners flying.

"It could mean that we're onto something," puffed Himmler when Koln had finished. "But it doesn't sound like the way the English operate. Herr Rahn, what do you think?"

"Well, Herr Reichsfuhrer, finding a Korr Stigmata is most exciting," Rahn said with nervous, mouse-like excitement. "To me it is a sign that we are getting close to something. These individuals probably have mercenary aims. The Grail possessor could command any price for his prize in today's world. Perhaps that is why they are following Colonel Streicher; they want us to find it, then they will try and take it for themselves and profit from the adventure."

Himmler took a labored puff on his cigar. "I agree that we are on to something, but I don't like the fact that Streicher let himself be bullied so easily, whoever and whatever that person is." He could not enjoy his smoke. He suddenly saw the Grail as his own property and the harassment by the Englanders as a personal affront, and it colored his perception of everything that was happening.

"Perhaps Streicher needs more support," Himmler puffed loudly. "Do we have anyone else over there who could help them with the annoying Englanders?"

Koln was caught off guard.

"Help them? We have Klein, his contact from Dorset, there for support," Koln said. "He created the diversion that enabled Colonel Streicher to get away."

"Klein?" Himmler groaned. "His best years are behind him. Who else do we have, with a little more wherewithal?"

Koln scratched his head.

"Uh, we have Mueller and his team outside of London, doing reconnaissance for the London phase of Operation Sea Lion," he said. "But Herr Reichsfuhrer, they have not been briefed on Operation Sangraal. Mueller and his team are hardly suited to something so esoteric." Mueller had a reputation for being aggressive and ruthless, and he had a long and bloody past as one of the Butcher *SS*.

"Perhaps Mueller and one of his team could be spared for a week or two," Himmler said. "Streicher could brief him on Operation Sangraal."

"Herr Reichsfuhrer, may I respectfully recommend that Colonel Mueller himself be allowed to continue his important work on the invasion?" Koln asked carefully. "His personnel are more than adequately qualified to lend Colonel Streicher the type of support he needs."

"Very well, so be it. Make the arrangements," puffed Himmler.

Herr Rahn was growing anxious listening to the discussion, especially when Mueller's name came up.

"May I remind everyone that this is a very different type of operation than most of the *SS* operatives have been trained for," Rahn said. "Discretion is of the utmost importance, and violence should be used only as a last resort. Sending out thugs to strong arm the English peasantry will almost certainly destroy our chances of finding it. It is against the very nature of the Grail: in the legends, only the purest of knights ever achieved it.

"Besides, whoever has assailed Colonel Streicher and his team could have taken far more severe action and did not. They would not appear to be too dangerous. In fact," Rahn paused a moment as he considered something, "they could be of service to us."

"Of course, Herr Rahn, of course," said Himmler. "That is clear. General Koln, make the arrangements, and be sure Mueller understands the nature of this assignment. And General, have a word with Colonel Streicher. He may be undercover, but he is still in the SS." The round spectacles flashed at Koln.

"Yes, Herr Reichsfuhrer," Koln replied smartly.

"Excellent, Herr Reichsfuhrer!" said Rahn. "Might I make one last suggestion?"

"Yes, Herr Rahn?" Himmler sighed.

"Perhaps they should rendezvous at the B Location. It is a site of tremendous potential that may not attract as much attention as Glastonbury, since it does not have as strong a Grail association, at least in popular history. In addition, it will allow things to cool a bit at Glastonbury." Rahn's palms started to perspire as he looked anxiously at Himmler. He knew there was a danger in making too many suggestions, especially after the disappointing results in the south of France.

"Very well, rendezvous at the B Location."

Grace and John stepped out of the tiny coffee shop and began to stroll down the street.

"I must say I'm a little embarrassed. I'm a graduate student and I still let myself get so caught up in this," she blurted out. "I should be smarter than that by now."

"Yes, me too." John replied, still confused. "It must have just been a remarkable coincidence that they knew about the connection of the historic Merlin and Ankerwyke Hill. After that I was ready to believe anything."

"Yes, the sword had me going," Grace said thoughtfully. "It must be some magician trick. The other strange thing is that they seem sincere enough—it's not like we're being conned out of money or anything. They just seem so intent on having us around…and I'm still not sure what help we really are to them."

He reached over and held Grace's hand. "Maybe we were just conned out of a ride to Glastonbury. If that's the case, then I'm happy to have done it but now must be moving on. Let's tell *Arthur* that when we meet, if that's his name."

They continued on in silence for two blocks, until John stopped suddenly.

"And yet, through all the years I've been studying," he whispered, as if he were speaking to himself, "there has been another part of me that always thought that Arthur would return." They were silent for a moment, and finally Grace replied.

"I'm sure all of us have had that thought."

He turned to her palely.

"But in the end we're left with the same horrible situation. The Germans really *are* going to invade England. It seems that our two friends are engaged somehow—don't ask me how—in efforts to prevent that. How will anything they're doing here matter in the final outcome?" He looked at her fair face lined with worry.

"I don't know, John. And for the life of me I can't imagine why they would want or need us to believe them to be—who they said they were." Grace felt it hard now to say their names. "This war seems to be causing a lot of people to lose their sanity." And as she pictured her mother's face quite clearly, she thought *I must be smarter.*

They had just arrived back at John's car. He sighed and looked at his watch.

"Well, I think it's time. Shall we meet our friend?"

"Yes," Grace answered, and they got in.

As they were driving, Grace saw another large wooden pub sign: The White Hart. It had a picture of a white stag with full antlers, framed by oak leaves. John saw it too, and found himself staring at the stag's large, black eyes which looked enigmatically at the viewer.

The eyes almost seem to follow you, he thought.

When Grace and John had finished exploring the town they drove back to the Tor, not at all sure if they would find Arthur. But when they pulled up Grace saw the tall, bearded figure in her father's raincoat just returning from the trail that disappeared around the foot of the hill.

"Is everything all right?" Grace asked Arthur as she got out of the car.

"Yes. I found what I was looking for. It is a cave, but it's too dark to see; I need a torch."

"But we need to be—" Grace began.

"I have one in the boot of the car," said John, and he quickly opened the trunk and produced a large flashlight.

Arthur puzzled over it for a moment. "That's not quite what I was expecting."

But he turned and started along a footpath that ran around the base of the hill.

"Follow me." John looked back at Grace apologetically, and she simply shrugged her shoulders. Ten minutes, she thought, then we really need to leave.

It was now late afternoon and Grace noticed an unmistakable hint of autumn in the air. She trudged along the path that skirted the bottom of the hill, passing fat sheep that looked up at her blankly before returning to their grazing. Finally they came to a crease between two hills, where the path went into a bushy area.

Arthur turned to the left between two large bushes and there, amongst a rocky outcropping, was a small tunnel opening. A few large rocks lying around the opening looked as if they had been recently disturbed.

"They have not been in here, not yet, because the tunnel was sealed off. I had to move away the rocks myself. And they had been in place a long time judging by the growth around them."

Arthur turned and looked at John.

"Torchbearer, lead the way!" he said with a smile.

John smiled weakly back at Arthur, then bent slightly and went into the tunnel. Arthur was behind him and Grace followed. She noticed the floor of the cave was a dirt path, but the sides and ceiling were jagged stone. Gradually the ceiling became higher so that first Grace, then John and Arthur, could stand up straight.

"This cave has been visited often," she remarked as he looked at the graffiti on the walls. The path was inclining, and the dirt path gave way to stone floor. But the daylight was diminishing with each step, and Grace began to fall behind.

"Be careful," John called back to her.

The tunnel bent around to the right, then opened into a small chamber, no more than twelve foot square. Grace stumbled in after Arthur, as John's light darted all around the small chamber. It was beginning to make her feel ill.

"May I?" she asked, holding out her hand for the flashlight.

"Of course," John replied.

She then placed the light on a rock outcropping so that it shone up to the ceiling and illuminated the small room.

"Much better." Arthur said, "Now, let's see what we have," and he began to examine the cave.

Grace and John tried to keep out of his way, which was a difficult task in the small chamber. After some time, Arthur stopped and sat on a larger stone protruding up from the floor. John also sat down while Grace leaned on a shallow ledge in the wall directly across from the chamber entrance.

"What are we looking for?" she asked.

"Anything. This is not a secret place, as we have seen," Arthur replied. "But you never know."

Just then the rock that Grace had been leaning on came loose. She had to catch herself as rocks and dirt fell onto the chamber floor. A cloud of dust filled the lower half of the cave, and Grace began to cough as it reached her face.

"Are you all right?" Arthur asked.

"Oh, yes, but I'm sorry, I didn't realize it might come loose," Grace said.

Arthur didn't reply. His attention was riveted on the spot in the wall that had just been exposed. Grace and John looked. The spot was about the size of a dinner plate and smooth, far too smooth to be natural. Bits of mortar still clung to it where the fallen rocks had been attached.

He took the flashlight from its place on the ledge and shined the light directly on the newly exposed surface. His eyes grew wide.

"Well, look what we have here," he said with a smile.

There on the stone was a pattern of five round dots, four forming the corners of a square, and the fifth, larger one in the very center.

"What is it?" asked John. Grace began to get a queer feeling in her stomach.

"This is the sign that the spies found in the tower above us," Arthur replied, still smiling, like he was seeing an old friend. "It has been associated with the Grail."

Grace felt faint, and it seemed to her as if the cave had started to spin around. She turned and started out of the tunnel, not waiting for Arthur and John.

"I need some air!" she called to them from the passage, and she staggered outside to the fresh air and daylight. It was twilight and noticeably cooler when Grace emerged from the cave, and it seemed to her she had never seen a sky so expansive or so beautiful.

On the hillside above her the bearded man from the pub in the broad-brimmed hat was just coming over the top of the hill toward the cave opening, when he saw Grace emerge. He stopped dead in his tracks.

"The woman from the pub last night! Is *she* after the grail too?" He was just starting down toward Grace, when John came out and ran up to Grace, touching her on the shoulder.

"Are you all right?" he asked, as she turned toward him.

"Yes, fine...I'm fine," Grace said. "I've never liked being in caves, and I think we just ran out of air in there."

"Are you quite sure?"

John suddenly had an overwhelming need to protect her, which he had never felt for anyone in quite the same way. It was as if Grace were a beautiful child who needed an adult to watch over her, or perhaps he was only now seeing the beautiful child inside her. Whatever it was, he was confused and did not know what to do or say. To Grace, John suddenly appeared to be strangely amorous.

"Yes, yes, quite sure," she said, eyeing him carefully.

"All right, then," John answered, and he embraced her, but she felt even more distant to him, and it was like a sweet, sharp stab in his heart. His feelings began to well up inside. He couldn't take it anymore; he had to do something.

Say something.

"I know we've technically been on only one date, but..." Grace watched him stammer, "b-but I think I love you." He looked like he had been caught off guard by his own words.

Grace looked up at him and smiled, and suddenly the distance between them vanished.

"I love you, too," she answered, surprised. She studied John's face as she smiled at him. It seemed to Grace as if she was hearing the words for the first time ever. She remembered the few times Roger had said he loved her—he always looked like it was being forced out of him. John had offered it to her openly, when it was the furthest thing from her mind.

Arthur came out holding the flashlight.

"Are you all right, Grace?"

"Yes, thank you. I'm sorry to act like such a child. I think I just ran out of air."

"Quite all right, you've both had a big day," Arthur said, but he was eyeing her curiously. "Let's head back."

John knew he should speak up. "Yes, about heading back, Grace and I—"

"Oh, I don't think I could stand a long car ride this afternoon," she said suddenly. John looked baffled but said nothing, he just stood looking at Grace as he scratched his head. She knew she would have to explain to him, as soon as she figured it out for herself.

They walked back to the car in the failing light and drove back to town as the stars were beginning to come out over the Tor. Watching from the hill above, the man in the broad-brimmed hat lit his cheroot with a puff, and watched the smoke billow into the evening sky.

"Apparently I am not the only one following the Germans," he said under his breath. "But why do these three risk so much? Is it possible they do not know how dangerous the Germans are?"

When the car was out of sight, he started slowly down the hill toward the little cave now hidden in the shadows.

Late that night at the roadside inn, Streicher slumped in front of the radio after receiving the new orders from headquarters. Dunst and Werner sat silently across the room.

"Mueller?" he repeated to himself in disbelief. "Why do we need a butcher like him?"

Suddenly Dunst spoke up. "He's the last person they should be sending us."

Streicher turned and looked at him, surprised that he had said anything.

"I mean, to find the Grail," Dunst offered. "Only the purest of knights was ever said to have attained it. In Chretien de Troyes or any of the Grail stories, someone like Mueller had no chance."

Streicher smiled for an instant, then began lighting a cigarette.

"Let's hope Chretien was wrong," he replied, standing up. "Whatever the case, orders are orders. In the morning, we leave for Location B. Let's take a look at your map, Lieutenant."

Werner handed him the folded map, which Streicher spread out on the bed. He began running his finger to the east along the paper, then stopped and began tapping his finger at one point.

"Winchester," he said as the smoke curled up around his eyes.

While sleeping on the floor of the room over the pub, John had an unusually clear dream. He was fishing at Lady's Well, when suddenly across the water he saw a magnificent white stag with a large set of antlers looking directly at him with its big, dark eyes. John dropped his pole and stood up, but the deer did not move or avert its gaze. It was as if the beautiful beast wanted something from him. John was drawn to it but frozen with confusion.

Suddenly Merlin was at John's elbow, dressed in the flowing robes they had first found him in, his large face full of urgency.

"You must follow it!" he whispered in John's ear.

The creature took a step into the trees, then stopped and looked back. He was trying to get John to follow! John started toward it, and with a flash of white and a rustling of leaves, the stag bolted into the woods. He started to run and at the same point at which the creature had vanished, he plunged into the forest. He looked up and saw that the white stag was already fifty yards ahead. John ran as fast as he could along the narrow winding path as branches whipped his arms and legs.

Suddenly John was aware of someone running immediately behind him. He was also chasing the white hart! Then the dream changed, and the winding path through the woods became a winding road on which John and the other pursuer were driving in automobiles as fast as they could. Both were desperate and drove with wild abandon. Just as his faceless opponent was pulling up alongside him to pass, John woke up.

He looked around the dark hotel room.

What a crazy dream, he thought, and he rolled over and went back to sleep.

Above him on the bed, Grace was wide awake. She was thinking of the time on the beach when she was seven, with just she and her grandparents, her late father's parents. She could remember it like it was yesterday. It was a warm summer day, the sun was shining on the waves and the beach was crowded with people. Her grandfather was helping her build sand castles.

He noticed the birthmark inside her right ankle and told her all about how special it was—how her father had had it on his ankle, too. Then he showed her the same birthmark there on his own ankle.

"Your great grandfather, my father had it on his ankle, and so did his father, your great great grandfather," he told her. "It has been in our family as long as anyone can remember, but you're the very first *girl* to have it."

She'd felt so special when he told her that, all those years ago. As time went by, it became more mundane, not so wonderfully significant as it had been that day on the beach. She had slowly come to think of it, after all, as just a birthmark on her skin—until that afternoon.

Grace kicked off the sheets and tried to look at her ankle in the dark room. The moonlight through the curtains provided her with just enough light to make it out: four dots forming a square, with one large dot in the very center.

Even though the fear in the pit of her stomach was still there, the memory of that day and how it had made her feel gave her the sense of being protected somehow from the insane, inexplicable situation she was finding herself in. She laid her head back on the pillow.

"Who *am* I?" she asked the darkness, and she fell asleep.

8. Return to Stokehill

The next morning was overcast, and a wet mist dripped onto the rooftops and hid the Tor in a cool gray cloak. Outside The King's Head, Arthur and Grace and John met as they had planned the night before. Before she had went into the little cave Grace thought it would be easy for she and John to part company with Arthur and Merlin. Now she was more confused than ever, and it no longer felt like something she could easily drive away from.

"I'm afraid I really must be getting back," Grace said stiffly to Arthur. "—to take care of my mother. Are you sure you'll be all right?"

Arthur didn't hesitate. "Of course. Don't worry about us."

Grace and John reluctantly got in the car while Arthur waited at the curb.

"Good bye for now, but you may hear from us. Be safe!" Arthur said with a wave, and John pulled out and they were on their way.

"How will we *hear* from them?" John wondered aloud as he drove through town.

"I don't know, but I feel like we're abandoning them," Grace said.

John turned east, onto the same road they had followed the spies on the day before.

He looked at Grace. Her face was long with worry, and he John wondered what had happened in the cave that so upset her. He was about to ask her about it, but he hesitated; it felt like something was blocking him from bringing it up.

She's probably just a little claustrophobic, he thought, and he shrugged it off.

Arthur made the trek back to the hidden wood and Merlin. A light rain had begun to fall as he turned onto the old footpath that led through the pastures. When he entered the damp wood, he saw Merlin brooding near the base of the yew tree, wearing his own robes and mantle. His eyes were slits, his beard dripped with rain, and he looked rooted to the earth as he stood beneath the canopy.

Merlin opened his eyes as Arthur approached. He looked as if he hadn't slept all night.

"Good morning," Arthur said.

"Good morning to you," Merlin replied, his mantle and robes covered with innumerable droplets of water. "How are our young ones?"

"They did have an encounter with the enemy, but they're all right. Grace has overstayed so they are now on their way home. " Arthur studied the ancient tree before him. "What have you learned, my friend?"

"Much, as we were told I would," Merlin said as he rubbed his tired face with his hands. He walked slowly over to a fallen log and sat down, and Arthur joined him. The wood was silent save for the gentle patting of raindrops on the leaves.

"The Grail party first settled here in secret all those centuries ago, in this wood initially, then near the Tor where the town is now. The Grail itself was kept in the cave under the Tor. But after time and generations passed, word slowly spread that this was more than just another holy place. Legends grew and the curious came. And so the Guardians, fearing they could no longer protect their charge, moved in great secrecy far, far away." Merlin paused, as if listening. His gaze seemed to follow that cloaked party on their slow, nighttime flight across the landscape of time.

"Does it still exist?" Arthur asked finally, betraying his own nagging doubts.

Merlin turned to him.

"Yes, but it has been lost. It had been safeguarded all those centuries, then somehow it slipped away from the safety of its guardians—I could not quite see how. I do know that the guardians believe again the same…misunderstanding that we struggled with. Maybe that had something to do with it." Arthur shook his head sadly.

"But the guardians have been looking desperately for twenty years, and now the enemy is trying to find it first. I don't know if the enemy realizes it is no longer in the safekeeping of the guardians, but he is after it nonetheless.

"And he has gotten closer to it than we thought. It could even be that his success in battle is a sign that it is destined that he to possess it. He seems to succeed at everything he tries, it all goes his way, and he aggressively presses his advantage. Late yesterday, Stokehill was bombed again."

Arthur's frustration was growing. "As we thought. Did Grace's—did the woman survive?"

"She did not."

"Where did the Grail move, all those years ago?"

"Different places, and at one time it was moved to the south of France, and the land was invaded by the Normans. But most recently it moved to Winchester—where it was lost," Merlin replied. "And although it was not revealed to me if it is there still, the enemy is on his way to Winchester as we speak. But that is where my knowledge ends; I can get no closer." He rubbed his face again and growled under his breath, irritated by his limitation. "My guess is that the way events are progressing, it is very likely there, somewhere."

Arthur's eyebrows widened. "They are headed there *now*? They are better informed than we thought."

"Yes! As I said, it could be their destiny; I do not know," Merlin replied, a fire suddenly in his eye. "But we cannot wait two days before going there. Things are developing too quickly. The fifteenth and the sixteenth of the month are pivotal for the air battle: the enemy will either be turned back or he will gain momentum and invade the country. The outcome was not revealed to me. But that is only two days away."

"And Grace," Merlin added, almost in a whisper, "Grace *is* the key."

Arthur rubbed his forehead.

"We explored the cave under the Tor yesterday afternoon, and some rocks fell away and she accidentally uncovered the sign. It was clear from her reaction that she recognized it," he said. "She nearly fainted."

"There is no doubt that she is the one, and it is increasingly dangerous to let her out of our sight. It all confirms the warning we received from—" Merlin's voice left him for a moment, then he continued.

"Grace is at least as important as the Grail itself."

"We must go now." Arthur stood, and together they took their leave of the great yew and the ancient wood and headed back down the footpath to Glastonbury.

Grace sat uncomfortably in the passenger seat as John barreled down the roads toward Stokehill, as if part of him was still racing with the Germans. Finally he stopped in a sunny, thatch-roofed village and used his remaining coupons for fuel, while Grace bought some bread and cheese for lunch at a small market.

As they sat in the car eating lunch, a tall, angular police constable came up to John's window.

"I'm afraid you can't park here," he said brusquely as he lowered his face to the open window. "Please move along."

John looked at him contemptuously for a moment.

"*Right*," he said sarcastically, his mouth full of bread. He choked down his food as he started the car and pulled out, annoyed that he couldn't finish eating in peace.

"What an idiot," he snarled after the last mouthful was on its way down.

Grace stopped eating and looked at him.

"Oh, John, he was just doing his job."

He looked back at Grace like he was about to argue the point, then he looked down and sighed. "I know."

"It's just my distrust of authority figures," he added flippantly, trying to make light of his reaction. "I learned all about it all in my undergrad Psychology class. It all stems from my relationship with my father, or lack thereof."

"Well, if that's the case, maybe it's a good thing you didn't enlist in the Army," Grace said half smiling. "It's nothing *but* authority figures."

They were soon up to speed, and after a while Grace spoke up again.

"Why do you think things didn't go well with you and your Dad?" she asked gently as she turned toward him again.

"I don't really know," he mused. "I suppose there were two sides to it, like everything. I remember the time when I was seven, and he and I were together in the back garden. I was playing with a stick, pretending it was a sword. Well, I ended up throwing the stick and hitting him in the thigh accidentally— pretty high up on the thigh, actually. You should have seen the look on his face," John said as his face flushed with the memory. "You'd have thought it was a real sword, the way he looked at me. Things were not the same after that."

Grace looked at the road ahead of them.

"Losing him at an early age didn't help matters either, I'm sure," she said. "You didn't have a chance to get to know each other as adults."

"I suppose," John said, and he continued driving in silence. Grace decided to let the matter drop.

They both watched the cars driving by. Most of the traffic on the road was going against them, away from the war.

"Are we crazy?" John asked as he watched the steady stream of oncoming traffic.

Grace didn't answer immediately; she was still afraid, but not as much. Her birthmark had been on her ankle her whole life, and only now did she begin to understand that it wasn't just a birthmark, it was a sign, waiting silently for her. She was meant to do all this, even if she didn't know where it was all leading, or what might happen to her before it was over.

"I suppose we are," she finally answered.

Grace reached over and held John's hand, then smiled at him. She would tell him about her birthmark, but not yet. She wasn't ready yet, and let out a sigh.

Who am I?

Dunst parked the car at the curb and the three men got out and looked around. It was a clear, sunny afternoon, and they had two hours before the rendezvous with Mueller's men, so they began to stroll through the town. On one end was the full-size statue of an old warrior-king, with his sword held high.

"Alfred the Great," Streicher said, with a tinge of admiration. "Their only monarch with that appellation. This was his capitol."

Dunst and Werner were also impressed. All three men had lived in England at some point in their lives and even then, in the middle of a war, there was much in the country that appealed to them.

"One wonders what it would be like to meet such a person, one of the old warrior-kings," Streicher mused.

"Indeed!" Dunst answered, intrigued by the idea. "A leader in the original sense of the word. I suppose he would feel quite out of place in our world. Still, it would be fascinating."

They continued up the main street, crossing a bridge under which flowed a beautiful rushing stream. Upstream they could see the green playing fields of a boys' school, stretching far into the distance.

A subtle feeling slowly stole over the three men as they strolled up the street. It was as if they were at the very heart of England, where somehow the essence of the land had been distilled and was floating invisible in the air, like some narcotic.

They continued walking in silence, but the feeling was so strong that they lingered here and there like tourists enjoying a holiday.

Further on up the high street, they turned into a short arched passage; when they emerged, they saw two rows of trees lining a path to a sprawling gothic cathedral. Streicher turned onto the path and the other two followed him. They entered the church and began looking casually around.

Streicher turned a corner and stopped. He pointed up. There, high on the wall, was an ancient depiction some twenty feet across of the Round Table, with Arthur's court seated around it. Streicher looked around to see if anyone was within earshot. They were alone.

"I have a good feeling about this place," he said quietly.

"We're almost home," John announced, waking up Grace, who had been asleep for some time.

She sat up and stretched. It was mid-afternoon and they were in the outskirts of Stokehill. Immediately Grace knew something was wrong. There was a chaotic rush of traffic leaving town, and the civil defense personnel and roadblocks were everywhere. One of the officers was directing traffic, and John rolled down his window and slowed down to speak with him as he went past.

"Excuse me. We've been away a few days. What's going on?"

The officer quickly removed the whistle from his mouth.

"The Germans dropped a few more bombs on us yesterday. One landed just down the street there," he said, pointing beyond some of the barricades.

John had to keep moving.

"Thanks," he shouted, and he rolled up his window. Grace sat silent for a moment, then felt a rush of panic.

"*Mum!*"

"I know—we'll go there right now."

He drove as quickly as traffic would allow, but it was painfully slow. They crossed over one of the small bridges the Culvert was piped under. Grace looked down and saw something she had not seen in all her life. It was dry.

"There's no water in the Culvert!" she cried.

"It's probably blocked by debris from one of these bloody bombs," John seethed.

As they approached Grace's street they saw it was barricaded and crowded with emergency vehicles.

"Oh my god!" she gasped. She felt like she was watching her worst nightmare come true. John pulled up to the civil defense officer posted at the barricade and parked the car. Grace burst out of the car.

"I live on this street! Can I get down to my house?"

"Which one is yours?" asked the uniformed man carefully.

Grace swallowed hard. "Number nine."

His face relaxed. "Yes, that one didn't get hit. You can go down, but please leave your car here."

Grace felt some of the weight lifted from her, but she knew her troubles were far from over. John reached over and held her hand.

"Thank you," he said to the officer, and they rushed down the lane of Victorian row houses.

The street curved such that they couldn't see any damage at first, but soon they saw what the barricades were for. There was a fire engine in the middle of the road in front of numbers 26 and 24. Then they saw why. The left side of number 26 and the right side of number 24 were completely gone. Below in piles lay black, charred brick and wood, and some barely recognizable items like chairs and tables, all burnt and broken. Shattered glass lay everywhere.

"Oh my god!" Grace said in shock. "Mrs. Davies! She's the old dear my mother and I were always visiting." John had a terrible feeling as he looked at the mass of debris from number 26.

Was her mother visiting Mrs. Davies when the bomb fell?

Grace went up to a stiff-looking female civil defense officer with carrot red hair tucked up under her uniform cap.

"Has anyone been hurt?"

The woman studied Grace as if from a great distance. "Yes, I'm afraid there were at least two casualties, one in each home. Where do you live?"

"Number nine," Grace answered as she tried to grasp the news. *Poor old Mrs. Davies!* she thought.

"Do you know who it was in number 26?" Grace asked.

"I'm afraid they haven't been identified yet—the bodies are nearly unrecognizable," the woman said gravely. "I just hope we don't find any more. There is still so much to dig through."

Grace felt faint and she gripped John's hand with all her might.

"Thank you," she said, and they hurried down to her own house. They reached the front door of number 9 and Grace burst in.

"Mum!" she called out. Dead silence. She ran into the kitchen, then dashed back and bounded up the stairs. Grace had nothing but anger for her mother for weeks, so that the nearly forgotten feeling of attachment to her mother, and the guilt at all her anger, hit her all at once like a strong punch in the stomach.

"*Mum*, are you here?" she shouted as she checked each room.

John heard the panic in Grace's shouts, and was expecting the worst as he peeked around every corner downstairs and outside in the small back garden. He was now very glad that his own family had gone to Wales, but had it been his own mother that they were looking for, he could not have wanted to find her more.

Grace rushed down the stairs as John was returning from the garden.

"Any sign?" she asked him out of breath, her face white with panic.

"None," he replied, trying to remain calm.

"I haven't seen her since yesterday," said a voice from the doorway.

They turned and saw the silhouette of a heavyset woman standing on the threshold. It was Mrs. Burke from next door.

"I was talking with her outside when the sirens started yesterday, and it really seemed to shake her up. But we both had to go back indoors. Then a little while later, the bomb went off just down the street, and I just thought the world was ending! It was horrible!" Mrs. Burke's voice was cracking and she covered her mouth for a moment.

"When they sounded the all-clear siren, we all went out to see what had happened, everyone on the street, but your mother never came out. I thought it was strange, but I didn't check on her at the time, because our houses weren't hit," she said haltingly. "I thought she was all right. But when I came by early this morning, she…wasn't here. Then I realized she hadn't been here since the bombs fell—she must have left *during* the bombing."

Grace was having a hard time figuring out what it all meant.

"*Why?* Why would she do that? Where on earth could she have gone?" she asked desperately, as she turned to John.

He felt so bad he had trouble getting the words out, and he plunged his hands deep into his pockets.

"I—I don't know," he stammered. John pictured Grace's mother running to Mrs. Davies' house to comfort her during the attack.

Grace thought about her mother, in a fragile emotional state, alone and terrified while bombs were dropped just a few yards from her own doorstep. She couldn't bear it any longer, and she started to cry. John took her in his arms.

Just then a low wail started in the distance, slowly building in pitch and volume.

"The air-raid sirens!" blurted Mrs. Burke, in a kind of controlled shriek. "It's starting again! Be careful, Grace!" She turned around and disappeared down the front steps.

The sirens soon started to fade, but all was not quiet. They heard a monotonous drone in the warm summer air, steadily increasing in volume. John looked out the front door at the blue sky, but he saw nothing.

Suddenly they heard the loud snarl of a fighter engine and high above, a vapor trail traced a huge arc in the sky. Soon other trails were formed as the first one started to slowly expand and fade. John and now Grace were riveted by the action in the sky above them. Finally, a white dot appeared against the blue heavens, gradually getting larger.

John pointed up. "Look! A parachute!"

Back in Glastonbury, Arthur and Merlin had walked back to town, discussing their predicament along the way. They turned onto the road heading east out of town and continued walking on the shoulder. It was warm and sunny, and they were both hungry.

"Care for another apple?" Arthur offered, producing two of the small apples from his pocket.

"Yes, although I don't suppose you have some roast beef in there as well?" Merlin asked with a smirk.

Arthur smiled and handed him an apple. A car was approaching from behind, getting loud as it got closer.

"This one?" Arthur asked.

"No," Merlin said without looking back. They continued walking along the gravel shoulder of the road as the car flew past them.

"Just as well," Merlin continued, "I never thought I'd have one of these apples."

Arthur swallowed a bite of apple.

"I never thought I'd come back, and I never thought I'd see you again, old friend. A lot is happening now that no one thought would happen; much of it bad, but maybe some of it will turn out good. Who knows," he said, looking at Merlin, "perhaps you will partake of more than just the apples someday."

They heard another car coming from behind them.

"This one?" Arthur asked impatiently.

"No," Merlin replied, again without looking back. They continued walking along the dusty shoulder as the second car zoomed by.

"Well," Merlin continued, "After I was allowed to visit Joseph and see with my own eyes the...well, my thirst for knowledge became unquenchable, and it was my undoing." He rubbed his forehead with a clenched fist and looked up to the high blue sky. The twinkle in his eye was gone and he looked to Arthur like a tired old man. Merlin continued.

"The power we both serve is mysterious and sometimes fickle: she tantalizes one with glimpses but rarely does she offer the whole picture. I thought I could develop my arts to a point where I could learn everything I wanted, not just what was revealed to me. That gnawed at me until . . . I was consumed by it." He sighed loudly, and they continued plodding along the road in silence.

"I know," Arthur finally replied. "But that was in ages past, and time heals all. And heaven knows, a lot of time has gone by."

They heard the sound of another engine coming from behind. Suddenly the sound changed—it was now a rough, mechanical staccato, and far too loud. Merlin turned around in an instant and saw a car driving on the gravel shoulder heading straight for them. He caught a glimpse of the driver in a black mackintosh bearing down on them.

Everything suddenly seemed to move in slow motion. With one hand Merlin grabbed Arthur by the arm and pulled him away from the road, and with the other he waved in a circular motion. The car was only ten feet away and still flying when its front wheels turned away from the two men. The black-clad driver looked at the steering wheel in his hand like it was betraying him as gravel and dust filled the air. Merlin and Arthur fell against the wire fence as the car passed them and the driver regained control. Merlin saw blood on Arthur's arm and back and looked at the fence: it was a barbed wire cattle fence, six feet high. The car stopped fifty yards down and turned around in the road.

"Here he comes!" Arthur cried. They heard its motor revving and saw the tires squeal and the driver's face fixing on them. Arthur and Merlin stood up against the fence as the car came barreling toward them on the shoulder of the road, a huge cloud of dust and gravel trailing behind it. The driver was steering the car up against the fence, the wire flexing as sparks flew off the car. The hideous screech of scratching metal filled the air, and it seemed to Arthur and Merlin like a demon was bearing down on them.

The car was only twenty yards away when Merlin waved his hand again, but even though the wheels turned, they lost their grip in the loose gravel and the car began to fishtail, coming at them with a sinister twisting motion. Merlin climbed on the fence, and the barbs dug into his hands and scratched his face. He saw a flash of light and looked for his companion.

Arthur was holding Excalibur out in front of him, crouched like a lion on the roadway in front of the oncoming vehicle, trying to get him to turn away from Merlin on the fence. Just before the car reached him, Arthur bounded back toward the fence and across and *over* its path, using the sword to vault over the passing car. Excalibur punctured the windshield and penetrated the interior, severing the right hand of the driver as Arthur flipped over, feet first and hit the gravel, sword in hand. Arthur was caught by the wire fence, and the rear panel of the car struck Merlin at the hip, and knocked him off the fence and onto the gravel as the car throttled past him.

The driver was clutching his bleeding limb, his face deathly white as he managed to stop the car twenty yards down from them. It was now perpendicular to the road. Merlin picked himself off the ground as Arthur dashed up to the idling car, brandishing Excalibur. The black driver saw him and accelerated in a panic, but the wheels spun wildly in the gravel. He finally got the car back on the road just as Arthur reached him, and as he tried to drive away he heard another loud metallic crash. Arthur had swung Excalibur and cut a long gash in the back of the car near the petrol tank.

The driver turned at the crossroads a hundred yards down and disappeared. Arthur rejoined Merlin and was about to say something when a loud *boom* shook them, and they saw a fireball rise over the fields a few hundred yards away. They stared at it for a moment and then looked at each other.

"The enemy's spies are everywhere," Arthur said. "He was the one who fired the shot back in town." But Merlin was staring open-mouthed at him.

"I never saw you do *that* before!" he said.

"I never faced one of *those* before." But he looked at his hands gripping the sword and he knew Merlin was right. *What else can I do?*

Another vehicle from town was coming down the road, and they both watched it anxiously.

"This is the one," Merlin said as his face brightened, waving at the vehicle.

They heard a loud squeak of brakes as it whooshed past. On the shoulder ahead of them, a lorry with some farm equipment in the back slowly pulled to a stop in a cloud of dust. Arthur and Merlin quickly ran up to the open passenger window.

"Where are you going?" asked the driver, peering at them over some boxes in the passenger seat.

"Winchester," Merlin smiled.

The driver looked surprised at them for a second. "Well, today's your lucky day. That's where I'm headed, although with everything going on, I wish I were going the other way. Get in, if you don't mind riding in the back."

"Not at all. Thank you very much," said Arthur, and they climbed into the back with the equipment.

They sat facing the rear with their backs against the cab, and settled in for a long drive. Arthur turned to Merlin whose eyes once again had the familiar twinkle.

"Good work, my friend. Good work."

Colonel Streicher stood on the cathedral lawn and lit another cigarette. Dunst and Werner stood awkwardly nearby, squinting into the afternoon sun.

Streicher was irritated; in his mind, he neither needed nor wanted more help. He was certain that they would only hinder him, and the kind of help they would provide would likely cause real trouble. He flicked the white cigarette ash onto the lawn with an angry jerk.

Finally they saw two men walking purposively toward them from across the street. Werner recognized one of them from a previous assignment, and he walked over to where Streicher was standing.

"Here they come, Herr Colonel," he said quietly.

Streicher put out his cigarette in the grass with a twist of his boot and watched the two men approach. They were younger, about the age of Dunst and Werner; one was short and stocky with a large roman nose and the other was taller, blond, and had a mouth full of crooked teeth. Neither looked familiar to him, but that didn't matter. If they were working with Mueller, he knew what to expect. The *SS* was full of that type.

You knew that when you joined, he thought, and he kicked at the smoldering cigarette butt. They came up to Streicher and stopped sharply, betraying an unmistakable deference to his rank.

"Is this the home of the Pendragon?" the shorter one recited, and waited for a reply.

Streicher just looked at them, making no effort to hide his disdain for them and the whole situation. Finally he spoke.

"He is gone, across the sea," he answered stiffly. Both men smiled weakly as Streicher continued examining them.

"Come this way," he said, and he turned and led them around the cathedral, past the boys' school, and out onto the empty playing fields where they would not be overheard. The school had been closed because of the war and the proximity of the air battles, and the campus was deserted.

Mueller's men followed close on either side of Streicher, while Dunst and Werner trailed behind. Acres and acres of green lawn spread out before them, framed by a line of trees that followed the stream on the left, and by the gothic stone buildings of the boys' school on their right.

"What are your names?" Streicher asked when he was certain they could not be overheard.

"Lieutenants Zimmer," said the shorter one, then nodded to his companion, "and List."

"Well, Zimmer and List, this is not like any assignment you've been on," Streicher said severely as they walked along. "We have had special training for this task, and we have made tremendous progress.

"Some local inhabitants at the A Location stumbled onto our work, so the high command sent you. But I want to be very clear." He stopped and turned toward the two. "I will not have the sensitivity and the success of this operation compromised by reckless behavior. If either of you steps out of line, I will see to it that your next assignment is not so pleasant. Do you understand?" Streicher had moved very close to both men and was glaring at them as if he would strike them if they gave the wrong answer.

"Yes, Herr colonel," they replied nervously. Streicher held his gaze.

I never threatened another officer in the Wehrmacht, he thought as he stared down the two young men in front of him. Now look at me.

Streicher shook his head, then turned abruptly and began walking quickly, as he began briefing them on his plan for the investigation of the cathedral. Zimmer and List were nearly skipping along beside him, trying to keep up. Before he could finish, they heard a low siren start, then build in pitch and volume.

"The air-raid siren," said Streicher. "We must return to the inn." And they turned back and headed across the field to the town.

9. Winchester

Later that afternoon, Grace and John heard the all-clear siren and bolted out of the house to search for Grace's mother. On their way to the car, they saw the redheaded civil defense woman standing rigidly in the street, writing on a clipboard. Grace dashed up and stood in front of her.

"Has anyone reported seeing Mrs. Arundel from number 9?" she asked anxiously. "She hasn't been home." The woman looked up efficiently from her clipboard.

"No, I'm terribly sorry, I'm afraid not." Then she hesitated a moment, and her complexion was suddenly more pale. "Could she have been in either of these two houses?"

Suddenly Grace felt a huge weight bearing down on her, and her gaze fell to the ground.

"I hope not," she managed to say. "She did visit Mrs. Davies in number 26 on occasion. We both did."

"Well, they're not done going through there yet, but let's assume the best," the woman replied, more warmly. "If she was home alone, she may have gone to a friend's house, or some other place where she felt safe. Perhaps you can try places like that. Good luck!"

"Thank you," replied Grace, and they hurried up the street to John's car.

Grace looked at John after they had settled in.

"Let's try St. Luke's. Maybe she was called in and forgot to leave a note." She crossed her arms protectively in front of her.

John drove as fast as he could on the east road, and they were soon at the small, whitewashed hospital at the edge of town. Grace directed John around to the emergency entrance, where he stopped the car.

"Wait here, all right?" she asked him as she opened the door.

"Yes, of course."

Grace strode up to the large open door and looked inside the emergency ward. The waiting area was nearly bursting with injured people, and all the doctors, nurses, and orderlies were rushing about with frantic, haggard faces. She looked everywhere, but there was no sign of her mother in all the chaos. Finally she saw the thin face of Mrs. Keegan, her mother's supervisor. Mrs. Keegan saw Grace and came up to her at once.

"Hello Grace, is everything all right?" she asked, sensing Grace's trouble. "How's your mother?" Grace noticed Mrs.

Keegan's face looked thinner than ever, but she still felt a glimmer of hope.

"I was hoping you could tell me," Grace cried. "I can't find her. One of the bombs dropped yesterday landed on our street, and I think she may have panicked and gone somewhere, but I have no idea where. There was no note or anything. I thought she might have been called in here."

Mrs. Keegan looked shocked for a moment. "She's not here, I'm afraid. What time did you notice her missing?" Grace felt her hope sink in her chest, and she had to force herself to speak loudly enough for Mrs. Keegan to hear her.

"Well, I didn't stay at home last night, so I really didn't find out until early this afternoon when I got back. But I talked to her on the phone yesterday afternoon, which must have been right before the attack, and she seemed fine."

"I have to get back to a patient now, but I'll spread the word around here, and if she turns up we'll ring you right away," she said kindly, her narrow features broadening into a smile.

"In the mean time, try friends' houses, or anywhere she might have felt safer. Try not to worry!" she added as she began to pull herself away.

"Thank you very much, Mrs. Keegan." Grace slipped out the door and back to John parked at the curb.

"Well?" he asked gently.

"She hasn't been there," Grace answered almost inaudibly, as she sank down in the car seat. "I feel really awful being away when this happened." She felt on the edge of bursting into tears. John reached over to hold her hand.

"Please don't blame yourself, Grace," he said. "Everything that's happening has really hit her hard, and your being home last night probably wouldn't have changed anything."

Grace kept seeing the pile of rubble from Mrs. Davies house in her mind's eye, and it was filling her with dread.

Is Mum at the bottom of all that? The thought of losing her mother had become her greatest fear when her father died, and it haunted her dreams growing up. Now it was staring her straight in the face. She tried to put it out of her mind as they drove off.

The sun had set and she knew it would be curfew soon, and she still had no idea where her mother was, whether she was safe or hurt, alive or dead. They had time to look at only one more place.

"Let's try my grandfather's," she said at last.

"That makes sense," John said with encouragement. "It's so close to her house."

They drove in silence back across town, crossing the little bridge over the dry Culvert, to an older cottage not far from Lady's Well. John pulled up to the curb and Grace led them up a garden path to the front door, past late-blooming roses and fragrant lavender. Grace knocked loudly on the front door, and they heard a muffled voice from inside.

"I'm coming, I'm coming."

After a moment the door opened, and Grace's grandfather appeared wearing the same green plaid shirt, with a surprised smile.

"Grace!"

"Hello, Granddad," Grace replied anxiously. "I'm looking for mother. She hasn't been seen since the bombing yesterday. Has she been here?"

The old man's expression changed from surprise to shock, and he suddenly aged before their eyes.

"She hasn't been *seen*? I haven't seen her."

Grace had already known in her heart that her mother had not been there, and she couldn't make herself tell him that her mother may have been with Mrs. Davies when the bomb fell. She felt the emptiness inside her growing as she stood on the front step in the failing light.

"Come in, please," he said opening the door.

Grace and John stepped into the parlor, where the radio was blaring. Her grandfather ambled slowly across the room and turned it off.

"I'm sure she's all right, Grace," he said as he straightened up from the radio. "Won't you sit down?"

"We really can't stay, Granddad. It's curfew now." Grace stood looking stiff and drawn. John sank his hands into his pockets.

"Oh, curfew." He stood smiling at Grace for a moment, trying to think of something to ease her mind. Then something occurred to him.

"Grace, can I give you something while you're here? It's something that I've been meaning to give you for a while." He went to the mantle and opened a dusty wooden box. He carefully took out an old photograph and brought it to her.

It was a picture of her father that Grace had not seen before. He was young and handsome, dressed in a dark suit and tie.

"He was twenty five in that picture," her grandfather said fondly. "Your age, Grace. It was taken for your parents' engagement . . . or some special occasion." He scratched his head, trying to remember.

Grace drank in every feature, every detail of the picture. Now the thought of their shared birthmark made her feel closer to her father than ever before.

"Thank you, Granddad," she said softly, and for a moment she felt better.

He looked at John.

"I suppose he was my son-in-law, but to me he was just my son," he said with a sad smile. John smiled at him in return.

Grace suddenly wondered if her father had ever had any duty or adventure because of the birthmark. There was so much about him she did not know. *Would Granddad know?*

There was no time to ask him now. Her thoughts rushed back to her mother, and Grace was again filled with dread. She took a step toward the door.

"We really must be leaving," she said as she motioned to John, who opened the door.

"All right," her grandfather said patiently. He went up and kissed her on the cheek.

"She'll turn up soon. Be strong, Grace," he said with a gleam in his eye, as if he could see something in her. Grace felt empty and not at all strong, but she managed a smile for him.

"I'll try," she replied, and she took a step out the door. John was already headed down the path.

"Call me when you find her." Her grandfather was smiling confidently from the doorway.

"We will," she answered as she followed John to the car. "Good bye, Granddad."

"Good bye, Grace. Good bye, John," he called out with a wave. Suddenly he was filled with sadness, and from the car Grace could not see him bite his lip.

"Lost for twenty years…"

The car pulled away as Grace waved to her grandfather through the window. John felt panic creeping in, and try as he might, he was powerless to stop it. He wanted to help Grace, but he was frustrated at his own inability to come up with the right thing to say or do.

"Maybe we should go back and ring all her friends, ring every phone number we can find," he said finally, but the words themselves sounded weak as he spoke them, and he went silent.

"Yes, all right," Grace replied, as she clutched the photograph to her chest. Then she began to cry.

She was too young when her father died to remember very much, but she couldn't imagine feeling any worse than she did at that moment. That biggest of fears that she had been fighting her whole life—losing a parent again—now appeared to be inevitable, and she felt herself ready to give up the fight. The dark sky seemed to be filling her soul, creating a black void that was getting deeper and deeper, and Grace felt like she was falling into it.

John reached over and held her hand again, but he felt it might be good to let her cry a bit and get it all out.

In only a minute or two, they were back at Grace's street, where they were allowed to drive the car past the barricades and up to Grace's house. John stopped the car and turned off the engine. Grace just sat there for a moment in the dark, not moving, tears streaming down her face. Then she looked out the car window at the house.

There was a light on, a warm, yellow glow coming invitingly from inside.

"She's home!" Grace exclaimed, and she bolted from the car, leaving the door open and John still sitting inside. She bounded up the steps and burst through the front door.

"Mum!" Grace shouted, "Is that you?"

"Grace? Where have you been?" said a voice.

It was her mother, coming out of the brightly lit kitchen in her bathrobe. They embraced tearfully as John came through the front door, and the heavy weight that Grace had been carrying all afternoon evaporated in the warm light of the Arundel home.

Grace and John sat at the kitchen table drinking tea while Grace's mother stood at the stove fixing dinner and relating the events of the past two days. John could not get over the change in Grace's mother. Since he and Grace had started dating, her mother had hardly looked at him, but now not only was she speaking to him, she was fussing over him like one of her own.

"John, how's your tea?" she asked him again.

"Fine, thanks," he replied, suddenly confident, and a smile lingered on his face. Then in a flash, the old Mrs. Arundel returned.

"Tell me again where you two were for two days?" Grace froze with the teacup at her lips and John's smile vanished.

I knew it wouldn't last, she thought. She heard John clear his throat.

"Glastonbury. I needed to do some field research for my degree, and Grace was good enough to go with me." He smiled and tried to nonchalantly set his cup down, but it hit the edge of the saucer with a *clank* and tea spilt onto the table. Mrs. Arundel stared intensely at him, then suddenly her face lightened and she returned to the frying pan on the stove.

"Oh," she replied, as if she had lost interest in what John just said. Grace looked at him in amazement. She was planning to make some excuse about not visiting her friend Beth, but there no longer seem to be any need. She just shrugged her shoulders and reached for a dishtowel to wipe up the tea. Her mother continued her story.

"When the bomb went off down the street, something inside me…snapped," she said sheepishly, "and I ran out the front door.

It felt like anything was better than to have the house collapse on me. When I went past the house of the Italian family around the corner, Mrs. D'Innocenti begged me to come in. I must have been quite a sight! And the strangest thing is, later, when she insisted that I spend the night, I agreed." She gave a puff of embarrassed laughter.

Grace knew how out of character that was for her mother. She had never spoken well of Mrs. D'Innocenti, and her favorite complaint was that the house smelled of garlic. She could see her mother clearly blushing as she stood over the stove, and she was careful to appear as if she didn't notice her embarrassment.

"Poor old Mrs. Davies!" her mother said suddenly, stopping what she was doing. She instinctively clutched her cross necklace. "The second I saw her house, I knew she was gone. God rest her soul." She shook her head, then returned to the stove.

"The poor old dear!" Grace added. She hadn't been able to think about anyone but her mother all afternoon, and the feeling of loss for her old friend came over her suddenly.

As she watched her mother stirring the pot, Grace felt like she had been away for months, not days, so much had happened and so much had changed. She slowly realized that in that short time *she* had changed. She watched her mother at the stove as she had thousands of times before, but this time she was looking at her differently, as if her mother was smaller somehow, and for the first time she and Grace were the same.

Then her mother stopped again, as if she had just remembered something. She put down the spoon and looked at them. John carefully put down his teacup and braced himself for another question.

"I'm going to stay with my cousin Elizabeth in York, Grace," she said, eyeing Grace's reaction. "You can come with me, if you like," she added. "But all this bombing is getting to be too much for me. I'm getting too old."

Grace stared dumbly at her mother for a moment.

No more fighting, no more spinster *barbs?* Grace realized she would finally be on her own, and something inside her leaped.

Don't cheer—say something mature.

"I'm glad to hear it, Mum," Grace said evenly. "It will do you a world of good." She looked at John, who smiled back at her.

"Yes," he added, "my mum and my younger brother have been in Aberystwyth in Wales with family for two weeks now, and I think it makes a lot of sense."

Mrs. Arundel looked at John as if he had just delivered another pearl.

Later that night, John returned to his spartan apartment to find his roommate at the kitchen table with a bottle of beer in his hand, reading a dry-looking periodical under the lone light bulb suspended over the table.

"Well, there you are," Dennis said when he came into the room.

"Hello," John answered. He opened the small ice box and retrieved a bottle of beer for himself.

"How was your trip?" Dennis asked with a grin, as John sat down at the table. "I'm going to have to start calling you John of Glastonbury."

"Ha!" John puffed at Dennis's historic reference. "That's a name I haven't heard in a long time." John quickly became lost in thought, but he took a sip and continued. "As for my little trip, Grace was good enough to go with me."

"Yes, I got your note." Dennis said enthusiastically, as he sat up in his chair. "You *are* getting to be quite the Romeo. Things are obviously going well." John usually wasn't fond of the banter about women that men engaged in, but this time he didn't mind.

"Yes, very well," he said. "But also very strange." He knew he couldn't tell Dennis everything, not by a long shot. "You know, the war and all."

"Oh, yes, I know," Dennis grumbled as he slumped back in his seat. "Did you hear the Germans bombed the Math and

Science building, and Dewey Hall yesterday? They may have solved your Mr. Martin problem for you—I heard he's one of the missing."

John sat in stunned silence, racked by guilt over his feelings toward his advisor. Suddenly the man didn't seem to John like such a bad chap after all.

"At any rate," Dennis continued, "that's the straw that broke the camel's back—they will have to close the university, at least for a semester or two."

John cradled his bottle of beer between his knees. "I guess it's the right thing to do," he said finally. "Stokehill is just too much in the middle of the war. We're putting Grace's mother on a train for York in the morning because of it."

"I have half a mind to get on a train myself, although I don't know where I would go," Dennis said matter-of-factly. He was from nearby Brighton, and things were no better there.

"We could enlist," John said, looking up from his beer at his roommate. "And fight the Germans."

"Yes," Dennis answered palely, "now that the university is closed, we may not have a choice." As if on cue, they both had a drink out of their beer bottles.

"Do you think we'll be able to hold off an invasion?" John asked after they had finished.

"I don't believe we can stop them on our own. If they're determined to invade England, then sooner or later they'll succeed. And they've built up so much momentum, it's more likely to be sooner. If Russia or America joined, that might be different. But if the Nazis are successful," he looked soberly at John, "they will pillage and plunder as they've been doing on the continent."

John looked up at him. "Plunder? Valuable art and such?"

"Yes," he replied, "the sacred and the profane, and everything in between. There are rumors that Herr Himmler has a taste for the occult and the mystical."

John had an odd feeling. "Such as...?"

"Well, if you believe in such things," Dennis answered as sat up and rested his elbows on the table, "they are going through a great deal of effort to find the Holy Grail! That's only a rumor, mind you. I heard it from a friend of a friend, who has French cousins in the Pyrenees, and it probably got garbled in the translation. But if it were true, could you imagine?"

John was frozen as he studied Dennis's expression.

Does he know what I've been up to? His roommate's expression looked innocent enough to John, and he decided that it must be coincidental, but he still could not get over the inexorable way events had been converging on him.

"Are you all right, old boy?" Dennis asked as he looked curiously at him.

"Yes, sorry, I must be more tired than I thought," John answered. "The Holy Grail?" he finally repeated. "Do you believe there is such a thing?"

"Of course not," Dennis guffawed. "Well, at least I think it's highly unlikely. I don't doubt that it must have existed at one time. But if it did still exist and the legends are true—"

Then he stopped and looked at John.

"Once again, of course, we're in your field, old boy. What do *you* think?"

John looked down into the half-empty beer bottle in his hands, as if it were a telescope peering at some dark, distant place.

"If it does *exist*, and if the legends are true," he repeated carefully, "they would be unstoppable."

That night Grace dreamt she was looking at a huge, flat expanse of lawn, framed by trees and a few scattered gothic buildings. It was the playing fields of some school, and in the distance she could see players in angel-white uniforms in a cricket match. Dappled sunlight filtered through the trees, and the white figures seemed to float just above the grass.

Suddenly Merlin was at her elbow. The scenery changed, and they were now standing on a straight path lined on both sides by tall trees, leading to an ancient gothic cathedral. Merlin's large whiskered face was directly in front of her.

"You must go here, by midday tomorrow," he said solemnly.

Grace was confused. "But I don't know where it is," she replied, yet as she spoke it began to look familiar. Then Merlin vanished, and Grace was alone on the path as the two rows of trees swayed in the wind. The wind was blowing through her hair, and it felt like it was blowing through her very soul, somehow blowing away the Grace she thought she knew, until it was gone, and she was left with just her soul.

She tried to call out, *Who am I?* but she had no voice, and she woke up with a start and looked around the dark room.

"Home," she said groggily, and she fell back to sleep.

In Winchester at that moment, armed with flashlights and dressed in dark clothes, Streicher and his men slipped out of their inn and over to the cathedral close. The streets were empty and all the lights of the town were blacked out.

They were able to enter the cathedral through an unlocked side door. Once inside, they split into two teams and began to explore. Werner and List began at the far end of the cathedral, while Streicher, Dunst and Zimmer stood below the picture of the Round Table high upon the wall.

"We'll need a ladder to get a closer look. See if you can find something," Streicher said quietly, and Dunst and a bored-looking Zimmer began looking for a ladder. Streicher lit a cigarette and casually strolled through the church, shining his torch as he walked along.

It was just after midnight when a constable on the street outside saw a light flicker, then vanish, in one of the cathedral windows. He strode calmly down the tree-lined path up to the main doors, and pulled on them to see if they were open.

Inside, the sudden noise of someone trying to open the main door gave Streicher a start. He immediately turned off the flashlight and put out his cigarette.

Someone saw our lights!

The others were in remote parts of the huge cathedral, and he couldn't tell whether they had heard the noise or not, or if their flashlights were still on. He waited, frozen, to see if the doors would open. When they did not, he darted down the dark aisle to where he thought the others might be.

On the far end of the cathedral, Dunst had gone outside to look for something that might house a ladder, with Zimmer straggling behind him. They could not hear the door being tried from outside and were unaware that anyone else was nearby.

Inside, Streicher heard one of the side doors being tried, and he realized that someone was going around the perimeter of the church checking all the doors. He was desperate to find the others to get the lights turned off and avoid detection. He scrambled around a corner to the nave and saw one of the flashlights throwing long shadows across the rows of chairs. The tall figures of Werner and List were examining an area of the floor. As he quickly ran up to them, a loud rattling sound made Werner jump. He immediately turned out his light as Streicher came up to them.

"Someone's checking the doors—they may have seen our lights," he whispered. "Hide somewhere until they're gone."

"Yes, Herr Colonel," they both whispered.

"Have you seen Dunst?" Streicher asked Werner.

"No, I have not, Herr Colonel."

"All right. Be careful—and quiet!" Streicher whispered sternly. "They won't find us at night in this place if we're quiet. And keep your light off until I tell you."

Outside, Dunst and Zimmer were still unaware that their search was slowly taking them toward the constable.

Back inside, Streicher realized that the door they had originally entered through could have been left open, so he dashed across the dark cathedral to try and close it before they were detected. He turned a corner and there, in the shadows, was the open door and a view of the moonlit lawn outside. Streicher ran up, grabbed the door and quietly pulled it to him, then he realized something.

"Dunst and Zimmer—they went outside!"

On the other side of the cathedral, the constable had just finished checking the last door on that side and was proceeding to the corner that would bring him around to the back. Dunst and Zimmer were coming to the same corner from the back side, still searching for a ladder and unaware of the approaching constable.

Streicher ran as fast as he could from the far side toward the back of the cathedral, trying not to lose his footing in the dark. He knew that the chances were now good that Dunst and Zimmer would encounter the watchman, but he the more he thought about it, the less concerned he was.

What's the worst that could happen? Tell him you came back to look for your camera or something you lost earlier today, he thought.

As Dunst approached the corner, his foot caught something and he fell flat on his face. He had tripped on a gas pipe sticking up out of the dark earth.

"Achhh du lieber!" he cried instinctively, just as the constable turned the corner, his tall figure outlined by the waning moon.

The constable clearly heard the exclamation in German and stood shocked for a moment as he saw Dunst get up and Zimmer appear behind him, suddenly ready for action.

Behind them, Streicher had just turned the far corner and saw the English police officer, Dunst on the ground, and Zimmer producing his long revolver with the silencer on the muzzle.

"What's all this?" the officer said, becoming outraged, but it was too late.

Dunst heard a muffled *pop* from behind and the wiz of a bullet pass his head. He watched the constable slowly slump to the ground, a bullet wound in his forehead.

Streicher had seen everything as he ran up to them. It was all he could do to keep from screaming at Zimmer, who looked at him with a smirk.

"Dumkopf!" Streicher seethed as he looked at the body. He knew he had to think quickly.

"Hurry," he said, picking up the feet. "We must move him to the other side, away from the street."

Dunst and Zimmer each took an arm and they began carrying the body back to the other side of the cathedral. Werner and List appeared from the shadows and rushed up.

"What happened?" Werner asked, gaping at the body.

"Never mind now," Streicher spat. Werner and List took the feet from Streicher and they carried the body to the far side. They turned the corner and laid it down in the deep shadows.

The next morning John, Grace, and Mrs. Arundel were motoring to the train station in calm silence. As they weaved their way through town, Grace marveled at the sudden lack of tension between she and her mother; she was actually enjoying her mother's company in a car.

It should have been this way all along.

When they arrived at the station, it was bedlam. People with luggage and boxes were everywhere, arriving, buying tickets, saying goodbye and milling about on the platforms. It looked like all of Stokehill was leaving.

They waited until she bought her ticket, then Grace and her mother embraced, tears welling up in their eyes.

"Please ring me as soon as you get there!" Grace choked.

"I will," she said.

She reached out her free hand to John, who clumsily took his own hand out of his jacket pocket and finally managed to grasp her waiting hand.

"Both of you take care of yourselves, and *be careful*! I had a good dream about you two last night, so please stay in one piece!" Grace and John were looking at each other quizzically when it seemed as if her mother had something else to say.

"Grace, there's been something I've been meaning to tell you since your birthday."

"My birthday? What is it?"

Her mother was suddenly uncomfortable and began looking down at her shoes. Suddenly the loudspeaker blared out the last call for her train.

"What *is* it, Mum?" she repeated. Grace knew it was something big, whatever it was, and she was beginning to feel uneasy. The conductor blew his whistle.

"Uh . . . there isn't time now. Ask your grandfather—he can tell you. The stubborn old mule won't come with me. He'll never leave Stokehill."

The conductor blew his whistle again and a loud metallic *bang* caused them all to turn and watch the train as it slowly began to move.

"Granddad? But what's it *about*?"

The train lurched forward and Mrs. Arundel pulled herself up onto the step as John handed her the suitcase. Then she looked at Grace for a moment with an expression on her face that Grace had not seen before. The train was moving gently down the platform.

"It's about your father." She was now twenty feet away and shouting.

"Good bye, Grace! Good bye John!"

10. The Grail Company

Grace stood stunned, waving weakly as her mother disappeared inside the train.

"My father?" she mumbled. "Good bye, Mum."

A few minutes later they were in the car passing the old stone buildings of the university. Grace was still puzzling over her mother's parting words when they saw rows of barricades, and something that made John stop the car.

"Look!" he gasped.

One of the buildings had a huge, gaping hole in its side that ran from the roof down to the first floor. There was an ugly pile of bricks and other debris below, and the whole area was littered with paper. A couple of workers were crawling over the rubble.

Grace and John stared at it for a while, dumbfounded. Finally they got out of the car and walked slowly up to the barricades. Several notices had been stapled on the barricades and John, still in shock, mechanically removed one and read it.

COLLEGES CLOSED UNTIL FURTHER NOTICE.

He stared at it for a second, then handed it to Grace.

"Dennis told me about this last night."

"I can't believe it," she said as she looked at the damaged building.

"I wonder if anyone we know was hurt," John said. "Or worse." He was picturing Mr. Martin bloodied and lifeless under a pile of rubble, and he felt another surge of guilt at the anger he had harbored toward him.

Grace gasped. "Professor Markson! I hope he wasn't...hurt."

"I hope no one was hurt, but that seems impossible."

"Let's get out of here," she groaned, and they returned to the car and headed back into the deserted town. Theirs was the only car moving on the empty streets. Soon the bombed ruins of the old Norman church appeared on their left, and John saw stray pieces of paper lying on the corner of the debris among the stones and timbers. It was the end of the church that had housed the old library, and he suddenly felt like he was in mourning, and needed to pay his respects to a departed friend.

"Grace, do you mind if we stop here for a moment?"

Her eyes were fixed on the rubble. "No, of course not."

He pulled over and they got out slowly and walked over to the broken walls and the piles of stone. Grace wandered off toward the other end. John saw a large piece of burnt parchment paper and leaned over to pick it up. His heart stopped when he recognized the sheet, and he slowly turned it over.

On Ankerwyke where the bodies heap'd...

He stood open mouthed.

"Of all the pieces of paper I could have found, I found this one." Finally he shook his head. "I no longer believe in coincidences." John was looking curiously at the page fluttering in the breeze, as Grace clambered over the pile of stones and debris.

"Did you say something, John?"

He took a deep breath then said in a shaky voice, "This is the document I was telling you about, the night on Ankerwyke Hill! The one I discovered 4 years ago." Grace could feel his excitement, but when she looked at the writing her face went blank.

"I can't read it."

"Oh, right!" John laughed nervously. "It's in Old English. It says,

"On Ankerwyke where the bodies heap'd
But for the one knock, his vigil keep
Would rouse him from his chamber deep
There waits Merlin, yet asleep."

"Merlin—on Ankerwyke!" Grace exclaimed. "I had no idea! And you found it four years ago?"

"Yes! Now you know why I was such a babbling idiot that night."

Grace was looking at the brown parchment and the florid handwriting, trying not to even breath on it. Then she realized it looked like two distinct groupings of verse.

"John, is there more?"

His blue eyes looked up from the document, and some of the excitement left his voice.

"Oh yes, but the second stanza is a little more ambiguous. It was really the first

one that got me going in grad school. But I can read the second if you like." Grace gave a quick nod and got closer, as if to follow along as he read.

"Alright," he said with a little cough, trying to recall his translation. "Um...oh yes.

"On that day the skies will moan
An enemy whose reach has grown.
Who pulls the sword from the stone?
She to whom the grail is known."

John gave an embarrassed smile. "I haven't read this recently, so I suppose the first two lines *could* apply to what's going on now."

"Yes!" Grace blurted out. "Now what about the next two lines, what does that mean?"

"That's where it gets ambiguous. The sword from the stone is an obvious reference to Arthur the pendragon, but the 'she' in the last line confuses things. Arthur isn't a she, so is it Arthur? Or a new pendragon? In the end I wrote it off as a vague reference to the divine feminine, and moved on to other things."

John scraped the ash off the page and carefully put the remainder in his jacket pocket, then they both began pulling other papers out of the cracks and crevices of the rubble. Grace looked at one half-blackened sheet from an old bible.

And Jacob rose up early in the morning, and took the
stone that he put for his pillow, and set it up for a pillar,

and poured oil upon the top of it. And he called the name of that place Bethel...

She discarded it and picked up another.

Early in the morning on the first day of the week, while it was still dark, Mary Magdalene came to the tomb. She saw that the stone had been moved away, so she ran off to Simon Peter and the other disciple...

A gust of wind came up and the sheet disintegrated in her hand. Grace brushed the pieces of ash from her hands as John began to climb over a pile of stone into what had been the library. Grace carefully followed him over the rubble. There one of the blocks of stone that had made up a support pillar lay on the floor, and one of its sides was strangely ajar. Grace stopped. The side of the stone was a door or a panel, and inside the stone had been hollowed out. It was a secret compartment and she could just see something in it. She nudged John in the rib, and he saw the little stone door. His eyes grew wide.

"I've never seen that before!"

John pulled open the little door, and there sat a sheaf of singed parchments. As he picked up the mass of papers, the blackened edges started to crumble in his hands. One of the papers was only slightly damaged: an ancient, formal-looking scripted document.

Thanks go to our most gracious benefactor, Squire Matthew Arundel, without whom the building of this fine church would not have been possible. Commemorated this Christmas Day 1287.

"Squire Matthew *Arundel*?" John said in disbelief. "I know every document and book in this old library, but I've never seen any of this! Did you know about this, Grace?"

"Me? I had no idea!" Grace's face flushed when she read the name on the document. "Arundel! So my ancestors built the church?!"

"It would seem so."

Then they saw amongst the papers a small book, which looked like a journal, and Grace carefully pulled the black pages away until she found something legible.

Already some in town have been talking to the new vicar, and he has been seen nosing about in the library. I will talk to the S.S. tomorrow about indoctrinating him, but this is becoming too frequent. The last buffoon was far too loose with his tongue, and the sharper folk in town now look differently at me.

"The S.S.?" The paper and the style of writing looked more or less contemporary. She looked inside the back cover, as John looked over her shoulder.

Property of Joseph Arundel

Grace looked as if she had just seen a ghost as she stood staring at the name carefully scripted in faded black ink.

"*Dad?* Why was this in the church? Was this what my mother was just talking about?"

"I—I don't know," he replied gently.

Together they carefully turned the pages, most of which were black and illegible. Finally they saw another entry.

Ma- -- 1920

I had a bad dream, about another war that will be fought in the skies over England. It will no longer be safe in Stokehill, and it must be moved now. The question is, where should it go? Godalming, Lyne, or further still?

Then they saw one last entry.

It will be moved again, after all these years. I'm afraid I've had a bit of a falling out with the S.S., and I'm on my own. I leave tomorrow for Winchester. Not even the General knows. I think I can trust ---

The page crumbled away in her hand.

"That must have been just before he died. But *what* must be moved again? And what is the *S.S.*?" she asked him. John had a strange expression.

"I don't know," he said hesitantly, "but I dreamt last night that Merlin wanted us to meet them in Winchester."

Grace gasped. "So did I! I didn't know where it was until you said that. He was telling me to go there today."

"Apparently that's what Arthur meant when he said *unless we heard from them*," John said. He felt his skin crawling.

"I think we should get going," Grace said mechanically, as her father's name still seemed to float in front of her. "But can we stop by my grandfather's house first? Whatever all this is, it had to be what my mother was talking about. Maybe he can explain it." She took the stack of documents with her, brushing off stray bits of ash as they walked to the car.

They drove to the little Doric-columned bank, where Grace was only allowed to withdraw a small amount of cash. As Grace was turning from the teller to leave, she felt someone nearby staring intently at her. Without looking directly, she was close enough to see out of the corner of her eye the familiar tweed jacket and expensive Oxford shoes.

It's no good ignoring him, she thought, and she bravely turned.

"Hello Roger," she swallowed. The tall, blonde young man with a prominent nose stood for a moment struggling to look dignified, but his cheeks were flushed red with hurt, like he could cry at any moment. Grace could feel everyone in the bank watching them, and she wanted to shrivel up and disappear.

"Hello," he said, composing himself and assuming his familiar aristocratic nonchalance. "I heard your mother left town. I'm surprised you didn't join her. But then maybe your mum lost out to John Perceval." Roger could sound snooty without trying, so the fact that he was trying made it easier for Grace to end the encounter.

"Word gets around," she replied. "But I still have a lot of things to do here in Stokehill, none of which I care to discuss in public. So if you'll excuse me." And without waiting for a reply Grace strode out of the bank and got in John's car at the curb.

For the first time as Grace sat in the passenger seat she was struck by the worn, tired condition of John's car, and she couldn't help recalling the countless hours she had spent in Roger's Bentley convertible. It was all fine leather and walnut paneling and power, and as she thought about it at that moment in that seat that felt more like sitting directly on metal springs, Grace felt doubt ooze into her like oil.

"Is everything alright?" John finally asked with an innocent smile.

"Fine, can we go?" she said more impatiently than she would have liked, but she wanted to leave before Roger came out and saw her with John. John looked momentarily stunned but started the car and drove off.

They returned home, where Grace packed her running bag again with a change of clothes and made sandwiches to bring along on the drive. Finally they made the short drive to her grandfather's cottage.

John pulled up to the curb, and before he could turn off the motor, Grace burst out of the car and dashed up the path with the bundle of blackened papers. She was knocking loudly on the front door as John came up the path. There was no answer.

"That's strange," she said as she knocked again. "He never leaves the house before noon. Where could he be?"

"I don't know, Grace, but I think we should get on the road. We'll just have to try and catch him when we return."

"I suppose you're right."

Grace turned reluctantly and John put his arm around her as they returned to the car. Within a few minutes they were on the road to Winchester.

There wasn't a cloud in the sky as they drove along the winding, rural highway. John was already eating one of the sandwiches with one hand as he steered the car with the other. Grace was carefully turning the burnt journal pages.

"Why would this have been hidden in the church?" she asked as they drove through the undulating farmland.

"I don't know," John said. "But this sudden convergence of signs, all pointing toward Winchester, is a little unnerving."

"Yes, and the role of my father in all of this is a little unnerving, too," Grace replied. "What would my mother have been so afraid to tell me?"

"I don't know," John replied. "But whatever he moved to Winchester, it must have been hidden in that secret compartment. And the dream he mentioned was …"

"Yes," Grace said, looking at him. "Eerily accurate."

John finished his sandwich. "It all seems to be coming to a head in Winchester."

"I remember Mum telling me that my father went there several times for business when I was an infant. Now I wonder what his business really was."

As he drove, John thought of her father's reference to the *S.S.* in the journal. He had heard of the name of Himmler's organization, and as improbable as the connection was, he could not put it out of his head.

But that's ridiculous, he thought. *Her father died twenty years ago!* Then the conversation with Dennis the night before came back to him. Himmler was going through a great deal of effort to locate the Grail. How long had he been engaged in those efforts? He knew the Nazis had been around for a long time—could it have been twenty years? John looked at Grace, carefully turning a page of her father's journal.

What was his business? Finally he shrugged, and as he looked at the road ahead, he recalled more of the conversation with Dennis.

"Hmm. John of Glastonbury."

"Sorry, what did you say?" Grace asked.

"Uh...nothing," he smiled absentmindedly, and he started driving faster.

That morning, Arthur and Merlin were just outside Winchester. The lorry driver had dropped them off late the night before at a farm a mile north of the city. After spending the night under a towering beech near the farm, they had begun the journey into town just after sunup, walking down a one-lane dirt road through the Hampshire countryside. It was another fine morning, with clear blue skies and a breeze that stirred the dry dirt around their feet.

"I find it ironic that the Saxons whom we fought so hard in our day are now the very people that we are trying to protect,"

Arthur mused, "and the new invaders are from the same part of the continent as the invaders of old."

"Yes," Merlin agreed wistfully, "Peoples come and go, but they change and are changed by the land they inhabit. It is the defining force."

"Aye, that's true," Arthur agreed. "And a powerful force she is."

The land began to rise as Merlin spoke again.

"There was a sacred grove here in our time. If it still exists, then whoever brought the Grail here may have been attracted to it."

They reached the top of a hill and a commanding view of the city lay at their feet. It was a sea of buildings and houses, and barely a tree could they see, but before long they spied the large cathedral rising from the center of the city. It dwarfed all the other structures.

"That looks like the place to start," Merlin said.

They finally arrived at the cathedral, and Merlin spent some time outside going around its perimeter while Arthur looked inside. He had finished and was just emerging from the front doors when Merlin came up to him in a great hurry.

"There was blood spilt here last night," he said grimly.

"Work of the enemy, no doubt," Arthur said. "Show me."

Merlin led him to the back corner, and there at the back of the cathedral, a small pile of freshly turned dirt lay in the sunshine. Arthur knelt down and pulled a handful of turf from beneath the pile. It was red with blood.

"Not much," said Arthur, examining the stain. Then he noticed a grayish, gelatinous substance underneath some of the turf. Merlin stood by silently.

"This looks like—" Arthur began.

"Like a life was taken," Merlin said. "We must heed the warning we received; we must find our two young friends."

"I know, but we have no choice: she must come here. Is there another way?" Arthur asked.

Merlin turned to him. "There is no other way. The ordeal will take place here."

Later that morning, Colonel Streicher slumped in front of the radio with his head in his hands. He was scheduled to report at midday and acknowledge the rendezvous with Mueller's team, and even though they had been able to dispose of the body of the police constable without incident, he was dreading the call. Streicher knew they could not now stay in Winchester for more than another day or two, depending on when the police found the body, and he was sure the High Command would not be pleased with another delay.

He was alone in the room. Werner and List were examining the crypt areas beneath the cathedral, and Dunst and Zimmer were out exploring the cathedral grounds.

Streicher looked at his watch again. It was time. He took a deep breath and began the procedure.

"Pendragon across the sea, reporting," he said. He waited for a moment, then repeated, "Pendragon across the sea, reporting."

After several seconds the radio crackled and a voice came on.

"Yes, Pendragon, go ahead."

It was not the usual voice. It took him a moment, but then Streicher recognized whose voice it was and his anxiety began to grow. It was General Koln. He took a pencil from the desk drawer and began nervously jabbing at the radio.

"Successful rendezvous at B Location with two from *Sea Lion*," he began.

The radio crackled again. "Acknowledged."

Streicher swallowed, then continued.

"There was an incident."

"What type of incident?"

"One of King Alfred's men was silenced. His other men are looking for him but have not yet found him. I would estimate another day at least, perhaps two, until they do." Streicher held his breath waiting for a reply.

Finally the radio crackled.

"I see." There was a long pause. "Is that all?"

Streicher's eyes brightened. "Yes. Nothing else at this time."

"The persons from the A Location. Any sign of them?"

"No sign."

"Good. Any more interference would be unacceptable. Do you understand?"

"Unacceptable? Yes, I understand."

"Continue your activities. Report back tomorrow. Same time." The transmission had ended. Streicher sat confused.

Why didn't Koln care about such a clumsy blunder? And *unacceptable*? Do they now want us to shoot the Englanders from Glastonbury? Is that why Koln took the call all of a sudden, to deliver the message? Whatever control Streicher had over the mission seemed to be slowly slipping away.

"Dunst is right. We'll never find it now." Streicher angrily threw the pencil across the room and watched it bounce off the wall, leaving a jagged black mark.

Grace and John drove along in John's car through open farmland, nearing Winchester from the southeast. Grace was reflecting silently on everything that had happened over the last few days, when suddenly something made her speak up.

"John, do you remember the sign that we saw in the cave with Arthur, the one he said was associated with the Grail?"

"Of course," John said. "I don't think I'll ever forget it."

"Well, that was not the first time I'd seen it."

"Really?! Why didn't you mention it before?" John asked impatiently as he looked at her. Then he saw that Grace had a very strange expression on her face and he went silent.

She gave no reply; she simply brought her right foot up and on to the top of her left knee and slowly rolled down her sock. There, on the inside of her right ankle, was the pattern of five dots, the same one they had seen in the cave with Arthur. John's jaw dropped.

"What is that, a tattoo?" he stammered, completely baffled.

"It's a birthmark," Grace replied calmly. "I've always had it. And it runs in my family." She felt emotion welling up inside her. "My father had it."

John was so confused that he pulled the car off the road and onto the shoulder. He turned off the engine and the silence began ringing in his ears. He ran both hands through his hair roughly, like one who is trying to shake himself of something.

"I don't get it. What does this mean? What *are* you, Grace?" he said, not sure she could even answer.

Grace hesitated. *That's a good question. Who* am *I?* But now she knew part of the answer.

"I don't know, but I presume that's why Arthur and Merlin have come to me," Grace said, coming to the realization only at that moment. "I have some connection with the Grail."

He looked dumbly at her. What was Grace and why was *he* mixed up with her now? He had known her practically his whole life and she had always seemed perfectly normal, but as soon as he got together with her she turned out to be…*what?* He was completely at a loss.

This is too much.

Grace had felt serene, but watching John in the quiet car grow visibly more agitated had suddenly ended her moment of calm. He was grimacing as he hurriedly rolled the window down for fresh air.

All was silent except for a bluebird chirping on the fence across the road, as Grace began to panic. *What if this is too much for him? What if he just wants an ordinary girlfriend?* It occurred to her that she could very well end up alone, with neither John nor Roger, and the word *spinster* re-appeared in the back of her mind.

"We're either both going insane, or this is so much bigger than we could have imagined that…I don't know," he said.

"I know," Grace replied patiently, watching his every move.

Just then they heard a low drone, steadily getting louder. It was the sound of aircraft approaching. John looked at her as Grace openly returned his gaze, waiting to see what he would do next.

"It's starting again," he announced finally. "We'd better get going."

I told her I *loved* her, for god's sake. He turned the key and the engine started loudly. John felt a lump form in his throat as he pulled the car back onto the road to Winchester, and he looked at her and smiled.

"In for a penny, in for a pound."

Soon they were on the outskirts of town. The air-raid siren was already winding down and they saw only a few people on the pavements. John turned onto the long, broad high street and immediately Grace noticed several policemen on both sides of the street.

"It looks like something bad has happened."

Presently they saw the cathedral on the right, set back a long way from the street. John pulled over and parked at the curb, and they both got out of the car. Grace left the stack of burned papers in the car under her seat.

The drone of airplanes was now oppressively loud, like a weight pushing down on her, although Grace couldn't see them in the high blue sky. She was beginning to get a queer feeling that she did not at all like, but she said nothing as they crossed the street. They walked across and into the dark passage, and when they emerged the cathedral loomed in front of them.

Two policemen standing by the main doors were having an animated conversation. As Grace and John got close, one of the constables started toward them in a great hurry. He ran past them and disappeared into the passage to the high street.

"Strange," John said, jumping out of his way.

"Yes, I wonder what's going on," Grace added.

Then the front doors to the cathedral creaked opened, and out burst two tall, bearded figures. It was Arthur and Merlin.

"There they are," said Grace cheerfully, and she waved. Arthur saw her and waved back, and Grace and John hurried down to greet them.

"We meet again," Arthur smiled, happy to see them.

"How's your mother?" Merlin asked Grace.

"She's fine, thank you, but she gave us a scare," Grace answered, not surprised that Merlin knew to ask about her mother, and she told them about their experience of the day before. When she mentioned the bombing of Mrs. Davies' home, Arthur turned and gave Merlin a brief look.

Then they heard the loud whine of a fighter engine above the din of the other aircraft, and overhead a huge, white arc formed in the sky.

"We are very glad that your mother *and* you two are safe," Arthur said, looking anxiously above. "These are dangerous days, indeed."

John watched the other police constable jog past them toward the high street.

"I wonder what happened?"

"Foul play: a constable is missing," Arthur replied gravely.

"And we have seen evidence of a murder committed near the cathedral," Merlin added. "It looks like the work of the enemy."

Grace's face turned white when she heard the word *murder*. How did I get mixed up in a business where people are being murdered?

"Come, let us go where we can speak," Arthur said. He let Merlin lead them back to the high street, around a corner and down a narrow lane with a high stone wall on the left and a row of small but attractive houses on the right.

The blue sky and warm air belied the sinister goings on, and Grace found herself wishing everything was over and she was taking a pleasant stroll in a quiet town under normal circumstances.

Normal, she thought. I don't even remember what that is.

They finally turned left down a narrow, mossy alley that was shaded by towering sycamores and which ended at a wooden door set in the stone wall. It looked like a dead end. Merlin opened the door and went through without hesitating, and the others followed single file. They were in a small, shady courtyard that appeared to be deserted. Three small stone buildings covered in green ivy faced the courtyard. There was a passage between two of the buildings, and Merlin went through it, with Arthur behind him, followed by John and Grace.

It opened up to a huge expanse of lawn, bathed in sunlight. Grace recognized it at once from her dream. It was the boys' school, and they had walked down to the far end of the school buildings and into the playing fields and the wooded area surrounding them. They continued under the tree canopy at the edge of the lawn area until Merlin finally stopped under a magnificent old oak tree with two park benches beneath it. He sat himself on one of the benches, and the others joined him.

The location was such that they could see a long way in all directions, under the tree canopy behind them and across the expanse of lawn. No one was around, and they would see anyone coming long before they could be overheard.

"You want to know about this sign, the five marks, is that right?" Merlin asked.

Grace was speechless, and she could only wonder how much more Merlin and Arthur knew about her and probably her father, too, and all her ancestors.

Finally John nudged her and she blurted out, "Yes!"

Merlin leaned forward and rested both elbows on his knees as he studied them both for a moment from under his bushy brow.

"The best place to start is usually the beginning," he said.

"The Grail story begins at the Last Supper, as you probably know. It is, in its most basic sense, the cup used by Christ at that meal. The story goes that Joseph of Arimethea kept the cup after the meal. The next day at the crucifixion, it was said that he caught the blood of Christ in the cup and somehow preserved it.

"Well, after everything was over some time later, Joseph and four others fled in a ship, and he had the cup, the Grail, with him. Their voyage took them many places, but eventually they came here to this island, before it was called England, and they settled at what is now Glastonbury, where we were just a few days ago."

"The five swore to keep safe and keep secret the Grail," Merlin continued impatiently, "especially from the Romans. They swore not only on their own lives, but their descendants' lives as well. Above all else, this became their purpose in life."

Grace felt her heart racing, and she shifted nervously on the bench. John reached over and held her hand.

"They devised a secret sign that would be recognizable, yet simple enough so as not to attract unwanted attention. It would identify without question their company and their descendants, then and for all time. It was the pattern of five marks, and it represented the five wounds of Christ: the four on His hands and feet, and the one in His side." Merlin paused a moment. "That much is certain."

"Some say it also represented the original Grail Company, the Five that braved the long and perilous voyage, Joseph's family, the Grail Family. That is likely, but I don't know." He sat up and placed his large hands on his knees, and it seemed to Grace that he was becoming uncomfortable with what he was telling them—or with what he was about to tell them. "In fact, some have said that—"

Suddenly Arthur stood up and began to pace, keenly eyeing something in the distance. John shot a glance at Grace, not sure if something was the matter.

"Excuse me," Arthur apologized. "I've always been a little restless. Please go on." Merlin looked at him and then appeared to change his mind.

"After a time, by some power, the sign that identified the keepers of the Grail began to show itself as a birthmark on certain descendants of the Five," Merlin said looking gravely at Grace.

Grace was staring at the ground as if in a trance. She saw her life as another link on a long chain that went back for ages.

"I am a descendant of one of the Five," Grace said to herself, unaware that she had spoken out loud.

John sat with his mouth open in awe, still squeezing her hand, but Grace did not notice. She was lost in her own past.

That was what my father, and all the Arundels, had hidden in that stone, she thought, picturing their little church telescoping back into the past. *They were the keepers of the Holy Grail!* She looked at John's hand holding her own as she pictured the burnt little journal under the car seat.

Then he moved it here, somewhere, twenty years ago. Grace looked up and saw the spire of the cathedral rising above the school buildings.

And now the Germans are after it!

Merlin shifted uncomfortably and cleared his throat.

"Yes, Grace, you are a direct descendant of the Grail Family."
He was eyeing Grace keenly, and it seemed to her as if Merlin
were looking for something in her reaction before he continued.

Is there something more he wants to tell me?

Just then Arthur, who had drifted ten or more yards from
where they were seated, called to them with urgency.

"There they are," he called, pointing across the playing
fields to the trees beyond that bordered the stream. There, in the
shadows on the way back to the cathedral, were four figures.
Neither John nor Grace could make them out from such a
distance.

"All I can see are four people," Grace puzzled. Everything
had suddenly turned chaotic, and she felt as if she had been
knocked off balance.

"One looks like the smaller one from the Tor," Arthur said.
"We need to see what they're up to," he said, looking at Merlin,
"—discreetly." He started off down the tree line on the near side,
without crossing out onto the playing fields.

"Let's go," John said, and without warning he had bolted
after Arthur. Before Merlin could say anything, Grace stood up
impulsively and dashed after Arthur and John.

"Wait!" Merlin said, exasperated. "I haven't told you the whole story yet," but Grace was now running to catch up with them.

"It is beginning," Merlin said, squinting into the distance. He got up slowly and started after them.

11. The Grail Lost

The playing fields were well over a hundred yards across and a quarter mile long, but unlike Grace's dream, there wasn't a soul on them. She followed closely behind Arthur and John in the shade of the tree line as they watched the four figures across the way. Finally Arthur stopped, giving Merlin a chance to catch up from behind.

"That's definitely the one from the top of the tower at Glastonbury, and the tall one we met on the street," he said as he studied the figures on the other side of the green field. "I don't recognize the other two."

Suddenly the group disbanded; two of the four were suddenly nowhere to be seen, while the other two began moving toward the cathedral until they, too, disappeared into the trees.

"Where did the first two go?" Arthur said to himself. Then he turned to Merlin. "We must follow them, before there's more mischief." He looked at Grace and John.

"I would feel better if you two were out of harm's way. Can you two please go the other direction, I don't care where, but away from the cathedral?"

"Of course," they both replied.

"Yes, please." Merlin added, "Meet us at the benches under the oak tree at sundown."

And with that Arthur and Merlin disappeared into the trees, leaving Grace and John suddenly alone. John squinted into the distance.

"Arthur has incredible eyesight," he said, but Grace wasn't listening. She was trying to absorb what Merlin had told her about her heritage, and what it meant now. Her head was spinning.

What is really *happening right now, in this country? And what will I be asked to do?* Grace knew she was still very much afraid, but there was something else. It was the sense of her own looming destiny, at once a mystery and yet strangely familiar and present throughout her life. And her father was a bigger part of it than she had ever imagined.

He was a keeper of the Holy Grail! She pictured again in her mind the photograph that her grandfather had shown her the day before, and she felt like she was dreaming.

"I say, are you all right, Grace?" John asked.

"Yes, sorry," she said. "He and Merlin both have extraordinary abilities."

"Yes," he replied, eyeing her. "Come on."

They moved out onto the playing field, heading away from the cathedral and the town. The slow pace together with the warm sun on her back helped Grace relax.

Arthur and Merlin had detoured down several narrow lanes, but finally found the cathedral, its spires bathed in the late summer sun.

"I wanted to follow the enemy, but I also sensed that you had given Grace enough to chew on for now," Arthur said as they crossed the lawn to the cathedral.

"Oh yes, I got that sense, too," Merlin replied. "And I just hope she doesn't choke on the next part that I have to give her."

"Aye."

They walked up to the front door of the cathedral as the droning of aircraft engines continued. Inside, the dark cathedral was quiet and apparently empty. The vestibule contained a baptismal font, a glass display case with old church relics, and a long table covered with stacks of church literature. Three large gothic arches led into the great nave, and the two men entered and started around the perimeter. It was deserted; every corner they turned was as quiet and empty as the one before. Finally Merlin whispered in Arthur's ear.

"It's odd that we don't see anyone," he said.

"Yes," Arthur replied, "perhaps they're somewhere where they cannot be seen."

Arthur came to a door just off the main altar. He tried it, but it was locked. He turned to Merlin.

"Can you give it a try?"

Arthur stepped aside as Merlin moved up and grabbed the doorknob. He held it in his hand without moving for a moment. Then there was a metallic click and Merlin let go of the knob and the door swung open. Arthur went through the open doorway, and Merlin followed him.

"Thank you," said Arthur as he went in. Merlin followed and closed the door behind him.

There were in an irregularly shaped room used by the ministers to change into vestments. The walls were lined with old oak closet doors and there was a large library table in the center of the room. The small, high windows left the room fairly dark, even in the middle of the afternoon, and the room smelled of mothballs and dust.

Arthur made his way around one side of the table while Merlin went around the other side, as both of them looked and listened carefully for anything that might divulge the presence of the German spies. The room bent around and to their left and ended at another dark, oaken door, scratched and scarred with time.

When they reached the door they found it unlocked, and upon opening it they saw a lower passage that led across the back of the main altar. They stepped down and quietly closed the door behind them. The passage was illuminated by a screen that ran down the left side at eye level, where the main altar could be seen through the grillwork. The air was still and cool, and they moved slowly down the passage.

Suddenly they noticed a small door on the right, exactly halfway down the passage, that was designed to blend into the woodwork. Arthur tried it—it was also unlocked, and it opened to a stone staircase that descended into darkness.

He stopped and listened for a long while before he spoke. "I don't hear anyone. Let's go."

"We'll need some light," Merlin whispered.

Arthur reached into his pocket and produced the flashlight from John's car. He fumbled with it for several seconds before turning it on, and a bright light flooded the dark passage.

"Will this do?" he said with a smile.

Merlin looked amazed for a moment then shook his head.

"You have more tricks than I do. I'll follow you."

Arthur descended the stairs in a crouch with Merlin immediately behind him.

Grace and John had finally come to the end of the playing fields when they began to hear the sound of the stream. The stream was lower than the level of the playing fields and they still could not see it. Grace touched his arm.

"Oh, John, let's follow it!"

"All right, it must be just down an embankment," he smiled. "Grace, your...birthmark, did your parents or anyone ever tell you anything about it?"

"Just that it has been in the family a long time—and that I was the first girl to have it." She turned to him. "But nothing more." His blue eyes were squinting carefully at her in the bright sun.

"Well, there are a few...controversial theories about who was in that Grail Family, aside from Joseph. One involves a baby."

Grace looked uneasily at him, so that she nearly tripped on the grass. Up ahead, Dunst and Zimmer had been following along the bank of the stream, and had just turned around and were beginning to head back to the cathedral. Suddenly, barely ten feet away, John and Grace appeared above them, nearly toppling down the small embankment as they tried to stop. Dunst looked up at them.

"The couple from Glastonbury!" he said to himself as much as to Zimmer.

Grace was shocked. It was indeed the man from the Tor again, and they were so close that they nearly fell into his lap. She froze like a statue.

224

Dunst pulled a revolver from his pocket and pointed it at them. Zimmer immediately produced his own revolver and glanced around quickly to see if anyone else was watching.

"Get down here, now!" he snarled.

Grace was so scared she felt like she would be sick right in front of them as she and John clambered down the short embankment, spreading a cloud of dirt and dust as they did.

"How did you know we were here?" Dunst barked at John. "Did you follow us?"

John was surprised that he was not more afraid.

"It was so obvious, everybody in the country knew you would come here," he said.

Grace looked at him in disbelief, but his cheekiness gave her courage.

"Oh, is that so?" said Dunst, not impressed by John's bravado. Zimmer fidgeted with his revolver.

"He's bluffing. Let's end this now and stop wasting time."

Dunst turned sharply to him. "No! None of that."

Grace was feeling bolder by the moment.

"Yes, the local police know all about the bloodshed last night. They're looking for you both right now." John looked at Grace, every bit as surprised as she had looked at him a moment earlier, and a smile played at his face, but she was far from being able to smile back at him.

Dunst blanched, unnerved that they knew about the incident with the police constable. The din of the aircraft was ringing in his ears.

"You two know too many things you shouldn't and are a little too cocky for being on the wrong end of a gun." he sneered as he turned to Zimmer. "Let's get them back to the room, where we can have a nice long talk."

He held his revolver inside his pocket but still pointed at Grace. Zimmer did the same, pointing his at John.

"Turn around now!" Dunst snapped. "Do as I say, and if you try anything, you'll end up like the constable. Now move!"

John and Grace marched slowly ahead with Dunst and Zimmer immediately behind, guns hidden but still trained on them. They crossed the fields and headed over to the other side, back the same way Grace and John had come.

Grace's face was flushed with fear and her stomach churned as they marched along. What would these men do to her and John? Would they be tortured? She was sure she would tell them everything she knew. Her palms were perspiring as they crossed the green grass, and her stomach was a knot of nerves. She wanted to scream out *Arthur! Merlin!* but she knew the men behind her had already killed, and she had no intention of doing anything to provoke them.

She looked at John marching next to her. His eyes were wide in panic. Would he try to do something foolish, especially now that they knew she was a descendant of the Grail family? It made sense that the enemy could very well find the Grail through her. What if he got himself hurt, or worse, trying to be heroic? The aircraft droning oppressively overhead only made her feel worse.

John was looking around wildly for any chance to get Grace away from the two men, but it was all lawn and trees. He simply couldn't let anything happen to her, whatever she was. *I've got to do something, and I can't wait much longer.*

They were heading directly toward the shade of the great oak tree with the benches underneath. John remembered the Tor, how his eyes had reacted coming from the blinding sun into the shade—it took several seconds to adjust. That was his chance! He would go for the one behind him first, then hopefully the other, while their eyes were adjusting to the shade. He knew he had to try. He would not get a second chance.

They were only twenty feet now from the shade of the great oak. John felt his heart starting to race. Ten feet. His breathing became more rapid and his arms became tense. The noise from the aircraft was almost becoming unbearable, and John felt his head pounding.

They must be in the shade, too, or it won't work, he reminded himself. One more step, and John and Grace were in the deep shade of the oak tree, their vision momentarily impaired.

Now! John crouched low and drove with his legs behind him and up, delivering a blow with his shoulder into the center of Dunst's chest. Dunst never saw him coming, and he was knocked off his feet and onto his back, gasping for breath. John landed on the ground on his side. Quickly he sprang up to his left and tackled Zimmer. Wrapping his arms around Zimmer's short, stocky legs and driving him to the ground, he called out to Grace with as much breath as he could spare.

"Grace, run!" He frantically wrestled with Zimmer for his revolver.

Grace was stunned at the sudden violence, but when John yelled she started off as fast as she could back toward the town.

"After her, Dunst!" Zimmer gasped. Dunst had been slow in getting up, but he finally started after Grace, who had gotten a good lead.

John surprised Zimmer by his strength and quickness, but soon the trained soldier had the upper hand. He had control of his revolver, and he would have liked nothing better than to take care of the young Englishman once and for all. Instead he brought the butt of the revolver down sharply on John's head, knocking him unconscious. John lay face down in the shadows as the winded Zimmer got up and jogged off after Grace and Dunst.

Grace was fast, and Dunst had only closed the gap a little as they dashed in and around the trees, heading back toward the buildings of the college and ultimately the town.

I *must* catch her, Dunst thought desperately. If word gets back that I couldn't catch a woman, I'll be laughed out of the SS—or worse.

Grace was sprinting wildly under the sprawling tree canopy, her arms flailing as she gulped and gasped for each breath. She struggled not to trip and fall headlong into the shadowy turf that was hiding a tangled mass of tree-roots, because she knew if she fell, he would catch her. A small, strangely quiet part of her mind saw the irony in the years she had spent practicing her upright, efficient running form and controlled pace, as she was now bounding along, her head jolting with each unseen lump underfoot. Grace was running for her life, and it felt like no race she had ever run.

Just let me get to the street!

She was desperate not to let John's brave act go for nothing, but Grace could hear the footsteps behind her—they were getting closer. The outbuildings of the college were just ahead, if she could just reach them and the street beyond. She felt a glimmer of hope and tried to lengthen her stride. Then she heard a voice, not five feet behind her.

"You are annoyingly fast!"

With a loud grunt Dunst dove forward for her legs, catching Grace by the ankles and tripping her. He quickly got on top of her as she struggled.

Somewhere in the blue sky above, the ear-splitting snarl of a fighter engine was the only sound that could be heard.

"John!" Grace screamed, but she could barely hear herself over the aircraft noise, and she knew he could not hear her. She tried to look back for John but she couldn't turn around. Zimmer caught up to them as Grace kicked and thrashed with Dunst on top of her.

"Save your breath, your boyfriend is out cold," Zimmer said as he bent down to help Dunst control Grace.

As she struggled, Zimmer noticed something that made him stop dead. He bent down and held Grace's right leg still so he could get a good look.

"Dunst!" he said in a strange voice. "Look at this."

The tone in Zimmer's voice made Dunst stop struggling and look behind. He spun around, keeping his weight on Grace as he looked at Zimmer, who had a curiously confused expression on his face. He was holding Grace's right leg above the ankle.

There, just where Grace's white sock had rolled down during the struggle, were five round marks forming a Korr Stigmata. Dunst's head started to swim as he looked closely. Was it a tattoo? He couldn't be sure. He looked up at Grace with a mystified expression.

"Who *are* you?" he asked breathlessly. She would not answer.

"I'll go check the boyfriend," said Zimmer, and he ran back to where John was still laying unconscious in the shadow of the great oak. He looked carefully at both John's ankles, then his arms, and then jogged back to where Dunst was holding Grace.

"He doesn't seem to have it," Zimmer said, out of breath.

"Leave him, for now," Dunst said, and they began marching Grace back to town.

On the same side of the field but further away from the school buildings, a dark figure in a broad-brimmed hat watched from behind a tree. He saw the two men examine Grace's ankle, but he could not make out what they had found from such a distance away.

Whatever it is, he thought, it's important enough to detain her.

"I must telephone now," he whispered as he watched them lead Grace away.

He made his way back to the lane that bordered the stone wall, and then to a red telephone booth at the far end. He entered it and closed the door. Inside the booth the plane noise was still loud but slightly better than outside. He fed coins into the machine with long, nervous fingers. Soon he was connected.

"They have the woman," he said immediately. He listened for a moment.

"Yes, they just took her away!" he snapped.

"And," he said hesitating, "they were examining her right ankle. There is something there of extreme interest to them."

He watched down the lane as he listened. "Yes, of course. Right away."

Arthur and Merlin reached the bottom of the stone stairs, to a chamber lit by the grillwork in the floor above. Arthur shut off the flashlight, and after a moment they found that the natural light was dim but serviceable. They were in a small stone chamber that opened to their rear, which was back toward the center of the cathedral. They turned and looked down a long passage that was also illuminated intermittently by grillwork in the cathedral floor above. The air was more chilly and slightly damp.

Arthur walked out of the chamber and found two smaller passages that ran off to the left and the right. Merlin came up and stood next to him.

"Which one do you want?" he asked.

"The left, I think."

"Then I'll take the right," Merlin said, and they both started off.

"Use the signal if you need to," Arthur called over his shoulder.

"Right," Merlin replied.

Merlin approached the right passage and found that it turned and ran to his left, paralleling the middle passage. It was deathly quiet. As he moved slowly along he saw row after row of stone burial crypts. He examined the first few closely, noting everything on them, but soon took to examining the walls and floors.

He had passed the row of crypts and come to a larger chamber when he suddenly gasped. There, lying on the stone floor, was a dead body, its long arms and legs askew and the face distorted in rage. It was the body of the police constable.

Merlin checked the corpse and saw the bullet wound in the center of the forehead. He lifted the stiffening arm and reckoned the body had been dead less than twenty-four hours. He shook his head.

"I hope we've done the right thing in bringing Grace here."

The left side of the passage was a mirror image of the right. Arthur soon found larger chambers that were open on the one side facing the passage and lined with crypts and stone statuary on the other three sides, all coated in centuries of dust and cobwebs. He glanced in each one but moved along more quickly than Merlin on the other side.

After a while, Arthur saw out of the corner of his eye the marble figure of a knight clutching a chalice to his chest. He walked up and looked closely at the chalice—the dust on it had been recently disturbed.

They've been here!

Just then two tall men sprang out from around the next corner, shining their flashlights in Arthur's face. It was Werner and List. Arthur squinted silently at the bright light.

"You *again*?" Werner said in disbelief.

"What do you think you are doing down here?" List demanded as he pointed his long revolver at Arthur.

Arthur stood up straight, annoyed by the bright light, but he did not answer. He closed his eyes, summoning himself for battle. The two young officers did not know what to make of him.

"Cat got your tongue, old man?" Werner sneered.

"Let's put the old eccentric out of his misery," List said with a toothy grin, fingering the trigger of his gun. "By the time they find him, we'll be long gone."

Werner did not respond; he knew Streicher didn't want any more violence, but it would be so easy . . .

Suddenly Arthur seemed to grow before their eyes. Werner thought it was a trick of the flashlights, and it unnerved him.

"Hold your light still!" he snapped.

"I *am*!" List growled back.

Arthur slowly opened his eyes. He still had the gun he had taken from them at the Tor, but he knew he could not match his enemy shot for shot. List extended his revolver, about to shoot.

In a flash, Arthur reached into his coat and produced Excalibur, holding it upright in front of him. It sparkled and shone like a jewel in the light of the torches, and Werner and List both took a step back.

"The ghost of the warrior-king!" Werner gasped, and his knees began to shake. Suddenly he had the feeling that someone was behind him. He turned quickly but there was only darkness, broken by the fleeting light of the torches.

"Snap out of it, Werner!" List was standing firm. He fired his revolver, but the muffled *pop* was accompanied by a metallic *clang* as the bullet ricocheted off the sword. Arthur stood his ground, ready for the next shot. List fired again, and another metallic *clang* told him that the sword had intercepted the second bullet as well.

"Who *are* you?" cried List as he, too, began to lose his nerve. Arthur took a step toward them. Then List saw light behind Arthur where there should have been only shadow. It was a figure in ancient battle gear, faint and silvery, as if it were illuminated by a light from another world. It had a sword of its own and a round shield, and beneath its helmet were only empty eye sockets and a hideous gaping mouth. He felt his skin crawling as he noticed out of the corner of his eye another silvery figure standing right next to him, its cold breath on his neck. Then he began to hear them all around, their wails and shrieks slowly filling the dead air. He managed a glance at Werner—his eyes were shut tight and the silvery host had surrounded him, their swords raised for battle.

Without waiting, List made a break for the stairway, with Werner on his heels. They covered their faces as they ran in panic down the now crowded passage, as the battalion of screaming dead swung their swords and battleaxes. At first it felt to them like cobwebs brushing their hands and faces as they passed, but quickly they began to feel stings, then cuts and lashes. Then they heard two sharp whistles behind them.

"A signal!" Werner cried. "There are more of them!"

They reached the bottom of the stairs, but when they turned to go up, there, at the top of the stairs, was a tall hooded figure with a long gray beard and flowing robes. In the irregular light he looked like death himself, and they were overcome with dread.

"You shall not pass!" It was Merlin with thunder in his voice, and the two Germans froze. Werner started crying like a child;

List's knees shook uncontrollably. Merlin started slowly down the steps, his right hand extended toward them, murmuring something barely audible. List started to raise his revolver to fire, but his will was quickly drowned in an overwhelming desire to sleep.

When Arthur came around the corner, he found the two men sprawled at the foot of the stairs, both fast asleep. He smiled up at Merlin above, and was about to say something when he noticed the expression on the druid's face. Something was wrong.

"What is it, Merlin?"

"Grace!" he gasped. "We must hurry."

Arthur stepped over the sleeping men and dashed up the stairs, closing the door behind him.

12. The Last of the Arundels

Colonel Streicher was smoking a cigarette when the door to the hotel room burst open and Dunst stumbled in dragging a woman, with Zimmer behind them. Zimmer carefully closed the door.

Streicher looked at her and nearly swallowed his cigarette. It was the young woman from Glastonbury.

"What is *this*?" he gagged. "Have you lost your mind? I say no more killing, so now we're taking *prisoners* instead? Dunst, what is the meaning of this?"

Dunst had never seen Streicher so angry and he knew he was on shaky ground with him already. Without speaking, he threw Grace down into a chair and grabbed her right leg, pushing her sock down.

"Look, Herr Colonel!"

Streicher noticed some freckles on her ankle and was about to rebuke Dunst again when he had a second look.

It was the pattern—the Korr Stigmata! He knelt down and looked closely.

"What is this?" he calmly asked Grace. She did not answer.

Streicher touched the dots with his fingertips, and Grace kicked her leg, but Dunst held it fast.

"Is this a tattoo?" he asked evenly. "Did you have this done yourself?"

Again Grace said nothing. She was determined not to tell them anything. If this was how she protected her family, her town, her country, then so be it. They could torture her, but she would not speak. Grace felt every muscle in her body tense up.

"You know my colleague here can get hardened soldiers to talk. What do you think he would do to you, hmm?" Zimmer grinned hungrily at Grace but she would not look at him. She closed her eyes.

Oh God. Here it comes.

Streicher wasn't sure what to make of Grace or the mark. He had rationalized their encounter on the Tor and on the street in Glastonbury as a run-in with some well-informed eccentrics—*Grail fanatics*, as he had come to refer to them in his own mind. What else could they be? And even if they were somehow able to follow his team to Winchester, they were still more a nuisance than a threat. But this mark was different, and something about it was not sitting well with him.

"Do the others have this mark, the two old men and your boyfriend?"

Grace immediately thought of John back under the oak tree, probably badly hurt. Would they go back to get him, just to look for the marking?

"I am the only one," Grace said, with a power in her voice that filled the room. She surprised herself as much as the three Germans.

Streicher eyed her curiously. "Well! You can speak. That is good."

"Her boyfriend did not have it, Herr Colonel, at least on his arms or ankles," Zimmer said. "But they both knew about the constable."

Streicher continued studying her. "Is that so? Very impressive—you should instruct the local police force."

He got up and retrieved a magnifying glass from his bag, then knelt close to Grace. The dots looked like natural moles to him, in a very unnatural configuration. Streicher himself had a tattoo and was familiar with their appearance, and these did not look to be that type of marking. He was almost certain that the larger dot in the center of the other four was a mole.

Most curious, he thought as he looked at Grace.

He stood up. "We must report this immediately," he said, and he sat down at the radio.

Somewhere to the west of London in a dark, smoky library, a tall athletic gentleman with a black moustache hung up the telephone.

"The Germans have detained the woman," he piped, "because of something they saw on her ankle."

He stood across from his visitor, an older man whose black hair was streaked with white. He was seated in the younger man's favorite chair, smoking a pipe.

"Her ankle? Could he tell what it was?" asked the visitor, taking the pipe out of his mouth.

"He's not sure," reported the younger man. "He was too far away. But he said they were looking intently at her right ankle."

The visitor did not answer, but sat looking at him with his mouth open and his pipe smoldering in his fist.

"That *must* be it," he said finally, standing up with a sudden burst of energy. The younger man looked at him wide-eyed through the cloud of smoke.

"I must contact the General immediately." The visitor put down his pipe in the ashtray and reached for the telephone. He dialed a number and waited as the phone rang on the other end. Finally a voice came on the line.

"Yes?"

"This is Korr. The Germans have detained the young woman," he paused, "and they were examining her right ankle. I believe she is the one!"

There was silence on the other end.

"Yes. She is the one," the voice croaked, slowly building in passion. "We must get her, at all costs!"

"I agree," Korr replied, and he hung up the receiver. He turned to the younger man standing in front of him. "Who do you have who can go now? We need the best."

The younger man took his revolver out of a drawer and began screwing the silencer on the muzzle. He began to smile, and he picked up a pair of dark glasses off the table and put them on.

"I'll go myself."

Back at SS headquarters, Herr Rahn was in his small office just preparing to leave for the day. He had spent nearly two days reviewing his various British materials.

This is clearly much more promising than the south of France, he thought. I should have had them start here first and not waste time and effort at Montsegur. It is all here: Glastonbury, the Chalice Well, Winchester, even Stonehenge and the Stone of Destiny.

"I can hardly wait to go there myself," he said to the empty room.

Just then the phone rang. It was the Reichsfuhrer's personal secretary. Rahn's palms immediately began to perspire.

"Yes," Rahn chirped nervously. "Yes, I'll come straight away." He hung up the receiver.

"*Another development*," he murmured, repeating the words just spoken to him by Himmler's secretary, as he hurried out of the office. He jogged down the hall and up a flight of stairs to Himmler's office.

Rahn entered the outer office breathing heavily, and Himmler's secretary looked up immediately from the work on her desk.

"Go in. He's expecting you," she said with more urgency than he had ever seen in her.

This must be big, he thought. *Did they find it?*

He knocked quietly on the door.

"Come in," said a voice from inside.

Rahn opened the door and awkwardly peered in. Himmler was seated behind his massive mahogany desk, and General Koln was seated in one of the two chairs directly in front of it.

"Please have a seat, Herr Rahn," Himmler said.

Rahn slid into the chair, looking at Koln as he did to see if there might be any clue in his expression that might divulge the nature of the 'development'. Koln simply nodded, then returned his attention to the Reichsfuhrer.

"There have been a couple of developments with Operation Sangraal at Winchester. General Koln, if you would be so kind," Himmler announced, turning to Koln.

"We have had two radio reports from Colonel Streicher today," Koln began.

Rahn interrupted, grinning. "Two in one day? My, things *are* moving along."

"Yes," Koln replied tersely.

"In the first one, Streicher reported a successful rendezvous with Mueller's men. Unfortunately, within twelve hours they had already dispatched a member of the local constabulary." Himmler was beaming like a proud father.

"Leave it to Mueller and his team to shake things up!" Rahn couldn't help but cringe.

"Herr Reichsfuhrer, may I respectfully remind you that the Grail was attained by only the most pure and noble of knights. If we have to shoot our way through England to look for it, we will never find it."

It occurred to Rahn that the shooting of a police officer might be the 'interesting development', in which case he had gotten excited for nothing. He relaxed in his chair.

Himmler looked like a youngster whose fun had been spoiled.

"Yes, of course, Herr Rahn," he sighed, becoming serious again. "But there is more. General, please."

"In the second communication," Koln continued, "Streicher reported that the four Englanders that had accosted him in Glastonbury had followed them to Winchester."

"Really?" Rahn said politely, but his interest level had fallen considerably. "Most interesting."

"And apparently while conducting their investigation outside the cathedral, the two younger Englanders stumbled onto two of Streicher's men. During the encounter, Streicher's men observed a very curious marking on the ankle of the young woman." Koln said and paused. Rahn sat up in his chair with renewed interest.

"Yes? What type of marking?"

"According to Colonel Streicher," Koln said, hesitating, "it looked exactly like--the Korr Stigmata."

Rahn stared blankly at Koln for a moment as if he did not understand him.

"Are you sure?"

"I took both calls from Colonel Streicher myself," said Koln. "He was quite sure."

Rahn continued to stare open-mouthed at Koln for a second, then sank back in his chair, lost in thought. Koln looked at him for a moment before continuing.

"They have detained the woman, of course. Streicher examined the markings himself and," Koln hesitated again, "and he does not believe they are tattoos or something artificial." Koln looked directly at Rahn. "He says they look like a birthmark."

Rahn was slouched in his chair, overwhelmed. Himmler finally broke in.

"What is the significance of this, Herr Rahn?" he prodded. "Should the woman be detained? Can she be of more use to us?"

Rahn looked at him, still distracted.

"Detain her? Yes, detain her," he replied, growing more excited by the second. "This could be the break we needed!" He was nearly out of his chair.

"I don't know exactly what it means, but we should most certainly detain her. I have never heard of the Korr Stigmata in the form of a birthmark." He scratched his head and looked down at the floor, still trying to make sense of the news.

"Father Gerald Korr was an Irish Jesuit who first documented the markings in France, which are the ones we saw, then again in Glastonbury. Since his rather complex paper was published some thirty years ago associating them with the Holy Grail, only two more have been identified, one of which was by Colonel Streicher at the Tor just a few days ago," Rahn looked up at Himmler.

"But the markings have all been on stones or stonework. Father Korr did not document markings on anything else, least of all on a person." He leaned forward in his chair, as if the different seating position might help him think more clearly.

Finally Rahn's expression changed, and he shook his head.

"With all due respect to Colonel Streicher, the Korr Stigmata as a birthmark just sounds too farfetched. I wonder if he could have been mistaken."

"Yes, most certainly," Koln said carefully as he looked at Himmler. "Despite what Streicher says, Herr Reichsfuhrer, they could have been artificially produced. We must keep that in mind."

"That does seem more plausible." Himmler shook his head. "Colonel Streicher continues to disappoint me. All right, who would mark themselves in such a way?"

Rahn hesitated for a moment.

"Perhaps she's a Knight Templar," he blurted.

"A Knight Templar?" asked Koln.

Himmler broke in.

"They were the warrior-priests whose charter was to protect the Temple of Solomon in Jerusalem during the Crusades," he piped in a high, excited voice, "but they have always been associated with the Grail. The order became too powerful and was eradicated centuries ago, but it has long been rumored that they have survived in secret."

Rahn waited a moment until he was sure Himmler was done speaking.

"Yes," he said, smiling politely. "There are several groups today calling themselves Templars, but most are middle-aged intellectuals afraid of their own shadows. Ironically, the historic Templars were the most fierce and courageous of warriors."

"Well, the young woman is neither a fierce warrior nor a middle-aged intellectual," General Koln said. "But the leader of the Englanders could fit that profile. And incidentally, our contact Klein did not report in yesterday from Glastonbury. It could be nothing, or it could be that he had an encounter with these Englanders, whatever they are."

"True," Himmler said as he tried to smile, but he was thinking about a secret order of knights, steeped in mystery and power through the centuries. *What kind of rituals would they have?* Rahn was only half listening.

"Yes, she doesn't sound like the type." He could not stop thinking about a birthmark. *How would she get that?* He was already picturing which texts on his bookshelf he would consult first.

"Whatever she is, this is clearly not coincidental," Rahn said. "She must know something that would be useful to us, and she should be detained."

"There is another complicating factor," said Koln, looking at Himmler as if to nudge him. "Operation Sea Lion."

Himmler seemed to shake himself at the mention of Operation Sea Lion and spoke up.

"Yes. The air war against the English has been dragging on for too long. It is already September the fourteenth, and if we continue sparring with the RAF as we have been doing, then the invasion will have to be postponed until after the winter.

"The Fuhrer does not want to do this," he continued. "It's now or never. Tomorrow, the fifteenth, we will launch the largest airstrike yet, to turn the struggle in our favor and allow the invasion to proceed.

"If this young woman is of value, then she must be safeguarded until the heavy airstrikes are completed. All of our espionage and reconnaissance activity will be curtailed for two or three days," Himmler added, looking directly at Rahn. "That includes Operation Sangraal."

"In fact," Himmler continued, "perhaps she would be safer with Mueller. Since everyone is laying low for a few days, that may be best. Streicher seems to attract a little too much attention. What do you think, General?" he asked Koln.

"Yes, Mueller's location will be safe from bombing, whereas Streicher has been moving and could move into danger," Koln answered.

Rahn groaned.

"Two or three *days*?"

"I'm sorry, Herr Rahn, it's for their own safety," Himmler replied indifferently.

"Of course," Rahn muttered.

"Very well. General, please proceed with that plan of action," Himmler snapped, turning to paperwork on his desk. Koln started to rise from his chair.

"I wonder if I might make a suggestion," said Rahn.

Himmler stopped. "What *is* it?"

"We have discussed on occasion how fitting it would be after the conquest of England to have the Fuhrer crowned sovereign on the Coronation Chair," Rahn began. Koln sat down again.

"You'll recall that the truly intriguing part of it is not the chair itself, but rather the Stone of Scone which it houses," Rahn said.

"Yes, of course I remember," piped Himmler.

Rahn watched the faraway look return to Himmler's eyes.

"All the English monarchs have been crowned seated on the Stone," Himmler began, as if he were giving a lecture. "The Coronation Chair was built by the English to hold the Stone. Before that, all the Scottish kings had been crowned on it until the English took it from its home at Scone. There it had always been called the Stone of Destiny. Before that the Irish had it, and legend says it was brought to that country by the Lost Tribes of Israel.

"Before that," Himmler continued, "it was said to be the Stone of Bethel, Jacob's Pillow upon which he was sleeping when he dreamt of the ladder to heaven." He stopped and looked up at Rahn as if he had lost track of the time.

"Quite right," smiled Rahn. "It is another mysterious artifact like the Grail, yet unlike the Grail, its location has always been known. It resides in St. Edward's Chapel in the Abbey at Westminster. If invasion is imminent, the English will surely move it to a secure place. They may have done so already. What I propose is that three or four of Mueller and Streicher's men try to retrieve the Stone if it is still there."

Himmler was intrigued.

"It's worth a try. Get the young woman secured first at Mueller's location, then proceed."

General Koln stood up. "Yes, Herr Reichsfuhrer."

John rose groggily from the ground, spitting dirt out of his mouth and rubbing his head. It felt like a nightmare, and he shook himself to try and wake up. He noticed that the shadows had gotten much longer.

How long have I been out? Then it all came back to him.

"Grace!" he moaned.

He looked around to get his bearings. He vaguely remembered a dark figure in a broad-brimmed hat in the shadows, watching him. He looked into the trees but saw no one. Then he looked out onto the playing fields.

There were two blurry figures coming slowly toward him from across the lawn. He blinked several times. Now it seemed they were in a hurry; they appeared to be jogging along. Then he recognized them: it was Arthur and Merlin.

John was rubbing his sore head as they came up to him.

"What happened?" Arthur asked, out of breath. John could hardly bear to answer.

"They have Grace."

Arthur's head hung down in despair. It was all he could do to keep from roaring in anguish like a wounded lion. Merlin approached John and examined his head.

"You have quite a bump here," he said, touching it lightly.

"Yes," John said. "We stumbled onto them, and they had us at gunpoint. Rather clumsy of me, I'm afraid. They were leading us back this way when I tried to have a go at them. One of them hit me with his revolver, and apparently I was out cold." His head sank down.

"And thanks to me, they now have Grace."

Arthur was heartened by John's honesty and his courage, and he laid a hand on his shoulder.

"Judging by the lump on your head, you put up a good fight. Besides, they may not realize who it is they have. But we must find her. Come on," he said, and they strode back toward town, walking along the perimeter of the playing fields.

John was soon lagging behind them. Not only was his head throbbing from the blow, his shoulder and hip were also stiff and sore. Arthur noticed him falling behind, and he stopped and handed John one of the small red apples.

"Eat this," he offered. "It will help you heal."

John was not in a mood to eat, but he thought anything that would help him feel better was worth a try.

"Thank you." John took a bite as they walked along under the branches of the big sycamores. Arthur and Merlin slowed their pace to match his.

"I believe she's all right, for the moment," Merlin began anxiously. "I only wish I knew *where* she was."

It was late afternoon as they walked back to the deserted high street and began going into every inn and public house they could find. There were a half dozen inns, and they inquired at the front desk of each one for Grace. No one had seen her.

They checked countless more pubs with the same result. It was dusk when Merlin and John stood on the pavement outside of *The Royal Oak* as Arthur came out of the open door. Even in the failing light, they could tell by his face that she had not been seen. John felt his hope deflate.

"No sign of her," he sighed. "And its nearly curfew time." They were not far from John's dark green sedan. He looked down the wide, straight high street.

"I can move the car to the end of the street where it leads out of town. Then we can at least watch to see if they try to leave with her," he suggested, even though it felt futile.

"That's a good idea," Arthur replied. "If you and Merlin position the car as you've said and watch for them, then I will continue looking on foot. This city is a labyrinth of lanes and passages."

"Right," Merlin added. "We'll keep a lookout."

"Good," Arthur said. "I'll check in with you after a few hours. Good luck." Arthur quickly disappeared while Merlin and John got in the car.

John turned around and drove back down the high street past the statue of King Alfred to the very end, where it turned sharply to the right. There a sign was posted:

To LONDON ROAD A30

John parked the car so that they could see both the road out of town, and back up the high street. As he turned off the engine and sat back in his seat, he suddenly noticed that his shoulder and hip felt much better, and his head had only a dull ache. He felt for the bump, but it was nearly gone.

"That was some apple!" Half of it was still uneaten in his jacket pocket. Merlin looked at him and smiled.

"That was a very special apple indeed. You are the first person in a long, long time from this world to have one. They are said to have the curative property of giving you whatever it is that you most need. You might find that it has some long-term benefits as well," he said, looking far up the high street. "It was from Avalon. Arthur brought them with him."

John was in awe. What did that mean? What was now coursing through his veins? He was feeling better by the minute, and although it was nearly suppertime and he usually would be starving, he felt completely satisfied. Merlin turned to him.

"You know, John," he began, "there is much that I can see, and much that I cannot. Unfortunately, it is not up to me to decide which is which. For example, today I knew Grace had not been hurt, but I could not tell exactly where she was, or where she is still."

John was riveted. Even though he was tired and upset, the chance to get a moment alone with Merlin and learn from him was a dream come true. But whether it was because he was injured or simply tired, he could not think of a single question to ask.

I wish I were in a more normal frame of mind, he thought. Is the apple making me sleepy? It was now evening and a mist was rising from the fields at the edge of town.

"I also know Grace's importance in this whole affair, and yours, too," Merlin continued. John felt his face flush in the darkening car.

"I began to tell you about both her birthmark and her heritage—but I did not finish," Merlin hesitated. "There is more."

"More?" John asked. "We found out more ourselves this morning in Stokehill." He then told Merlin about the journal and the sheaf of papers under the seat that they had discovered in the bombed church. Merlin listened intently, and when John had finished he sat silent and still like a great wizened oak, as if he were still listening. Finally he spoke.

"That was twenty years ago—also around the time he died, is that right?"

"Yes."

"So Grace's father lost the Grail and perhaps his life as a result," he mused. "I wonder what the circumstances were that brought it about. Was it simply some kind of accident, or were some other forces involved?" He stopped abruptly and looked at John.

"Well, what I have to say goes back before the church, before there were any Arundels, back to the Grail Company. The Grail Party of five were represented by the five marks of the sign they devised: four forming a square and a larger one in the center. The marks also represented the wounds of Christ, as I said earlier, but I'm fairly sure the original five members of the party were each represented.

"One was Joseph of Arimethea, the leader of the party, the Grail Family. They used his vessel on the voyage. The next was James, the brother of Jesus. The third was the mother of Christ, Mary," Merlin said with a faraway look in his eyes.

John was beginning to see why he had begun using the word family.

"The fourth," Merlin hesitated, "was Mary Magdalene."

As Merlin was speaking, John saw a small, rounded foreign car emerge from the mist onto the high street. As the car got within a block, John noticed that the driver wore a dark, broad-brimmed hat.

"Look!" he said suddenly. "I've seen that man before."

Merlin peered at the car drifting toward them. Its headlights were off, and it was the only vehicle of any kind moving on the now foggy high street. It was going very slowly, as if the driver was looking for something. He had a short black beard and wore a black, broad-brimmed hat, and he was looking from one side of the road to the other, only occasionally glancing at the road ahead of him. Suddenly he made a sharp turn onto another side street barely fifteen yards in front of them and vanished.

"Where have you seen him?" Merlin asked.

John scratched his head.

"I'm not exactly sure, that's the strange thing. But I know I've seen him." John was surprised that he could not remember, since he was usually very good at placing faces.

"Could he be from Stokehill?" Merlin asked.

"I don't think so," John said as he struggled to remember. Suddenly his expression changed and he looked at Merlin palely.

"I remember now—I saw him in the pub in Glastonbury! He must have followed the Germans here as we did." Excitement lit Merlin's face.

"If he finds them, he will lead us to Grace. Let's follow him!"

John started the engine. "I'll try to keep some distance between us."

He pulled out onto the high street and turned right down the foggy side street after the small car. Up ahead they could see it moving slowly along the dark lane. It crossed a bridge and turned slowly to the left and vanished. The dark green sedan crept across the bridge and made the left turn. The small car was about a block ahead when suddenly it sped up.

"He's seen us!" Merlin cried.

John hit the gas and the car sputtered for a second, then lurched forward. Merlin was thrown back in his seat and he groped around for something to hold onto. The car ahead quickly went out of sight as the street bent around to the right and began to rise.

"I hope we don't wake up the whole town!" John said as they went loudly up the hill. Merlin was holding on to the door handle with white knuckles as they barreled along the narrow street. The small car was still out of sight.

They reached the top of the hill, where the road split off two ways. They were now out of the fog, but there was no sign of the small foreign car and its dark driver.

"Left is back toward the center of town," John said as he slowed down.

"Let's try it," Merlin said, and John veered off to the left, down a misty lane with small shops on both sides.

"I don't see him," John said, as he drove more slowly. "We may have lost him."

"It's odd that he ran from us," Merlin pondered. Then he relaxed his grip and sat up in his seat. "Still, we should return to our position near the road out of town. We can keep an eye out for him there."

John stopped, turned around on the small lane and drove back the way they had come, descending into the mist.

"Who would be following the Germans?" he asked. Merlin looked gravely at him.

"I don't know, but whoever he is, I sense death following him. He has killed before, or I am much mistaken. If we encounter him again, we must be careful. Very careful."

John didn't realize how tired he had become until they broke off the chase and he began to relax again. He had to force his eyes open as he drove back down the hill.

I could fall asleep right now.

He began to think about what Merlin had been saying earlier. He knew Merlin was headed somewhere with all of it, and whether it was because he was tired or injured, he was getting a bad feeling about it. He parked the car in the same way he had done before, with a view of the high street and the road to London. Merlin looked at him when John had turned off the engine.

"I was telling you earlier about the Grail family," he began, as the mist drifted back to the car.

"Yes, I remember" he answered as he rubbed his eyes. Merlin was watching John, who look like he could doze off at any second, then changed his mind.

"Hmm. What is really important for you to know is that Grace is not just another descendent," Merlin said.

"All right," John said quietly. He was now too tired to respond any other way.

"This invasion that is about to take place was foreseen long ago," Merlin squinted into the fog. "As was the lost Grail."

As he looked at Merlin half asleep, John felt the uncomfortable feeling inside him grow more pronounced.

"John, this land in vulnerable as long as the Grail is lost," Merlin said.

John heard what Merlin said, but he felt his eyes completely close and for a moment he was asleep. He opened his eyes with a start and shook himself.

"Quite simply, one very special descendent of the Grail Family, *must* find the Grail, or the invasion will succeed."

Merlin could see that John was having trouble accepting what he was saying as much as he was having trouble staying awake, so he stopped to give John a chance to take it in. The occasional street lamp illuminated the mist drifting up the high street, and John felt the silence pressing on his ears. Merlin waited a moment, until something told him to continue.

He put his hand on John's arm.

"Grace is –

Before Merlin could finish John roughly shook off his hand. He looked at Merlin as if hurt.

This is too much. John felt trapped in the small car. All of it: this invasion, Arthur and Merlin and the Grail, Grace being whatever she was, was so overwhelming he couldn't accept it. The tinge of nostalgia and even romance that his study of history had so often brought him were nowhere to be found in the coarse, hairy old man seated next to him, or in anything he was telling him.

"Then *why* on earth did we bring her here, and put her in jeopardy?!" he shouted, surprising Merlin with his outburst.

"I'm sorry, but you said yourself the Grail is lost, so it is just as likely to be back in Stokehill. Why not let her live her life *as it was?*"

Merlin's eyebrows sharpened and there was a fire in his eyes.

"Because one of the things I *do* know," he snapped, "is that had things been allowed to continue for Grace, she would not have survived the bombing of a few days ago on her street. She would have been in the old woman's house when that bomb was dropped, and she would have been killed! Arthur and I knew that from the start."

John would not look at him; he remained slumped in his seat. He felt as angry as he had when he'd gotten into the shouting match with Mr. Martin several months before. He knew he was lucky his advisor hadn't had him kicked out of the doctoral program then and there.

That little outburst could have set me back months.

But it felt like both they and the Germans were trying to take Grace away from him. He felt heat radiating off his face as he battled for self-control, and he crossed his arms and sunk further down in his seat.

Merlin looked at the exhausted young man seated next to him.

He's upset about Grace, he told himself as he took a deep breath.

"And Grace is the last one," he continued more evenly, "so if she did not survive then the bloodline would have run out."

John tried not to think of it, but Dennis's words hung silently in front of him as if on a billboard. *The last of the Arundels.*

"Unfortunately, I could not see how things would develop once we came, and I don't know how the Grail itself works if the Germans reach it on their own. It could serve them apart from Grace, or she may be integral to it, or it may be that Grace is the only important thing. I can't yet *tell*," Merlin grunted, reminded again of his own limitations.

John did not appear interested. His eyes were getting heavy. Merlin looked at him slumped in his seat, tired and emotionally spent.

I don't blame him.

"At the end of the day, I'm still a man, struggling like you," Merlin sighed, as he looked up the high street into the fog. "So is Arthur. The only difference is our relationship to this land, and the powers that underlie it. It is they who summoned us. And for every gift they give us, like this language, they take one away."

Merlin looked back at John. "Arthur and I are now as mortal as you and Grace and everyone else in this world. We had to accept mortality in order to return."

"Well, I really don't know about all that," John said softly, as if he were talking in his sleep.

"I love Grace, so I'll do whatever I can to get her back. When we get out of all this, I'll marry her, if she'll have me. But all this other stuff, I really don't know…"

Merlin turned to say something more, but John's eyes were closed. He had fallen asleep.

"That's all you really need to know," he whispered, and he kept lookout while John slept.

Grace was having the worst night's sleep of her life. They had tied her hands and feet, and she was so uncomfortable she couldn't sleep more than twenty or thirty minutes without waking up. When she did manage to sleep, her dreams were so tortured and unpleasant that she felt she was better off staying awake. Finally, just when she was sleeping restfully, someone was shaking her.

"Wake up, we're leaving," said a voice.

She woke groggily and looked up. It was the head spy, the Colonel. The others had addressed him that way the night before.

He untied Grace's feet and made her stand up, but she was so sleepy she nearly fell over. She had no idea what time it was; it felt like the middle of the night.

"We're going for a little car ride. Now if you are good and keep quiet, we will let your boyfriend go," Streicher said. He threw an overcoat over her shoulders and begun collecting his things.

They do have John somewhere, Grace thought in panic, and she was suddenly wide awake.

"Do you promise?" she asked him.

Streicher stopped what he was doing. "Yes, I promise," he said, looking at her. There was something about her that he could not put his finger on.

Soon she was in the black car, with Zimmer in the front seat watching her. They were waiting for someone. Outside, Streicher was talking to Dunst on the dark and empty street. Dawn was not far off and the mist lingered only in patches.

"We can't wait much longer," he said. "Go check List's hotel room again to see if they came back and fell asleep. We'll go back to the cathedral. Meet us there in ten minutes."

"Yes, Herr Colonel," Dunst replied, and he disappeared into the night.

Streicher got in behind the wheel. He went quickly to the cathedral, driving without lights and as quietly as possible. He parked close to the tree-lined footpath, which had a waist-high blanket of mist drifting around it.

"Check around the perimeter of the cathedral," Streicher said to Zimmer, "I'll look inside." Zimmer nodded and got out of the car.

"You need to accompany me into the cathedral," he said to Grace as he opened her door and helped her out of the car. "Please be good."

Grace was so tired that she had been dozing in the car. Now the cool night air woke her up again, but she was still sore and too tired to talk. As she stood up, she saw a hint of dawn showing itself in the east.

Streicher walked them quickly down the misty path to the cathedral, where he produced a key and quietly opened one of the large main doors. He led Grace inside to the vestibule. She immediately sat on the edge of the long table covered with stacks of church pamphlets.

I could fall asleep right here. She didn't even notice that Streicher had disappeared into the church.

Her eyes rested lazily on the old glass display case just across the way. Dusty old crosses and bibles, vestments and gold chalices littered the glass shelves. Little white placards with writing on them were placed near each item.

Grace felt so comfortable that she didn't want to move. Behind her, dawn was slowly creeping in through the tall stained glass windows. The sun was not yet up, but light was filling the chamber around her, warming Grace and making her content.

"There it is," someone said in Grace's ear, making her jump up off the table.

She turned around quickly but there was no one there. It was far too real to be a dream—she had heard a voice, she was sure of it. Had she heard that voice before? She walked around the vestibule and looked under the long table, but there was no one else in sight.

"Now I'm going mad," she said to herself as she sat down again on the edge of the table.

She saw a small, greenish-gray ceramic chalice at the bottom corner of the glass case that she had not noticed before. It was out of place with all the other bigger, more beautiful gold chalices in the case, and it looked like it had been relegated to a dark corner and forgotten. Just then Streicher bustled in from the cathedral.

"Well, I can't find them," he grumbled to himself.

"Come along, we must go," he said to Grace as he took her by the arm, but she did not hear him.

There it is, she thought to herself, mouthing the words, the beautiful words, even though she dared not speak them out loud. The clutter of the old display case had seemingly disappeared, and only the small green cup remained, radiant and perfect in its simplicity.

Grace was filled with such peace and contentment that it seemed to flow out of her and fill the room. She felt it increasing, as if her contentment had somehow filled the room, then the cathedral, and was now flowing out into the sleepy town.

She let Streicher take her away and bundle her into the car, but it did not matter. It was as if she was watching herself from above the treetops. Grace knew that from that moment on, she was beyond harm; they could still torture her or worse, but it simply did not matter what the Germans or anyone did to her ever again.

There it is, she thought again as she pictured the little ceramic cup in her mind's eye, and she sank back into the car seat and fell into a deep, dreamless sleep.

13. Something Vast in the Dark

Merlin sat alert in the passenger seat with his window slightly open. The sound of the nearby stream drifted slowly through the open window like the cool mist that was lingering around the car. It was now getting light; dawn was nigh.

Suddenly he heard the quiet sound of a car engine in the distance. There, coming down the high street, was a black sedan with its lights off.

"There it is," he whispered.

As he spoke the words, he was struck with a strange and powerful feeling, as if he had brushed up against something vast in the dark that he could not see. He felt his pulse quicken.

What has happened?

John woke with a start, rising slowly in the car seat.

"Stay down," said a voice from the back seat. It was Arthur.

He must have come in some time during the night, John realized.

The car sound got louder until the tires could be heard squealing slightly. They had made the turn and were headed out of town.

"Wait, we don't want to follow too closely," Arthur said. John slowly rose in his seat until he could just see the road. The black sedan was getting smaller as it headed toward London.

"Alright," Arthur said, and John started the car. He pulled onto the road and accelerated slowly, but soon was up to speed. It was getting lighter by the minute; the sun would soon be up. The black car was now well ahead of them but clearly visible.

Back in town, the small foreign car was stopped by a phone booth, where the dark figure in the broad-brimmed hat was craning his neck to see down the High street.

"Yes, hurry! They're heading toward London." He burst out of the phone booth and jumped into his small car, starting it with a roar. He flew down the High street, made a screeching turn onto the London Road past where John's car had been parked, and barreled down the highway.

John did not feel like talking. Even though he had gotten an unusually good night's sleep for sitting in a car, to have Grace in such danger left him upset and angry.

And that other bit Merlin had said, well, that was just . . .

John's thought was choked off in a tangle of emotion. The sun's first rays hit his eyes through his side window. Arthur and Merlin were silent.

That figures, he thought. *They got Grace in this mess and suddenly they've run out of things to say. I wonder how much of what they've told us is true, and how much isn't.* John knew his anger was rising up inside him again, but being aware of it didn't seem to help him much.

He tried to find something to look at that would calm him down. Sunlight was now bathing the rolling countryside and throwing long shadows across the road. Up ahead, the black car was still just in sight. He sighed. At least he could see her, and that made him feel a little better. Finally Arthur spoke.

"Today is the day. The enemy is making an all-out effort. Already they are in the sky."

What? John couldn't hear anything other than the car. He rolled his window down an inch, and immediately he heard the familiar drone of aircraft engines in the distance. He rolled the window back up.

Whatever he is, Arthur certainly has sharp senses.

"How's your head?" Arthur asked John.

My head! John felt so good physically that he had completely forgotten about his injuries, and when felt his head for the lump he could find no trace of it.

"Good as new," he replied in astonishment.

"Good," said Arthur.

"That was quite an apple you gave me. Thank you," John said.

He actually felt stronger than he could ever remember. He gripped the steering wheel firmly with both hands, and it seemed that with very little additional effort he could rip it off the steering column. *Remarkable apples.*

"You know, John," Arthur continued, "whatever happens, we will get Grace back safely. I promise you that," he said, his voice reverberating in the car.

John looked in the rearview mirror and saw Arthur's face fixed on him with a power that seemed to loosen John's anger.

That was a promise not lightly made.

"Thank you," was all he could answer. John felt his anger fall from him in pieces, and he drove along feeling lighter and yet more determined to rescue Grace, whatever was in store for them.

That afternoon, the black car pulled off the A30 into the village of Englefield Green, just at the edge of the forest at

Windsor, less than an hour outside London. John saw them make the turn but made sure to keep his distance.

"They've just turned off," he announced.

"Good," Arthur said. "Let's be careful."

John turned off the highway, which emptied directly onto the high street of the small town. The black car was nowhere in sight.

"We've lost them," John groaned.

"That's all right," Arthur replied. "This is a small town and there don't appear to be many cars. We'll find them."

John took the first left and followed the narrow lane as it bent around to the right, passing dreary brick row houses on both sides. There were no cars like the one they were following, and John was getting more anxious by the minute.. They ended up back at the high street and crossed at a roundabout over to a lane on the other side of the village.

The lane went for about two hundred yards before it ended at the forest, and there, at the last row house on the left, was the black sedan. It was parked at the curb behind another almost identical brown sedan.

John stopped with a lurch and pulled over to the curb behind another car at the entrance to the street, near the roundabout. He turned off the engine, and immediately he heard the loud noise of fighter planes. In the distance, they all heard the unmistakable sound of bombs going off.

"The war is close now," said John.

Grace watched Lieutenant Colonel Mueller pace back and forth like a caged animal. He had curly black hair and was powerfully built, and everyone's eyes were on him going back and forth across the tiled kitchen floor, at the back of the brick row house. She was seated in a chair at the old wooden kitchen table, her hands no longer tied, with Colonel Streicher seated next to her. Dunst and Zimmer were in the next room with another of Mueller's men.

Streicher was the senior officer, but the house was Mueller's base of operation. When they arrived, Mueller had saluted Streicher according to military protocol, but the hint of a smirk on his face betrayed his arrogance. Streicher disliked him, but he had to be careful. He was a favorite of Himmler's, and they both knew it. Mueller was dangerous in many ways.

Grace had felt all day that she could face anything, even torture, but they had done nothing to her. She had slept most of the way in the car, and had woken up feeling stiff but surprisingly refreshed. And the thought of that unassuming ceramic cup sitting safely back in Winchester made her glow with serenity.

It was right under their noses, right under *everyone's* nose, in a glass case for the entire world to see, and only she knew what it was. Twenty years it had been sitting there collecting dust, and she could not begin to guess how many thousands of people had looked upon it without having the slightest idea what it really was. Did her father intend it to be on display, even if anonymously? She knew it did not matter.

There it is, she mouthed again, remembering that voice just behind her shoulder. Have I heard that voice before? Grace wondered as she looked at Streicher smoking a cigarette. He was the only one there, she thought. Was it his voice?

"We'll need at least three men to go to the Abbey," Streicher said. "The Stone weighs well over three hundred pounds. Four men would be better. Do you have a hand truck here?" Grace couldn't help turning to Streicher, but she was determined to remain silent. She turned back again, trying to puzzle it out. *Westminster* Abbey? What stone in Westminster Abbey is so valuable that they'll risk their lives to get it?

"Yes," snapped Mueller, not trying to hide his irritation. "First I am housebound, then I am a babysitter, now I am moving rocks."

Dunst looked up from the next room, surprised that Streicher was allowing Mueller to speak to him in such a way.

"Well," replied Streicher with a puff, "you could remain here as just a housebound babysitter and let the rest of us be rock movers." He was enjoying Mueller's predicament.

"We'll wait for nightfall," said Arthur. "If you need to stretch your legs, go ahead. Just be careful; they could be in the village."

"I might go for a short walk in the forest," Merlin replied. "But I'll try to find an entrance back that way." He looked behind them toward the trees.

"I'm fine at the moment," John said. "Although I think I'll finish my apple," and he produced it from his pocket.

"I'll be back shortly," Merlin said as he got out of the car stiffly. He headed back to the high street and disappeared around the corner. Arthur and John sank down in their seats just far enough that they could still see the front door of the last house.

John had just finished his apple and was putting the core back in his pocket when they heard a car from behind go past them and down to the end of the street. It was also brown, and identical to the other two. They both sat up enough to be sure they could see it.

It parked at the end of the street, across from the house they were watching. The doors swung opened and out came Werner and List, looking back down the street to see if anyone was watching them.

"Those are the two Merlin and I encountered in the cathedral cellar," Arthur said as he peered down the street. "It doesn't look like they've seen us."

List quickly crossed the street and headed into the house, with Werner behind him. Arthur waited a moment before opening the door.

"I'm going to find Merlin. Wait here and keep your eye on the house."

"I will," John said nervously, and Arthur closed the door and was gone.

It was less than a minute after Arthur had left when John got the sudden urge to walk. It surprised him, especially since Arthur had just told him to keep watch, but the impulse nagged at him.

"I can watch from the high street," he told himself, and he got out of the car and walked back to the high street, looking over his shoulder every few steps as he did. He crossed to the other side of the street at the roundabout, where he could still see the house. The air was shaking with the noise of planes as a few people on the street hurried nervously about.

Arthur had gone about a hundred yards further up the high street when he came to an entrance to the forest at the end of the village with a sign overhead: *Kingsgate*. It was bordered by village houses on one side and a high stone wall that ran off into the distance on the other. The view through the gate was one of solid trees. He entered and made for his left where the land was rising. Up ahead he saw Merlin at the top of the rise, motionless.

"The two we met in the cathedral cellar have arrived," Arthur said as he came up to him. "There must be at least six of them now, probably more."

"If they were all in one room, I could put the sleep on them," Merlin offered.

"Not likely," Arthur replied, listening to the noise of aircraft that filled the woods.

"This morning," Merlin began, dropping his voice to almost a whisper, "just before their car drove past us, something happened." He looked at Arthur.

"With Grace?" Arthur asked, swallowing hard.

"Yes. She may have found it. I didn't mention it earlier because of our young friend in the car," he motioned down the slope toward John. "I think we have already told him more than he can handle, at least for now."

"The Grail?" Arthur asked, surprised. "But she has been captive since yesterday. How would she have been able to look for it?" He paused for a moment. "Does the enemy have it?"

Merlin looked troubled.

"A great awakening has occurred—or a great sundering. What I felt was too big to be anything else. I have never in all my days felt anything more powerful.

"Something is still in Winchester, somewhere, that must be the Grail cup." He turned to Arthur. "But something is here, too. I can feel it now, and it is stronger than what was left behind in Winchester. It is Grace.

"I know now that she is integral with the Grail. She needed to come into contact with it to awaken the power we are now experiencing, however that happened. It could not be found without her: the two are connected, Grace and the Grail." Merlin swallowed, then continued.

"So even though the cup is in Winchester, the enemy has the Grail, because he has Grace. And so it may be a great sundering we are feeling, a foreshadowing of a historic disaster, and a change in the world order."

He put his hand on Arthur's shoulder.

"We must get her out of there now. I don't believe we can wait. Whoever has Grace has the Grail, and whoever has the Grail will win today's battle, and the war as a result. And this war will touch everyone on earth before it is over." Merlin tightened his grip on Arthur's shoulder.

"And Grace must be alive. If she does not survive, all is lost."

Arthur felt something rising within him, something he had not felt in a very long time.

"That's *it?* One girl decides the fate of the land and the course of *history?*" His voice was growing, and Merlin watched Arthur begin to change before his eyes. His gaze was fixed and his breathing was becoming rapid, and he was somehow expanding, or was he gradually rising? Merlin wasn't sure.

"I cannot stand by and watch," Arthur said, his voice carrying throughout the forest. *"I will not!"* Suddenly he drew Excalibur and thrust it toward the battle in the sky. Merlin took a step back.

"You must help me, Merlin! Help me lead that battle, up there!" Merlin looked mystified for a moment, then he realized something.

"You do not need me," he said, looking at Arthur. "That is what She meant, back on the street corner in Glastonbury. You are *not* the same!" Merlin thrust both hands into the air and his eyes were shut tight. Arthur grasped the hilt of the great sword with both hands over his head, and he shut his own eyes.

Suddenly Arthur felt himself rising into the air, and he clearly saw himself and Merlin face to face in the forest below his feet, getting smaller and smaller. He looked across the treetops and saw a mighty castle on a hill at the other end of the forest. He turned toward the southeast, and there was the battle playing out before him: hundreds of planes engaged in a desperate fight, spread out over a vast area of land and sea.

In a flash he was in their midst. He not only knew the enemy planes by the Iron Cross on their wing tips, he somehow knew there were 200 Messerschmitt fighters and Junker bombers. With the speed of a thought, Arthur was in the cockpit of the Spitfire piloted by Major Thomas Stevenson. Stevenson's plane had the deepest penetration into the German assault, but his courage was beginning to waver.

At the same instant, Arthur was also in the cockpit of the Hurricane piloted by Captain Terence Walsh on the northern phalanx of the British defense, and with Lieutenant Alvin Woodham to the south, and Captain Peter McDougal over Canterbury, and a score of other men, each of them in a critical position in the battle. They could not see him but each of them said afterward that they felt someone there with them, and several swore they heard a voice.

Give the thought of your own death no weight—keep it light as a feather. Now fight for your home! Fight for Britain!

Inside the house, Werner and List were reporting on the events of the last twenty-four hours. They had gone over it all carefully in the car on the way in, and they knew they could not say anything that would sound fantastic or childish. They knew how things said were taken and twisted in the *SS*.

"Are you sure they didn't follow you?" Mueller asked, glaring at them. Streicher was still sitting quietly at the table next to Grace, who had a plate of food in front of her that she had not touched. Grace felt evil surround Colonel Mueller like she had never felt before. The more time she spent in the presence of Mueller, the more Grace felt like her life was at risk. And yet she did not feel petrified inside as she did when they were stuck in traffic on the high street in Glastonbury.

I've changed—or I am changing. She couldn't tell which, but she knew something was different. *Who am I?*

"Yes, I'm sure," blurted Werner nervously. He and List were standing at attention in the middle of the kitchen, while Mueller continued pacing.

"Zimmer!" Mueller barked. Zimmer dashed in from the next room.

"Yes, Herr Colonel?" he said, snapping to attention.

"Check outside to make sure they weren't followed. Check all the cars on the street," Mueller said without taking his eyes off List.

"Yes, Herr Colonel!" he said and he dashed out the front door.

"Now, tell me about the one with the broadsword again," Mueller said, looking at List's mouthful of bad teeth.

"He wielded it with a skill I have not seen," List mumbled. "I fired two shots at him, and he deflected them both with it."

Mueller eyed him carefully.

"Are you sure you didn't just *miss*?"

"Quite sure, Herr Colonel," List croaked.

"The man we encountered in Glastonbury had no broadsword, at least at that time," Streicher said as he casually lit another cigarette. "We would have seen such a large weapon."

"It was the same man, Herr Colonel," Werner said to Streicher as his voice cracked. "I am sure of it!"

A few minutes later they heard the front door open and close, and Zimmer came back into the room.

"No sign of anyone on the street, Herr Colonel," he said. "All the vehicles were empty." Mueller nodded to him, then stood directly in front of Werner, looking up into his face.

"Werner," Mueller snapped. "Why did you run after the two shots were fired?"

"We heard him signal to his accomplice," he recited, as he had practiced on the drive from Winchester. "I was trying to prevent his escape."

"And that was when the accomplice put you both to *sleep*?" Mueller exclaimed.

"It must have been some type of hypnosis, Herr Colonel," List whined, as a bead of perspiration formed on his forehead.

"Are you sure one of them did not somehow drug you?" Mueller asked.

"I don't know how they would have, Herr Colonel," Werner said. "Neither one of them touched us!"

Streicher put down his cigarette.

"This is going nowhere. We have another job we have been given, and we need to get started. Those persons, whoever and whatever they are, are clever and tenacious. They followed us to Winchester, and we must assume they will follow us here looking for her." He motioned to Grace as he stood up.

"We leave now for Westminster Abbey, and we will bring the girl."

Grace had sat impassively during the interrogation, looking at the floor, but now she looked up at Streicher.

Going to the heart of London today is suicide. She looked at him, but Streicher would not look back at her.

Mueller was speechless for a second, caught off guard by Streicher's sudden interruption. Then he looked directly at him.

"My men are perfectly capable of keeping her here safely," he sneered, abandoning any protocol. Streicher was aware of the slight and he answered Mueller sharply without looking at him.

"Then they should be just as capable of keeping her safe in the car! Two of your men will join us, Colonel, I don't care who," he snapped as he got Grace up. *"Dunst!"* he shouted, "please join us."

Mueller stood for a moment as everyone sprang into action, then he barked out, *"List!* Get the hand truck. You and I will go." Mueller glared at Streicher, then went to another room to retrieve his weapon.

John had wandered a short way down the street to a newsstand to have a glance at the day's paper. The street was now deserted amidst the drone of aircraft and the regular sound of bombs going off in the distance. John was reading the headlines when suddenly he noticed a small, foreign car coming up the street from the highway. As it approached, he saw that the driver wore a black, broad-brimmed hat. It was the dark man from Winchester, and he was looking directly at John.

"He followed us!" John realized, frozen as the small car drove by. The man continued to look steadily at John as he drove past, and John felt like a prey animal in the sights of a hunter.

Just then John heard a second car from behind, passing the small, foreign car close to where he stood. It was heading the other way, toward the highway.

"I'd better get back!" He dropped the newspaper on top of the stack.

As the second car passed him he looked up. It was the black sedan, and Grace was in the back seat. His heart sank like a stone as he watched them make a left turn toward London.

"Oh God!" John gasped as he ran across the street and back to the car. He felt like he could cry, but there was no time. Up the high street, Arthur and Merlin were returning from the forest. John waved both arms at them as he sprinted to his car.

"*Hurry!* We must follow them!" he called out, pointing down the empty street toward the London road.

They both started to run but John did not wait. He ran to the car, jumped in, and started the engine, which sputtered badly before it roared to life.

Both doors on the passenger side opened as Arthur quickly got into the front seat and Merlin fell into the back, barely able to get the door closed as the car jolted into motion. John reversed all the way to the roundabout, then hit the brakes hard and threw the car into first, his tires squealing as they roared down the high street.

In his excitement John had forgotten about the dark man in the small foreign car, who went up the high street and pulled up next to another parked car, and rolled down his window. He was talking to the driver of the parked car, a man with a black moustache, in a brown fedora and dark glasses, and was gesturing frantically down the side street toward Colonel Mueller's house. The man in the parked car barked something, then jerked his thumb sharply toward the highway. Without hesitating the dark man nodded, then turned his car around and flew back down the high street, while the man in dark glasses turned off his engine and waited before carefully getting out and locking the car.

"What happened?" Arthur asked as he held on tightly to the door handle.

John was so ashamed and upset all at one time that he could not answer. If he did, he was sure he would start crying like a child. He made the left turn onto the highway and hit the accelerator, still not speaking.

John looked over at Arthur. He was waiting. Arthur was simply waiting, as if he had all the time in the world to wait. John glanced in the mirror, and Merlin was listening equally patiently from the back seat.

John was completely taken aback. Who were these two, his companions with whom he now found himself? If what they had been saying was true, then his inattention a few minutes ago could cost everything. And yet they sat patiently, waiting for him to gather himself and respond. What person had he ever known, be it a teacher or an advisor or a parent, with only a fraction as much hanging in the balance, who would have acted so calmly and clearly? Whoever and whatever they truly were, they were unlike anyone he had ever known in his life.

"I'd gone down to look at the paper when they all drove past in the black car with Grace in the back," he said finally. "That was stupid. I'm sorry. I left for only a moment."

"It's all right," Arthur replied evenly. "If you had been waiting in the car, they might have seen you." He paused for a second as he looked ahead. "Look, there they are."

They had come onto a long straight section of road and, John could just make out the black sedan, about a quarter mile ahead of them, still heading toward London.

"*Thank God!*" he yelled. "Why do you think they're going into London?"

"I have no idea," said Arthur as he watched the black car.

John looked in the rear view mirror at Merlin, who had not said a word since returning from the forest. Now his eyes looked like they were nearly closed. John looked back at the road in front of him and the black car ahead in the distance.

"The Stone of Destiny," Merlin said suddenly, opening his eyes. "They mean to take it."

"The Stone of Destiny?" John asked. "Do you mean the Coronation Stone?"

"Yes," Merlin answered, looking at John in the mirror. "They want to make sure it is not taken away and hidden from them. They plan to consummate their invasion by crowning their leader on it."

Arthur's face tightened in anger.

"Not if I have anything to say about it," he growled.

John drove fast until the gap between the two cars was about two hundred yards. There was no traffic going into London, only the steady stream of lorries and automobiles heading out of town. The bombing was now so close that they could clearly hear it inside the car as they drove.

Behind them, the small, foreign car was keeping pace. John was so absorbed with Grace in the black sedan in front of them that he completely forgot about the man in the broad-brimmed hat he had just seen on the high street, and he did not notice the small car following them.

Up ahead, Dunst was driving with Colonel Mueller seated next to him. In the back, Grace sat in the middle between Streicher and List. She was hungry and getting more uncomfortable by the minute in the crowded car, and in a detached way she knew it was likely she would not survive the trip into London.

They were in the outskirts of town when Dunst noticed the dull green car behind them in the rear view mirror.

Odd that someone else is fool enough to be going into London, he thought as he watched it closely. Then he recognized it—it was the same car from Glastonbury.

"Colonel Streicher!" Dunst exclaimed, still looking into the mirror. "You won't believe who's following us."

Immediately the other three men in the car turned to look behind them. Grace felt a smile on her face for the first time in nearly two days.

"They are tenacious," said Streicher as he turned around again in his seat.

"They are *foolish*," Mueller snarled. "We have a hostage."

"We are not to harm her!" Streicher snapped.

"But *they* don't know that," Mueller said quickly to Streicher. He gave Streicher a surly look.

He's nothing but an antiquarian and a relic chaser, Mueller thought. The girl will be a casualty of war, if I have anything to say about it.

"By bringing her, you expose her to more harm than if she had been left behind." Mueller looked at Grace with a disturbing grin as he mulled over his new idea. Grace continued to look straight ahead, but her stomach began to turn.

"Perhaps," replied Streicher as he looked out the window. In the distance, smoke from innumerable fires filled the sky.

Suddenly a bomb went off so close by that they all jumped.

"We're in the middle of it now," Mueller said with a smirk.

Back at *SS* headquarters, Herr Rahn was in his small office pouring over a worn, bound academic treatise. He was wearing white gloves so as not to touch the paper with his hands.

The Occurrence and Historic Significance of Certain Markings at Sights Associated with the Holy Grail

By Rev. Gerald Korr, SJ

"Why would an Englishwoman have the Korr Stigmata as a birthmark?" he muttered for the hundredth time, his reading glasses perched on the end of his nose.

He had been reading and re-reading all day, and his eyes were tired. He stopped to take off his glasses and rub his eyes.

When he put his glasses back on, he saw something that made him stop.

The exegesis thou knowest will wynd away
The bloodline shall rule on Judgment Day.

"*Bloodline.*" Rahn looked up, openmouthed. "Bloodline! *Could it be?*" He felt a mixture of excitement and panic crash over him like a wave.

He tried to pick up the telephone, but his hands were shaking so badly he dropped the receiver on his desk. Finally he managed to pick it up and dial the number.

"I must see the Reichsfuhrer right away!" he said as his voice cracked.

On the other end of the line, Himmler's secretary was unimpressed. "He can't see anyone; he's busy all day."

Rahn's excitement boiled over. "It's a matter of the highest importance!" he shouted into the receiver.

Within twenty minutes, Rahn was seated in the Reichsfuhrer's office at Himmler's desk, which was covered in paper. Himmler and General Koln listened skeptically as Rahn blathered about his revelation. He knew he had to calm himself before he was thrown out of Himmler's office, but he could not slow down.

Koln looked confused.

"But Herr Rahn, why would we bring the woman here if the Grail is in England?"

"Because, gentlemen," Rahn said, finally composing himself, "She may *be* the Grail." Despite his calm voice, his face was pale and his hands were still trembling.

Himmler and Koln looked at each other.

"How could she *be* the Grail, Herr Rahn?" Himmler asked, impatiently tapping his pen on a stack of papers.

"I believe there exists the Grail, the vessel that Christ used at the Last Supper, that was secured by Joseph of Arimethea and spirited off to England by way of Montsegur. But it was important because it contained the Holy Blood in the cup from the crucifixion. It was important as the *vessel* of Christ's blood. That is the story we all know. But if the blood of Christ was the really important thing, how long would it have lasted in the cup? If we found the cup, the Grail today, do we really think it would still contain His blood?

"But what if Christ had a wife, never mentioned as such in the scriptures? What if He had children? They would be vessels of His blood, in a very real sense. What if this *bloodline* was what Joseph of Arimethea spirited away to England for safekeeping from the Romans?

"Gentlemen, I know we have very little time," Rahn said passionately, "But I have reason to believe that the Korr Stigmata on this young woman could identify her as a direct descendent of Christ. As such, she will be of *far* greater value to us here."

"Herr Reichsfuhrer," Rahn said standing up, his voice hushed, "this woman could ensure the destiny of the Thousand Year Reich!"

General Koln looked skeptically at Rahn.

"I thought we agreed it was most likely an artificial marking, Herr Rahn. When did you decide it was really a birthmark?"

But Himmler was not listening to Koln; instead, he had fallen back in his chair, dumbstruck. Finally he spoke.

"General, she is still in Mueller's custody, is that correct?"

"Yes, as of the last report," Koln said.

"Make sure of it," Himmler said, his voice growing louder and higher with excitement.

"And make arrangements to get that young woman back here before the invasion!" He was shouting as he picked up the second phone on his desk, the private line to the Fuhrer.

"I don't care how you do it, just get it done!"

14. The Stone of Destiny

John was now less than two hundred yards behind the black sedan. They were moving more slowly, as driving was becoming more and more dangerous. Cars going the other way pulled suddenly into John's lane to pass; he narrowly avoided a head-on collision at one point by swerving up and onto the concrete pavement. On their right, a street was barricaded, and as they drove past, John had a glimpse of a long section of houses decimated by the bombs.

The further they went, the worse things got. The sky was overcast with smoke, and the noise of planes and bombs was so loud they had to shout to hear each other. There were more and more destroyed buildings and piles of smoldering brick and debris with rescue workers crawling all over some of them.

"It looks like the world is ending," John groaned.

Suddenly they heard a loud whistling. John instinctively hit the brakes and a bomb exploded barely thirty yards in front of them, rocking the car and blasting them with smoke and dust.

"Is everyone all right?" Arthur asked after a moment. John looked at all the car windows: they were intact.

"Yes," Merlin replied from the back seat.

"Yes, I think the car is all right, but we can't go yet," John said. They were in a dense cloud of smoke, and he couldn't see a thing.

Up ahead, the explosion had rocked the black car and all of its passengers were looking behind to see if their pursuers had survived. Dunst stopped the car so they could all watch, but all they saw was a swirling cloud of smoke and dust and nothing emerging from it.

"It doesn't look good for your rescuers, my dear," said Streicher as he looked behind them. "Dunst, let's go!" he barked as he turned around again in his seat. Dunst put the car in gear and they were moving again.

Grace did not know what to think. She heard the bomb and saw the smoke, but her mind went blank, and the last light of hope in her flickered out.

Am I alone now?

Well behind John's car, the small, foreign car had stopped when the bomb went off. Without hesitating, the driver pulled onto a side street, then turned and drove parallel to the main road for two blocks, passing the site of the bombing. He then turned back onto the main road again and toward the middle of London, leaving John's car and its occupants behind. He was closing in on the black sedan.

Back at the house in Englefield Green, Werner, Zimmer, and Guenther, Mueller's other officer, were sitting at the kitchen table playing cards. Suddenly from the other room they heard the unmistakable sound of the front door being opened.

"Back already?!" Werner said under his breath, and the three of them scrambled to clear the table of all the cards, stuffing them into their trouser pockets. They stood at attention around the table, expecting Colonel Mueller to burst into the room, as usual. But there was no heavy footfall, and just as Zimmer and Guenther realized that it could not be Mueller, a tall, athletic man with a black mustache and dark glasses was standing in the kitchen doorway. He looked well-dressed but had a drawn, sinister expression, and he was pointing a large revolver with a silencer on the muzzle directly at them.

"What's all this?!" Werner began. "What do you want?" On Werner's right Zimmer was slowly edging his hand down to his own revolver at his side.

"Don't try it!" the man shouted at Zimmer, who froze but did not withdraw his hand. Guenther stood nervously biting his lip. Suddenly two loud mechanical beeps came from the back room.

"What's that?" the man barked.

"It's the radio," Werner replied, feeling more comfortable that the intruder had been put off by the noise. "There are more coming here right now. Whatever it is you're after, you won't get away with it."

"I'm after the girl. Where is she?"

Werner looked at Guenther and Zimmer quizzically, and he began to smirk. "Girl? What girl?" *Beep, beep* sounded again from the other room.

Zimmer figured the man couldn't take all three of them, and as his hand had reached the gun handle, he had gone past the point of no return. His finger found the trigger and he was just pulling the muzzle up, but it was not soon enough. One shot from the intruder's gun went off with a familiar, muffled pop, and hit Zimmer with surgical precision straight in the heart. He crashed noisily into a kitchen chair before falling in a heap onto the floor, nearly knocking Guenther off his feet.

"Don't shoot! Don't shoot!" both Werner and Guenther were suddenly shouting hysterically. *Beep, beep* went the radio from the other room.

"Now tell me," the man snarled, "*where is the girl?*"

Guenther instinctively tried to catch Zimmer, but as luck would have it he ended up catching Zimmer's gun in his left hand. He tried to drop it but it was too late, and another shot went off. Guenther also fell dead from a shot to the heart, landing on top of Zimmer's body.

Werner was white as a sheet, and he raised his hands as high as he possibly could. The intruder didn't speak, he simply turned to Werner, waiting for an answer. *Beep, beep* went the radio signal.

"Westminster Abbey, in London!" He croaked. "They took the girl there!"

"Thank you," said the man, and he dispatched Werner with a third shot. Then he began to search the rest of the house, and stopped when he saw the telephone near the beeping radio. Immediately he picked up the receiver and dialed with the same hand, keeping his weapon ready. After a brief conversation that ended with an emphatic, "Right!", he bolted out of the house and ran to his car, not bothering to hide his revolver, as a few frightened inhabitants of Englefield Green watched from their windows. He jumped into his car and roared down the high street toward London.

At SS headquarters, General Koln was pacing by the radio operator.

"Where are they? Can't someone operate the radio?" he demanded.

"Perhaps they all went into London," said the operator.

"With the *woman*?!" Koln shouted. "*The Fuhrer himself wants her!*"

The cloud of smoke was just starting to dissipate when John had an idea.

"I know another way to the Abbey," he said suddenly. "I bet they'll think the bomb hit us if we're no longer following them."

Arthur turned to John and slapped him on the shoulder.

"Good idea. Let's go."

John felt himself smile as he backed up a short way then turned onto an empty and undamaged side street. Up ahead, Dunst kept an eye on the rear view mirror as he drove.

"Still no sign of them," he said.

They had to go even more slowly as rescue vehicles came into their lane, forcing Dunst to pull over and let them go by. The sound of aircraft and bombs was now deafening, and the car was rocked again by another explosion. Streicher turned to Grace.

"I hope we don't end up like your friends."

Grace did not respond, but continued to sit stunned in the middle of the back seat. *Is John gone, and Arthur and Merlin?* She couldn't think of anything. She felt as if she were sitting in the very middle of the war, and all the bombs and smoke and destruction were swirling around her, but somehow she was at the still point in the very center, in the calm eye of a huge hurricane of fire and smoke and devastation.

Finally they came to a large square, and there were the buildings of Parliament, barricaded and guarded by dozens of soldiers. Across one of the streets were the lofty towers of

Westminster Abbey, also barricaded, with a few soldiers around its perimeter. Dunst parked along the side of the cathedral and towards the rear.

"Check your weapons, gentlemen," Mueller said calmly, and the metallic clicks of revolvers being loaded filled the car as the din of war continued outside.

"Colonel Mueller," said Streicher, "you will need to gain access before we bring our guest. We cannot leave her in the car. Signal us when you do."

Mueller looked at him smugly.

"Oh, I will."

When he opened the door, the volume of aircraft and bomb noise instantly doubled, and Grace felt herself flinch. Across the way at the Parliament buildings, soldiers were coming and going chaotically, and no one seemed to notice the Germans in their car. At the Abbey two soldiers stood in front, and another stood forlornly by a large side door toward the back, only thirty feet or so from their car. He appeared distracted by all the activity at the Parliament buildings.

Mueller walked directly up to him.

"May I get in, please," he said smiling. The soldier looked at him as if he were mad.

"It's *closed!*"

"Oh, I see," said Mueller, and he turned slowly as if to leave, then turned back suddenly with his long muzzled revolver pointed directly at the soldier.

"Open the door," Mueller said coolly. The soldier suddenly went pale.

"It's o-open," he stuttered.

"Inside, please," said Mueller.

The soldier turned and opened the door; as soon as he crossed the threshold, Mueller shot him in the back of the head. The soldier fell in a lifeless heap, and the blood from his wound began to pool on the stone floor. Mueller dragged the body to one side. Then he looked back at the car and nonchalantly waved his hand.

"Quickly!" Streicher barked, and they all got out of the car and hurried toward the open door. No one at the Parliament buildings or at the front of the Abbey seemed to notice what was going on. Soon they were all inside, and Dunst closed the door with a bang.

"Not another church," List said wearily.

It was considerably quieter inside the Abbey, although the noise of the war outside was echoing in a strange way, as if the old building were moaning in pain at all the destruction in the city around it. They were in an ordinary-looking room used for deliveries and other practical matters. Dunst took the lead.

"St. Edward's chapel is this way," he said.

Mueller followed him, then List, then Grace and Streicher. She felt sick when she saw the pool of blood by the head of the soldier and her legs felt suddenly rubbery, but Streicher pushed her ahead. They went through a doorway that opened up to the main part of the church, and the ceiling soared over their heads.

Behind them, the black-suited man in the broad-brimmed hat had watched the group enter the cathedral. They had not noticed the small, foreign car following them, and they did not see him now as he crept up to the side entrance with his revolver drawn. He opened the door and glanced at the body of the British soldier at his feet, then slipped into the church.

Dunst led them around a choir section toward the center of the Abbey. All along the walls there were memorials, crypts, and grave markers for many of the most famous people in English history. It was as if all of them were watching to see what would happen next.

Dunst led them through a doorway in an ornate wooden screen that partitioned off a small room at the very heart of the building.

"This is St. Edward's Chapel," he announced as he looked around. Then he saw something that made him gasp.

Grace's eyes became as wide as saucers. Streicher looked, and the hair on the back of his neck stood up.

The Coronation Chair was against the far wall facing them. It was an old oaken chair in the gothic style with a large, empty shelf under the seat. In the center of the chapel floor was a large block of stone, the stone for which the shelf and the Coronation Chair had been made. It was the Stone of Destiny, ageless and inscrutable, and it had been removed from the chair and placed in the middle of the floor.

But the sight that made them all stop was a large shining sword that had somehow been imbedded halfway down into the very center of the stone. It was Excalibur, sparkling like a beacon in the dim light, and it was impaled directly into the rock.

Grace did not move, but the glow that she had felt that morning in Winchester was rekindled, and she stood serenely on the cool stone floor. Dunst was frozen where he stood, his mouth agape, while Streicher and the others crept slowly toward the sword in the stone.

Streicher carefully examined the stone and the sword without touching them, utterly baffled by what he was seeing. Mueller slowly went up to the stone and arrogantly grasped the sword by the hilt and pulled on it, his eyes suddenly wide with excitement. It did not budge.

"This has to be some sort of trick!" he cried, frustrated. "Who *did* this?"

Before anyone else could speak, the smoke parted somewhere in the skies to the west of the Abbey, and a shaft of sunlight came through the large windows and landed on another doorway across the chapel. Standing there, silhouetted by the brilliant sunlight, was a broad-shouldered man, standing defiantly in the opening.

"The warrior-king!" gasped List.

Grace smiled as the sunlight moved and encompassed her as well, illuminating her in the midst of all the darkness.

"It is Arthur," she said in a voice so clear and bright that it rang through the cathedral like a bell. They were all motionless, confused and spellbound by what they were seeing.

"Arthur!" Dunst said as his voice trembled. *"What have we done?"*

"Arthur?" Streicher sneered. "Dunst, don't be an idiot!" But he recognized the man he had encountered on the street in Glastonbury, and his crusty, callous exterior was pierced for a moment by the possibility that it somehow could be *the* Arthur. He felt frozen, as if his feet were cemented to the floor.

Mueller had to shake his head.

"It's a trick," he repeated to himself over and over as he slowly raised his revolver.

Just then the sun vanished and the light through the windows was gone. *Pop! Pop!* Mueller fired his revolver at the doorway but Arthur had vanished. The smile vanished from Grace's face and she instinctively covered her head as she tried to look around. *Where's John?*

306

The shots caused Streicher to leap into action.

"List! Watch her! Dunst, come with me," Streicher shouted, and he went back out the doorway they had come in with Dunst immediately behind him.

List grabbed her by the arm as Grace watched Mueller run to the opening where Arthur had stood and look through the doorway into the church. He was just behind the main altar. He began to creep around to his left, when suddenly Grace saw a large hand appear from the other side and clamp down on Mueller's arm. It was Arthur, lunging for the weapon.

Mueller tried to turn away from him to protect the gun, and Arthur threw all his weight on Mueller, causing them both to crash to the floor and sending the gun sliding underneath a marble bench.

"Not bad for an old man," Mueller said getting up, impressed by Arthur's strength and at the same time annoyed that he had let himself be disarmed.

He flew at Arthur, driving into his midsection. Arthur turned to try to avoid the direct blow, and they grappled with each other in the shadows. Mueller had a concealed dagger that he was trying to get into position to use, but he could not yet free his hand to reach it. Grace tried to watch but they disappeared behind the wooden partition, so she scanned all around as best she could for John or Merlin, while List continued gripping her arm.

Maybe he and Merlin didn't survive that bomb blast, she thought, and she felt despair grip her like the hold on her arm.

Streicher and Dunst had just turned the corner when the two grappling men crashed into them. They were too close and too tangled to fire at, so Streicher and Dunst grabbed Arthur, and with Mueller, began to bring him under control. Then Arthur gave a low grunt and with a burst of energy the three men suddenly exploded off him, as if they had been shot out of a cannon. They landed dazed on their backs on the stone floor. Dunst was stunned and Streicher looked in amazement at Arthur towering over them.

How did he do that?

"Impressive," sneered Mueller, "but you can't keep this up. You're twice my age."

Arthur resisted the urge to rub the back of his neck. "And then some."

Just behind the wooden screen, John was looking frantically around for Merlin who had just disappeared. He was nowhere to be seen, and with the tall German just about to round the corner, John knew he had to act. Since his last encounter did not go as well as he would have liked when he went low at his opponent, John decided he would go high. He knew there was no time to think about what he had to do.

Just then Grace saw a figure out of the corner of her eye on the other side of the partition opening. It was John! But she saw that determined look on his face, the same one he had when they were being led across the playing fields in Windsor, and her fear suddenly doubled. *What's he going to do now?! They have guns!*

With a surge of adrenalin, John flew around the corner and jumped on List's back, wrapping his right forearm across List's throat. Grace jumped when she saw John leap onto List's back, and for a moment felt frozen, unable to help but also unable to stop watching. The tall German turned and grasped John's arm, but John's left hand held his right in place, and kept pressure on List's throat. John held on harder than anything he had ever held on in his whole life, as List tried to fling him off his back. He slammed John into the partition with a loud bang but John barely felt it; he simply continued to hold on like it was the last thing he had to do in the world.

When they heard the bang, Streicher and Mueller jumped up.

"Go!" Mueller snarled to Streicher as he produced his dagger. "Leave him to me."

Streicher ran back to the chapel and Dunst followed him. Grace watched helplessly as List staggered around the floor with John piggybacked on him, choking him with his arm lock. Streicher raised his gun but John and List finally tumbled onto the floor, and Streicher couldn't get a clean shot. He and Dunst pulled John off, but List did not move.

"Filthy English!" Streicher hissed as he raised his gun to John's head. Grace watched horrified and was about to lunge at Streicher when a voice boomed out.

"Do not harm him!"

It was Merlin, standing just behind the sword in the stone with his long arms outstretched, but he seemed far larger, far more menacing than any ordinary man could be. He was easily ten feet tall and growing before their eyes. Streicher watched him in amazement; Dunst was terrified.

"Leave this sacred place now," Merlin said, his powerful voice rivaling the din of war from outside the Abbey. He was now over fifteen feet tall and a mist that seemed to emanate from him was beginning to fill the chapel.

"You will not take this stone, nor the young woman, nor this land!"

He pointed his huge right hand at them as if to strike them dead. Dunst ran screaming through the chapel doorway and out the Abbey door into the war outside. They never saw him again.

For the first time in his memory, Streicher was unnerved. He desperately scrambled away, shooting wildly at the huge figure as he ran out of the chapel. He disappeared somewhere toward the back of the Abbey. Grace and John embraced fiercely, with the lifeless figure of List at their feet.

"Are you all right?" John asked Grace as Merlin, his form again normal, went after Streicher.

"Yes, yes!" she answered. "Where is Arthur?"

The dark figure in the broad-brimmed hat had seen glimpses of what had happened from his place in the shadows. He watched Streicher and Merlin leave, and saw his chance. He moved toward the chapel, toward John and Grace.

On the main altar, Arthur and Mueller were again grappling with each other for the dagger, neither able to gain the advantage. When the shot rang out, Arthur hesitated for an instant and his grip relaxed on Mueller's hand holding the knife.

"Grace!" he gasped.

Finally! Mueller freed his hand and lunged with the dagger at Arthur's chest. Arthur barely reached up in time to deflect the blow, but the knife found Arthur's shoulder, causing a long gash that bled freely.

Grace and John had heard him and instinctively ran across the chapel to the doorway of the main altar. The dark man had reached them just as they ran off, his long revolver drawn.

Grace saw the knife and the blood on Arthur's shoulder and was horrified; everything began going in slow motion again. John lurched through the doorway but then hesitated.

The dark man stepped over List and crept through the chapel around the stone, toward the doorway to the main altar.

"Stay with her!" Arthur shouted to John as he grappled with the German.

When Mueller lunged with the knife, Arthur was able to reach up with his other hand and grab him by the throat, even as he was being stabbed. Arthur growled with anger as he directed all his remaining strength to his grip on Mueller's throat. Mueller instinctively flung himself backward, but as he did, Arthur grabbed the knife from him with his other hand.

Just then, Streicher emerged from the shadows outside the chapel, pointing his gun at John and Grace.

"Drop the knife now or I will shoot her!" he shouted at Arthur.

John and Grace stood frozen while Arthur held his position, maintaining his grip on Mueller or the knife.

"*Shoot him!*" Mueller managed to scream. Streicher hesitated.

"I said drop the knife!" he shouted again.

Suddenly a ghostly figure emerged silently from the shadows behind Streicher. It was Merlin, his robes flowing behind him as he glided up to Streicher. Streicher turned and fired wildly, grazing Merlin's left arm, but he was too late. As he fired, Merlin had reached out and touched his arm, and Streicher fell to the floor as if dead.

Mueller screamed desperately and made a go for the knife. Arthur let go of his throat, and with both hands on the knife, pushed it deep into Mueller's chest. Mueller choked blood and gasped, then slowly stopped struggling.

Arthur rolled off Mueller's body and stood up, breathing heavily and clutching his bloody shoulder. Grace felt like she could finally relax enough to take a breath, but it didn't last long.

"Do not move!" said a hoarse voice. Grace turned slowly to her left. It was List at the main altar, holding his throat with one hand while he pointed his revolver at her with the other.

"Come here, my dear," he croaked, and Arthur, John, and Merlin looked helplessly at her as Grace walked over to him. List grabbed her and pointed the gun at her head.

"We will take her, or no one will." Grace was ashen as she felt the muzzle of the gun press against her head. She went stiff with panic.

Never in his existence had Arthur felt so helpless.

If I make a move, he will shoot her and if I don't, he may shoot her anyway.

There was movement in the shadows behind List, and they heard *pop! pop!* Grace jumped at the sound.

John could not breath. *Did he shoot Grace?* Grace couldn't feel anything for a second, and she realized that she didn't feel anything because she had not been shot. She felt List slide heavily down her side to the floor. Then she began to get a strange, light feeling, like she was never in any danger, even when the gun was pressed against her head. But she was distracted by someone standing right behind her.

It was the dark man in the broad-brimmed hat, his revolver smoldering. He quickly checked List's body.

"He's dead."

They all stared silently as the dark man put his revolver inside his black jacket. Finally Arthur spoke.

"Thank you, stranger," he gasped. "May I ask who you are and who sent you?"

"I am also a protector of the Grail," answered the man in an accent that Grace could not quite place.

"I have been sent by the superiors of my Order to watch the Germans and track their efforts to find the Grail. I followed them here as you did."

"What Order is that?" Arthur asked.

"I cannot say more about my Order," he said quietly. "It is a secret society."

Merlin eyed him curiously as he spoke.

"Do you know where the Grail is?" he asked. The man looked at Merlin.

"It has been lost for twenty years, and we have looked endlessly, but have not found it," he said. "We thought perhaps the Germans might find it for us—but that has been a dangerous game, as you have seen."

Lost for twenty years. Grace looked silently at the dark man next to her as she pictured the small ceramic cup in her mind.

"It is safe," she said suddenly. All four men turned and looked at her awestruck, and the dark man took off his hat. Finally Arthur spoke.

"That is all we need to know."

"Yes," said the dark man as he bowed his head. "I must leave now, and I suggest you do the same. It is not safe in this city. Let us not tempt fate."

And with that he disappeared into the shadows.

15. Excalibur

Arthur walked over to Grace and gently patted her cheek. She felt her cheek flush crimson and she smiled and held Arthur's hand, her dark hair falling onto their grasp.

"I am glad to see you are safe, Grace," he said smiling. Then he turned to John, who had come over to stand next to Grace. He put his hand on John's shoulder.

"Good work, John Perceval."

"Thank you." John looked at Arthur's shoulder. "Are you all right?"

"It needs some care, but I should be all right," Arthur replied.

They went over to where Merlin stood, holding his left arm. Streicher was snoring quietly at his feet.

"How is your arm?" Arthur asked him.

"It's nothing," Merlin said, stepping over the sleeping German. He looked at Arthur's shoulder.

"It's bleeding badly. You're getting too old for this, you know."

"Yes, I know," Arthur smiled painfully.

"Come over here; there's something we can try," Merlin said, and he led Arthur through the doorway back into St. Edward's chapel.

Excalibur was still impaled in the stone, looking as if it had always been there. Merlin led Arthur up to the stone and helped him carefully remove his bloody coat, while Grace and John stood by. The noise of the war outside still filtered into the Abbey as dusk approached.

Merlin tore the sleeve off Arthur's shirt so that the wound was exposed. Grace and John gasped. It was very deep and still bleeding freely. He had to act quickly.

Merlin held out his hand. "Grace, come here please."

Grace looked at John in surprise but walked over to where Arthur and Merlin were standing. It was as close as she had been to the stone and Excalibur, and she could not stop looking at them in the dim light. They almost seemed to be carrying an electric charge.

"Grace," Merlin said solemnly. "Remove the sword."

She looked at him in disbelief. She wanted to speak, to object, but she knew there was no time. Without hesitating further, Grace reached out to the stone and grasped the great sword by the hilt. She took a deep breath, then with both hands pulled Excalibur out with one graceful, even motion. The weight of the sword impressed her as much as the shining brightness of the metal.

John watched her in silent amazement, and his mind was reeling. *Who pulls the sword from the stone?* Grace pointed the heavy sword upward as she turned to Merlin and Arthur.

"Place the blade flat against the wound," Merlin said.

She carefully lowered Excalibur and gently pressed the width of the blade against Arthur's bleeding shoulder. Merlin held the sword in place with his hand for a moment, then slowly removed it. He wiped the blood from the area carefully with the shirtsleeve, and then stood back. The bleeding had stopped.

"It worked!" Merlin gasped.

Grace and John breathed a sigh of relief. Merlin quickly tore the bloody coat and fashioned a sling for Arthur's arm.

"The kingly power to heal resides in both Excalibur and the stone, but I wasn't sure how to tap it," he said, wiping his brow.

"You were the key, Grace," Merlin said softly, turning to her. "Besides Arthur, only you could have pulled Excalibur from the stone."

Arthur lightly touched his wound, then looked at Grace

"I was never able to do that," he said. John was holding his right hand on top of his head as he looked at Grace holding the sword. *She to whom the Grail is known.*

Grace looked in wonder at the glimmering sword in her hand, then turned to Arthur and presented Excalibur to him. Arthur took the sword and Merlin helped him wrap it in what remained of the coat. It almost seemed to disappear in the fabric.

"I'm sorry about your father's clothes, Grace," Arthur said.

"That's all right," she said smiling, "he doesn't need them."

Then she laughed for what seemed like the first time in weeks and John responded by embracing her, but carefully, like he was holding the most precious thing he had ever known.

"Time to return the stone to its resting place," Arthur said. All four of them stood by a corner of the great stone, then reached down and lifted it as if it were made of paper. They slid it back onto the shelf in the Coronation Chair.

"It's time to go," Arthur said looking around. It was now dark and the noise of war from outside had finally subsided.

"Go ahead," Merlin said. "I'll be right there."

As the other three went out to the car, Merlin went over to where Streicher was sleeping. He knelt down by the sleeping man and began to softly speak strange, ancient words in his ear.

Streicher was suddenly aware of the bearded man bending over him but he was paralyzed with sleep and, try as he might, he could not wake himself up.

"Go back and tell them everything that has happened here," said Merlin, his large bearded face hovering in the darkness. "You cannot invade this land."

"Yes," Streicher felt himself answer wordlessly.

Streicher tried to ask, "Was that *King* Arthur?" but still he couldn't speak.

"Yes," answered the old man's grinning face. "And I am Merlin."

With that, Streicher fell back into a deep sleep.

Merlin dashed out of the church to the car where the others were waiting. John turned the car around in the square and started the long journey out of London and home as searchlights crossed back and forth in the dark sky. Arthur closed his eyes and appeared to fall asleep almost immediately, while Grace sat next to John holding his hand as he drove the car through the bombed city.

After some time, Streicher woke with a start. It was nearly pitch black and he was disoriented, but he managed to stand up and make his way around. He stumbled on Mueller's body near the entrance to the chapel, then he went through the doorway. He noticed the stone was no longer in the middle of the floor, but it was too dark to see if it had been returned to its place in the Coronation Chair.

He staggered into the service room, past the body of the British soldier, and went out the Abbey door. Night had fallen and searchlights patrolled the sky, but he heard few aircraft, and no more bombs. They were done for the day. He climbed into the black car and drove off, and everything that had happened slowly came back to him.

Something inside him was no longer the same. Whatever had really happened in that church had shaken him down to his core. Could they have staged it? Possibly, he thought, but all that, just for one woman? Not likely, and now Mueller was dead, Dunst and List were missing and probably dead, and he had lost the girl.

"Unbelievable," he said to the black sky.

He was finished, that was certain. He knew that as surely as he knew his own name. But he would report in when he got back to Mueller's place, and he would tell them everything. They would court martial him, maybe execute him on the spot, but it didn't matter.

As he drove west with the searchlights dueling in the sky above, Streicher thought back to when he had first taken the assignment. The idea of somehow getting close to the Holy Grail had intrigued him. He felt a strange, forgotten attraction to the Grail that he had not felt since he was young, a connection that had been slumbering deep inside him, only to be awakened at that most unlikely of times. In his youth Streicher had a mystical bent, and had even considered the priesthood for a while, but the first war left little room for any of that, and he joined the army and became as pragmatic as the next officer. But *Operation Sangraal* rekindled his mystical side, and although this nagging attraction to something as mystical as the Holy Grail was at odds with his adult view of himself, he had thrown himself into his work and stopped thinking about it. Soon it became more than enough for him that achieving the Grail would be the pinnacle of atonement for all that had happened to his country in the First War. It would be their crowning achievement, their destiny, and everything seemed to be leading up to it.

But now he knew that he had been wrong. What had seemed like a quest for the ultimate validation of their national spirit he now saw plainly as an exercise in ambition and audacity.

"And I was no different," he whispered to himself, as his own life crystallized before him. "That was why I joined the SS—ugly ambition. I turned my back on a noble profession and joined a pack of wolves."

He thought back to his days as a young officer candidate in Hannover, and to his circle of friends. Pezold, Kiesel, and Stauffenberg had symbolized for him the best chance for atonement and the real hope for his country. Stauffenberg especially was not only a model of leadership and a top officer, but an intellectual and even a mystic, and Streicher had felt a strong kinship with him. When Streicher later joined the *SS*, Stauffenberg's blunt disapproval had stung him, and they went their separate ways.

"I wonder where his path will lead," he mused, as something foreign to him began to blur his vision. "Someplace better than mine, I hope."

He knew in his heart that the advantage in the air war had shifted that day to the British, and that an invasion would not succeed. And for the first time, he had a very bad feeling about his country's destiny in the war.

He lit a cigarette and enjoyed it immensely as he drove along in solitude. He saw the image of Grace's face in the windshield in front of him, as clearly as if she were there with him, her fair face and red lips surrounded by the mass of black hair that now merged with the dark London sky.

Who was she, *what* was she, the woman that he'd had in his custody? He felt again the nagging connection deep inside him, only this time to the strange young woman with the improbable birthmark.

I'll likely never know what she really was, he thought, *but I believe we were very close to what we were seeking.*

"Unbelievable."

On the road headed west out of London, the small foreign car lurched to a stop at a telephone booth. The man in the broad-brimmed hat climbed out of the car and went into the booth to make a call.

In a dark room somewhere in the south of England, the telephone rang. An old gentleman got out of his chair with much effort to answer it.

"Yes?" he said.

The man in the broad-brimmed hat hesitated.

"Is this the General?" he asked awkwardly. He couldn't believe he was actually speaking to the General after all these years, and suddenly his throat started to tighten.

"Who *is* this?" the General asked sharply.

"Octavos," he stammered. "Dedalus s-said I should contact you directly. He stayed in Englefield Green while I followed them into London."

"Yes, yes, he reported in. Go ahead," replied the old man impatiently.

"The young woman is safe. The Germans have been eradicated, at least the four that took her into London," he said, fingering a crosslet on a chain around his neck with long, nervous fingers.

The General relaxed and looked up to the ceiling.

"Thank god," he said with a loud sigh. "Good work. The ones in Englefield Green have been eradicated as well. Where is she now?"

"They are driving out of London," answered Octavos. "She was with young Perceval, as we know, but the two older men she is with…" Octavos struggled to find the words to report things he wasn't even sure he had seen correctly.

"What is it?" the General snapped, suddenly agitated again. *"Tell me everything!"*

Outside London, along a heavily wooded stretch of road, John pulled over at a filling station for fuel.

"We need petrol, but I'm out of coupons," he said to Grace.

Arthur slept while Merlin sat up in his seat.

"Don't worry," Merlin said as a teenage boy came up to John's window. Grace watched John's expression brighten, and she sensed that maybe a little bit of fun was on the way.

"Fill it up, please." he smiled.

"Yes, sir," the young attendant answered. "Uh, can I have your coupons, please?"

"I'm afraid I've used them all," John answered cheerfully.

The boy stood silent for a moment as if he were losing his equilibrium, then he slowly went over and began filling the tank. When he was finished, he walked sleepily away. John turned and smiled at Grace.

"Thank you," he said to Merlin smiling in the back seat.

"You're welcome," Merlin chuckled. Arthur's eyes were still closed but a smile played across his face.

They flew down the highway to Stokehill. As John drove, Grace remembered the documents under her seat, and she turned to John.

"Did you tell Merlin about the papers we found hidden in the church library?"

"Yes," John replied. *We talked about a lot of things*, he thought as he looked back at her.

"So my father, after having a premonition about the bombings in Stokehill, apparently moved the Grail to Winchester," she said. Even though she was exhausted, being able to talk about her father made Grace's skin tingle with excitement. She felt closer to him than she could ever remember.

"Yes, secretly," Merlin added. "And that was when something happened he did not plan, to him and the Grail."

Grace pictured the ceramic cup on public display in the cathedral.

"The Grail was in public view in the glass display case in the vestibule of the cathedral, along with other relics," she said. "It was as if whoever put it there didn't know what it really was. Perhaps my father died before he could put it in a more secure place."

"It would seem so," Merlin said, and he fell silent. He was tired, and he slumped in his seat as he looked out the window in silence. Dark images flitted by, and he flashed back to his long, dark sleep under Ankerwyke Hill. Disquieted, he seemed to experience again the barren, black confinement—barren, except what was that trickling sound? All that time he had been aware of something, but his mind could not stir itself to recognize it. Now he knew—it was the clear sound of water. Like diamonds dropping from somewhere, from someone, only the presence of water had given him any relief in all those long ages. He sat up in his seat.

From someone. *For every gift they take away, they give one.* He looked to John and Grace in the front seat.

"John. The hill where you found me—is there water there?"

John looked in his rearview mirror.

"Yes, a spring. It's the source of the Culvert."

Later that night, General Koln and Herr Rahn drove to the High Command building where an agitated Himmler was preparing for a late meeting with the Fuhrer. They were able to get Himmler alone for a few minutes to brief him on Colonel Streicher's report.

"What shall I tell the Fuhrer?" Himmler snapped, as the stress and strain of more bad news took its toll on him. The reports from the Luftwaffe that day had not been good. Sixty planes had been lost.

"That we *had* the Holy Grail," he shouted, "the heir to Christ and the guarantee of the supremacy of the Reich forever, and we let her *get away*?! He'll shoot me himself!" He took off his glasses and rubbed his eyes.

"That w-was only a theory, Herr Reichsfuhrer," said Rahn, stuttering fearfully. "The birthmark could have been purely coincidental. As for the bearded men, they could simply have been English eccentrics who had a talent for hypnosis."

"Someone obviously thought it was more than just theories— Mueller and four men dead, and one missing! Colonel Mueller was *not* hypnotized and beaten by a small group of English *eccentrics*," he spat. "Even Streicher, who is clearly not what he once was, barely managed to get away. How did he do that if he was hypnotized too? Besides, I *know* him. You said yourself that during his report, he was calm and rational, not like someone under hypnosis."

Rahn and Koln sat silent. Rahn had never seen Himmler so angry; the veneer of civility had been stripped away and Himmler was shouting at him like he was a child. Himmler put his glasses back on.

"I even told him about the plan to capture the Stone of Destiny! What a fool I was to rely on such a group of bumblers!" Himmler tried to compose himself as he stood up. He wiped his mouth with a starched white handkerchief.

"Well, I must meet with the Fuhrer now, unless there is something else you wish to tell me," he said sarcastically.

"Nothing, Herr Reichsfuhrer," they both mumbled.

Two days later, Herr Rahn went for an afternoon drive in the mountains to look at the fall color and gather his thoughts. He never returned. The next day, two boy scouts found his abandoned car by the road, and his body on a little hilltop in the woods. There was a bullet wound in his head, from a shot that appeared to have been fired from close range.

The bombings would continue for several months more, and the war for another five years, but the tide of battle had turned that day. Germany's largest aerial assault on England to date had been turned back, and two days later, on September the seventeenth, the Fuhrer issued Directive Number 19, indefinitely postponing Operation Sea Lion.

16. The Secret of the Grail

That night, while sleeping on Grace's sofa, John dreamt he was running through the forest again, and the white hart was only ten tantalizing yards ahead of him. With one giant leap of his will he threw himself bodily at the animal and closed the gap, but as he looked around excitedly for the white hart, he realized that it inexplicably had become Grace. She looked radiant in flowing white robes as her dark hair cascaded around her shoulders. Her lips were the color of ripe strawberries as she smiled at him, and there were snow-white apple blossoms in her hair. John smiled back at her and as the dream ended, they walked hand in hand into the deep, lush, green woods.

The next morning Grace woke up early, in her own bed, in no hurry to get up. After what seemed like ages she finally had time alone, and she was basking in the luxurious solitude. She lay there turning everything over in her mind: Arthur at Lady's Well, her father's journal hidden in the church, the voice in Winchester, and the way she healed Arthur with Excalibur. Just being a descendent of the Grail family, as Merlin said, and a *keeper* of the Grail like her father—that didn't explain how she was able to make the bleeding stop. And then there was the bit John said on the lawn, just before their encounter with the Germans, about one of the Grail Party being a baby.

Grace turned onto her side facing her night stand. There, propped up against the alarm clock, was the photograph of her father that her grandfather had given her just a few days before.

"Who am I?" She asked the handsome, familiar face, and it felt to her for the first time like an answer was close to her, closer than ever before.

Just then she heard noises coming from downstairs. Someone was shuffling around the kitchen. Grace threw on her robe and went downstairs, not quite sure what or who she would find there. She first saw John in the parlor on the sofa, still asleep. His shoes were on the floor by the front door and his big stocking feet were sticking out from underneath the throw blanket he was covered with. Grace looked at his placid face, and she realized in that calm moment that she really loved him, however quickly things had happened to get her to that point. In some way she knew—with everything else going on—that was the most important thing. She felt herself smiling. In four years with Roger, she thought, it never felt like this. She turned and went into the kitchen to find Arthur and Merlin seated at the kitchen table.

"Good morning," Arthur said.

"Good morning," Grace replied. "How did you sleep?"

"Fine," he and Merlin answered in unison.

"Would you like something to eat?" she asked, as she started moving about the kitchen.

"Yes!"

Grace began to gather what she could find, starting with eggs and bacon from the fridge. As she reached into the cupboard for a bowl, she noticed her mother had left her cross necklace on the window sill.

"That's funny, she never takes it off," she said under her breath, and she was about to slip it into her pocket when she stopped. Grace had not held the necklace since she was a little girl, and she had never noticed that the center stone was a little larger than the other four. At the table Merlin suddenly noticed Grace holding the cross and studying it intently.

Just like my birthmark. Grace was staring at the stones in the cross that were an exact copy of her birthmark. She couldn't believe she never made the connection before, and she felt at once inexcusably dimwitted, but gloriously enlightened.

My birthmark is a cross!

Grace could feel the final piece of her puzzle slip silently into place. She mechanically began to fry the bacon in a pan but was barely aware of it. The eggs seemed to crack themselves into the bowl as she pictured the four of them again under the oak tree in Winchester, as Merlin was telling her about her ancestry.

I am a descendant of the Grail Family, she thought, *but what member would have been designated by a cross?* Something was coming at Grace that was so huge she wanted to turn and run from the idea, but that was the old Grace. Now she quietly considered it.

Am I more than just a guardian? Merlin continued to watch her very carefully out of the corner of his eye, and now Arthur too was aware that Grace had made some discovery. He was about to say something, but the smell of the bacon cooking had started to drift through the house, and just then John wandered in from the living room.

"Good morning," he yawned.

"Good morning," they all responded, and Grace seemed to put her thoughts aside, and quickly finished cooking the meal. Soon all four of them were eating their breakfast hungrily as sunlight slowly filtered into the kitchen. Arthur was the first to finish.

"Well," he said with a sad smile, "our time here is done."

Grace just looked at him. Then she got up silently from the table and went upstairs to change, while the three men quickly got ready and waited outside by the car.

The morning air was cool and crisp, and although the remaining inhabitants of Stokehill were quiet, there was a chorus of birds heralding the morning with their song. Soon Grace appeared on the step and all three men turned toward her.

She felt strangely radiant, and they looked at her like they were seeing her for the first time. John noticed that she was wearing her scarlet track warm-up suit, but it barely registered with him. All he seemed to see was Grace's almost glowing white skin contrasted with the scarlet suit and her black hair.

"I'm ready," she said. They slowly got into the car and John turned the key and coaxed the old engine to life.

"Lady's Well, please, John," Arthur said from the back seat.

They made the short drive to Lady's Well, where they got out of the car and marched down the footpath, Arthur carrying the sword still bundled in the torn, bloody coat. They soon came to the clearing and stood silently at the shore of the small lake. Grace noticed that the pipe out of which the Culvert emptied into the lake was dry.

Arthur slowly unwrapped Excalibur from the bloodstained coat as the other three watched, and they were surprised to see that it was as spotless and as clean as if it had just been polished. He held the sword in both hands for a moment, then he unexpectedly grasped the sword by the blade and extended the handle to John. John and Grace were surprised; even Merlin had not expected it.

"John," Arthur said, "take Excalibur and cast it into the water."

John looked confused and took a half step back. "Are you *sure*?" But Grace gently touched John's arm and turned to Arthur.

"May I?" She slowly raised both hands out in front of her. Merlin's eyes widened and a smile broke over his face.

"Yes," Arthur answered, also smiling at her. "Of course." As he handed the sword to Grace, they could just hear him say under his breath, "Goodbye, my old friend."

Grace slowly took the sword in both hands, marveling again at its weight and flawlessness. It was sparkling like crystal in the morning sun. She held it upright with the blade just inches from her face, but instead of casting Excalibur into the lake, she slowly stepped into the water.

John let out a loud gasp. "Grace!" But she continued to slowly, carefully wade into the water that was now above the knees of her track suit, as Arthur and Merlin watched, speechless.

Just then a graceful hand clothed in white fabric emerged from near the center of the lake. Grace's heart felt like it was glowing as she continued down into the lake, the water now above her waist, raising the great sword straight up over her head. As she neared the hand she saw that the white fabric was trimmed in a bead of red and black, but the swirling water was too murky to see anything else below the surface. The hand moved gently toward her, and opened slowly. Grace's arms began to shake as she lowered the sword and carefully placed the handle into the waiting hand. It grasped the great sword and silently pulled it into the water.

Grace stood there, cheeks aflame and water still above her waist, then turned carefully and began to move out of the lake. It was like she was watching herself from above the treetops, just like in Winchester, as she waded up the slope, and she could not feel the water pouring off her as she stood on the shore. Arthur and Merlin stood reverently, almost like priests, but John was open-mouthed, eyes bulging and completely in awe.

"Good lord!" he cried, and he looked as if he felt like he no longer belonged in her company. Grace said nothing but stood in silence. She was lost in her thoughts. She later wondered how long she stood there without speaking, the other three watching her closely as water dripped off her and back into the lake.

All the time she had spent playing at that small lake as a child and the special fondness she had always felt for it and the Culvert which fed it, all of that crystallized with everything that had happened over the previous two weeks. Indeed, all of her life was crystallizing before her eyes as she watched the water ripple out from her wake, and from where Excalibur had been returned: her birthmark, her father and all her Arundel ancestry, the war, Arthur and Merlin, and somehow even the Lady of the Lake, whatever she really was. But then she looked at John. He had been there all along, the outspoken historian, always just offstage in her life but now stepping in at the right time.

I honestly don't think I could have made it through the last two weeks without him. Just thinking the words nearly made Grace choke with emotion, and she snapped out of her reverie. Arthur took a step toward her.

"Well done," he said as he put his hand on Grace's shoulder.

They all stood for a moment, then turned to go to the car. Suddenly they saw an old man standing there, not twenty yards away. He wore a green plaid shirt with a large cross on a chain around his neck, and he had seen everything.

"Granddad!" Grace exclaimed. She turned to Arthur and Merlin.

"That's my granddad," she repeated. They did not seem surprised or the least bit concerned at his presence. As her grandfather walked slowly toward them, Grace gasped when she noticed the cross around his neck was a larger version of the one her mother wore.

"That's odd," she said to them, "I didn't know he had—I've never seen that before." But for some reason it didn't surprise Grace at all, even if she couldn't say at that moment exactly how Granddad fit into it all. He came up and embraced her emotionally.

"Hello, Granddad," she said, still surprised. "How did you know I was here?"

"I had a feeling," he said, choking up. Arthur, Merlin, and John looked on silently.

"Oh," Grace said, turning to Arthur and Merlin, "this is my grandfather. Granddad, this is, uh, Arthur and Merlin, and you know John."

They nodded to the old man. Grace's grandfather smiled at them awkwardly. He was clearly overwhelmed and he looked like he could burst at any moment.

"What is that cross you're wearing?" she finally asked him. "I've never seen it before. It's like Mum's, isn't it?"

"Yes. It's been called an engrailed cross," he blurted, holding it out toward her. "It was a variation of a Templar cross." Merlin looked at Arthur.

"A Templar cross?" Grace said. "I'm confused."

"So am I," John added.

Merlin spoke up. "We were helped by a dark man in a broad-brimmed hat, who spoke with an accent. He said his superiors sent him. Are you his superior?"

"Yes," said Grace's grandfather modestly. "I am the Father General of the Secret Scion of the Knights Templar."

Grace looked at him in astonishment. "You're the *what*?"

"It's a secret order, Grace," he said. "We are the protectors of the Holy Grail. I have belonged to it since I was twenty-five, as did my father before me, and his father, going back a long, long way."

"But, the Knights Templar," John said, bewildered. "They're not a secret, are they?"

"You may have read about them in your history books, John," said Grace's grandfather. "Historically the order protected the temple of Salomon during the crusades, but the real charter has always been to protect the Holy Grail and the Secret of the Grail. And even though the Order was officially eradicated centuries ago, different groups have called themselves Templars, even to this day. But my branch has an unbroken line back to the original Knights, and it has always been secret, because it has always been close to the Secret of the Grail." Grace saw Arthur turned to Merlin and smile...was it a sad smile?

Then John remembered the cryptic journal reference. "The *S.S.*—Secret Scion!"

Her grandfather nodded. "Yes, for short."

"Father General—does that mean you're a *priest*?" Grace asked.

"No," he laughed, "I am no priest, although there is one in our number who is a priest. He joined us nearly twenty years ago, right after your father—" Then he stopped and smiled sadly at Grace.

"Your father also belonged, Grace. My family and the Arundels, *your families*, have been closely allied for many, many generations. We have belonged to the secret order, and they have *been* the secret that we have protected. And many of them have belonged as well."

Her grandfather affectionately touched Grace's hand.

"The picture I gave you the other evening was not taken to commemorate your father's engagement to your mother, it was taken when your father joined the Order."

"So you've known all along about me," she said. "Why haven't you told me, Granddad?"

"Of course I've known. You are the first child of a union between our two families, at least as long as anyone can remember. So you see, Grace, even though you've felt guilty about being the last of the Arundels, it's really a new beginning. The Arundel name is not the most important thing. It's you, Grace, and what you are inside, that matter the most."

Grace could see a light shining on part of her soul that had always been in shadow. She felt herself smiling as her grandfather continued.

"When you turned twenty-five, I planned to tell you about it, but I was going to do that slowly, over the course of six months or so. It's not something you just drop on someone all at once. But then apparently you met these two gentlemen," he nodded nervously toward Arthur and Merlin, "and you were caught up in the events of the past week or two, and you found out before I could tell you."

"What about my mother?" Grace asked. "Why hasn't she ever said anything?"

Her grandfather sighed.

"Grace, when your father died, your mother was still very young, and she had a very hard time with it. Part of her blamed the Order—it's very complicated. As a result she hasn't wanted anything to do with it since."

Grace began to understand her mother a little bit better. Her mother knew that she would lose Grace to the Order now that she was twenty-five, the same Order that she had lost her husband to. No wonder she had been so upset lately, especially with the war on top of it all. Grace's heart went out to her.

Oh, Mum!

"Does your order know the whereabouts of the Grail itself?" Arthur asked him.

"We did, until Grace's father died in a car accident some twenty years ago. He was determined to move it away from Stokehill because of a premonition he had, and I was dead set against it. I'm afraid we fought over it terribly," he said, shaking his head with remorse. "Finally he took it upon himself, which he was well within his rights to do, but unfortunately he died before he could tell anyone where he had moved it. We've been looking for it ever since."

Grace gently touched his arm.

"Winchester, Granddad," she said simply. "It is safe, in the cathedral in Winchester. I saw it myself." She watched a tear begin to form in her grandfather's eye.

"Thank goodness!" he choked.

"Aye," said Arthur, and they were all silent. Finally Arthur spoke again.

"And now if you'll excuse us, our time here is done."

Grace's grandfather looked frozen, as if he wanted desperately to say something, but was unable. Arthur walked over to him and took his hand.

"You and your Order have done a great service to us, to the Grail, and to this land. Thank you," he said, looking him in the eye.

"Aye," Merlin smiled. "Thank you."

Grace's grandfather looked as if he might burst into tears as he stood shaking Arthur's hand. Finally managed to blurt out, "Thank you very much indeed!"

Then her grandfather then gave Grace a kiss on the cheek and disappeared down the path back to his home.

The four of them left the car and walked to the beach, and went out to the same spot where Grace had first met Arthur the week before. The wind blew their hair as they climbed down to the sand. The beach was empty save for a few crying seagulls, and they stood silently for a moment watching the waves crash onto the beach.

"Look!" said John suddenly. A small boat with a single sail appeared about a quarter mile out, making its way toward them. There were three figures in it. Arthur turned to them, his hair and beard blowing in the wind.

"It is time." Then for the first time since she met him, Grace saw Arthur take a deep breath.

"Grace, I know what you just heard from your grandfather, but you must know what you really are." Grace felt herself swallow. *Now what?*

"You've heard the stories about *our* search for the Holy Grail," he nodded to Merlin. "Well, it wasn't the cup we were after. That was never in question." Much to Grace's alarm, he took another deep breath as he looked at the approaching boat.

"I don't have much time, but…we believed that Christ had an heir, that came to this land with Joseph of Arimethea as part of the Grail Party. It was a rumor, a legend, that had been around a long time, and we decided if it was true, then of course we needed to find any descendent. We spent our best years searching for any living descendants, and soon it was to the exclusion of all else. I was consumed by it…"

"As was I," Merlin added, shaking his head. Arthur smiled sadly then continued.

"The kingdom became a wasteland, and I knew it, but I couldn't stop. Finally, late one night, after years of frustration, I did something that I had never done. I took a drink of water from the Grail cup, as a desperate prayer for help.

"I remember sitting there on the throne after I had finished, holding the cup, alone, in the middle of the night, and Merlin came into the room." Merlin smiled. "I had just had a dream, the likes of which I haven't had before or since. In short, I was shown a way to go back to Joseph's day, to the Grail Party when they arrived, and see the truth for myself. Arthur sat me in the throne, and although I did not travel in body, I was sent back in my mind and I was there when they arrived on these shores, in their little sailboat, as clearly as I am here with you now."

Grace could picture everything Merlin was saying, to the point where she almost felt transported too.

"Well, there was no child, no offspring in the Grail Family," Merlin sighed. "I knew then that the Grail was the cup, nothing more, and everything else had been an illusion." Arthur continued.

"And although it was painful for Merlin and I to admit we had been disillusioned for so long, the truth was like a drink of clear water to one who had been dying of thirst. And the sign, *your* sign, Grace…it was only then that it began to appear. And it designates a descendent of Joseph, no one else—and a guardian of the Grail."

"Then I am a descendent of Joseph," Grace said evenly. She somehow knew deep inside this was right, but she also knew she had to share it with her grandfather. *That* won't be easy, she thought.

"Yes," Arthur added, "but there is more." He slowly raised his right arm, then with his left hand pulled down his right sleeve. There on the inside of his right wrist was the sign, exactly like the one Grace had on her ankle. Grace stood speechless while Arthur and Merlin both beamed at her. John began to sputter like his old car, this time with both hands on his head.

"J-John of Glastonbury!"

Arthur looked at him a little confused. "Sorry, John—what?"

John still had both hands on top of his head, as if to keep his mind from exploding. "H-He was a monk in the 1300s whose claim to fame was that he said you," he nodded to Arthur, "were descended from Joseph of Arimethea." The three of them watched John kindly, but curiously. "That's all," he smiled sheepishly. Arthur continued.

"I was the first one to have the sign, and I was not born with it, because it appeared shortly after Merlin's return. You Grace, are a descendent of mine!"

"And so was my father, and grandfather, and great grandfather, all the way back. Is that right?"

"Yes, that's right. But you are something that none of them ever were." Arthur looked at Merlin.

Merlin smiled. "You were and are the one descendant at this most critical moment in history that was destined to protect against this invasion. Only you could have done over the last few days what had to be done. You Grace, are the Pendragon, and you are only the second one, after Arthur."

"And," Arthur added, "as good as you have done, your work is not over. The war is far from being finished."

Grace felt a strange mixture of emotions: the glowing feeling inside she had experienced in Winchester had returned, but it was surrounded with a great, sweet sadness. She felt closer to her father than she could ever remember, but the two men who had brought her closer to him were leaving her life, probably for good. She felt tears streaming down her face.

"John," Arthur said as he took his hand, "thank you for your bravery and your trust." He looked at him with such sincerity that John felt a tear form in the corner of his eye.

"I would ask you to take good care of Grace," Arthur said quietly, as they continued shaking hands, "but I know you will."

"Thank you, Arthur, thank you for everything," John answered, wishing he could think of more to say as tears began to blur his vision.

The small boat was much closer. John could just make out three regal-looking women dressed in strange, beautiful gowns.

Arthur turned to Grace, whose face was covered with tears. "Grace," he began, and without waiting she wrapped her arms around him. Arthur returned her embrace, smiling.

"Grace," he said into her ear, "you've been given a huge responsibility and you have borne it well, and this land will remain free as a result. I've seen you grow as a woman in the past two weeks, and I could not be more proud of you if you were my own daughter." That was it for Grace, who began to cry freely.

"Never forget your heritage and your special charge, and be brave in the trials ahead!" he said as he let go of her.

"I won't forget, but I'm not sure how brave I'll be," Grace said, sobbing. "Will we ever see you again?"

"You never know," Arthur said smiling, "you never know!"

He turned and began walking to the boat, which had now reached shore.

Grace and John looked at each other in shock, for Arthur had left without saying a word to Merlin. Merlin stood silently with the wind blowing his hair and beard, looking deeply hurt. Arthur had waded out to the boat and climbing in when the woman in the center, dressed in a white gown with black and red trim, extended her right hand to Merlin, beckoning him.

"The Lady of the Lake!" Merlin gasped.

Arthur stood up in the boat and also extended his hand in welcome to Merlin. John and Grace's faces went from anguish to joy, as Merlin now turned to them.

"John," he said as Grace moved off a few steps, "take good care of her."

"I will," John replied. "But how shall I *treat* her?" he asked anxiously

Merlin laughed. "Grace is indeed a special person, but she is still a *person*, no different than you or me. Treat her as you like to be treated—I find that approach works best."

Then John remembered something. "What will happen to you and Arthur, now that you're mortal again?" Merlin thought for a moment as he looked at the boat. He faced a mystery about which he knew absolutely nothing and he realized that in his past, he would have searched desperately for any bit of knowledge that would prepare him for the journey. Now he simply smiled contentedly.

"I honestly don't know, but I'm sure I'll find out in good time."

He walked over to Grace, and she embraced him as she had Arthur.

"Farewell, Grace," he said, surprised at the gesture. "In Winchester, how did you know it was the Grail?"

Grace felt the glow fill her again. She looked up at him.

"A voice helped me realize it." She tried to remember the sound of the voice.

"I thought perhaps that it might have been your voice," she said to him, smiling, but he looked surprised.

"A voice? It wasn't mine. Remember I told you that was one of the things that was hidden to me?"

Grace looked puzzled. "Yes, I remember."

"You were the *only* one who could find the Grail, Grace. Now you must keep it safe," he said.

"I will," Grace said, remembering the dusty earthen vessel sitting unnoticed and forgotten in the glass case.

"As for the voice," Merlin continued, "only one of your lineage could have known the Grail." He looked at her carefully.

"Grace, the voice may have been your father," he said gently, as he turned to leave.

Grace realized he was right. She *had* heard that voice before! A dim memory from her childhood had survived: the voice reading to her in bed at night, and comforting her when she fell, and all those other times. The memory of her father's voice had stayed with her. He was with her in Winchester, and he had been with her all along. Grace was so happy she stopped crying.

"Goodbye, Merlin! Thank you," Grace said.

"Goodbye," Merlin said as he walked across the sand to the boat.

Then he turned and shouted over his shoulder. "Oh, and John, plant a few apple trees!"

John felt for the apple core: it was still in his jacket pocket. They both waved as Merlin waded out to the boat and climbed in. They saw Arthur clasp Merlin's hand as he helped him on board.

Then the Lady looked directly at Grace, who was immediately paralyzed, as if someone had switched on a powerful electric current. Grace heard her speaking clearly—even though she was fifty yards away and her lips were not moving—as clearly as if the lady were standing next to her, whispering in her ear.

"Who am I?"

Grace gasped. The very question she had been asking herself over and over lately was now being put *to her*, taken straight out of her deepest, most guarded thoughts. Her skin prickled. She suddenly felt incredibly small, like a grain of sand in front of a mighty snow-capped mountain. And she knew she was never more vulnerable at any time in her life than at that moment—somehow with one word it could all end. But Grace knew she had to answer, and from somewhere inside she found the voice to reply.

"You are the Lady of the Lake."

Grace saw her smile. "You are the one, Grace Arundel. Generation upon generation of your ancestors have all been building toward you and this moment in history. It was destined for you to summon Arthur, and to find the lost Grail when you least expected it, purely and without ambition, and thus awaken the power that had been slumbering within you. You are the Pendragon, and although there are trials still ahead, you have blessed your land with freedom." Then she raised her arms and her voice to the sky, and it sounded to Grace like trumpets, filling her up with the sound. At that moment Grace felt somehow released, and her spirit soared.

The small craft moved quickly but effortlessly away, seeming to glide over the waves through no effort of anyone on board. Soon it was out of sight, and John and Grace were left standing on the empty beach. They embraced for a long time without speaking, as the waves crashed and the seagulls cried.

Then John looked at her, smiling, and it felt to him like the heavens opened up overhead as he spoke.

"It's time for me to enlist, Grace. If I do, will you wait for me?" His face brimmed with emotion. "Will you marry me, Grace Arundel?"

Grace did not seem at all surprised, but beamed at him.

"Of course I will, John Perceval!" He took her arm and they started back to the car. "If you take me back to Winchester. There is something there I must get."

Just north of Stokehill, workmen had just finished clearing the last section of the Culvert that had been blocked by debris, and the water surged down the little channel and into the center of town. One by one the townspeople on the pavements and in the shops noticed it, and a cheer slowly rose up from them until Grace and John heard it as they were reaching the car.

"I wonder what's going on?" John asked, out of breath.

Grace smiled. "Maybe they're cheering for us."

THE END

Made in United States
North Haven, CT
18 December 2021

13233644R00212